THE PRO

THE
PROPOSAL
ANGELA HUNT

Tyndale House Publishers, Inc.
WHEATON, ILLINOIS

Scripture quotations from Isaiah 41 are taken from the *Holy Bible,* New Living Translation, copyright © 1996. Used by permission of Tyndale House Publishers, Inc., Wheaton, Illinois 60189. All rights reserved.

Library of Congress Cataloging-in-Publication Data

Hunt, Angela Elwell, date
   The proposal / Angela Hunt.
      p.   cm.
   ISBN 0-8423-4950-2 (sc)
   1. Breast—Cancer—Research—Fiction.   2. Authors and publishers—Fiction.
3. Medicine—Authorship—Fiction.   4. Women authors—Fiction.   5. Abortion—Fiction.
I. Title.
PS3558.U46747P76   1996
813'.54—dc20   96-133

Printed in the United States of America

03   02   01   00   99   98   97   96
 9   8   7   6   5   4   3   2

It is not the lie that passeth through the mind,

but the lie that sinketh in,

and settleth in it, that doth the hurt.

—FRANCIS BACON, *"Of Truth"*

AUTHOR'S NOTE

The idea for this book germinated when, at a convention, I received a telephone message from a well-known editor who had intended to reach another writer. . . . Truth is far stranger than fiction.

I also must express a multitude of thanks to Karen Ball, Ron Beers, Ken Petersen, Scott Somerville, and Rick Blanchette. Without their insights, this book would fall far short of its intended mark.

And finally, though the characters within the pages of this novel are fictitious and not intended to represent any actual person, references to abortion, breast cancer, fetal-cell research, and the National Institutes of Health are based on fact. After all, as Theodora says, truth is truth.

If only the world had ears to hear . . .

PROLOGUE

Theodore Marshall Russell, recent darling of the *New York Times Book Review* and best-selling novelist, scowled at the chirping telephone on his desk. His agent had prophesied that Russell's phone would "ring off the wall" after the success of his recent book, but the disturbing calls he'd been receiving in the last few days had not come from those offering congratulations.

Frustrated, Russell snatched the phone from its cradle. "Hello?"

Silence. Then the slow, disquieting sound of heavy breathing in his ear.

Russell's temper flared. "Listen, you freak, stop calling me! I don't know why you're doing this, but the police are tracing this call. They're probably on their way to find you right now!"

A soft, masculine laugh echoed from the black receiver. Russell snorted in disgust and slammed the phone down. Within thirty seconds, the chirping began again. Moving to the bar, Russell poured himself a strong drink. He didn't need this.

Madison Whitlow, his agent, had promised that life would be good after the success of *Out of the Darkness, Into the Light.* "You'll be able to name your price from the best of the big publishers, the crème de la crème," Madison had promised. In addition, he'd predicted that the suddenly famous author would be a fixture on *Oprah* and *Nightline.* Russell smirked, recalling that the agent had been as excited as a dog with two tails when, the day after the advance copies hit the street, Barbara Walters had called and begged to interview Russell.

Though the attention was nice, Russell hadn't accepted a single television offer. There was no author picture on the dust jacket of his book, no acknowledgment of his hometown, his college, his background. The only personal information in the *Darkness* blurb was a brief mention that the book was Russell's first novel and was based on months of painstaking research and interviews with people struggling to cope with the suicides of their loved ones. As an afterthought, the editor had added that Russell lived in the southeastern United States with two parrots. Russell had thought about cutting even that vague note, but the book went to press before he had a chance to tell his editor to ax it.

Theo Russell liked his privacy. His anonymity had enabled him to gather the interviews that formed the basis for *Darkness*. Most people whose lives had been affected by trauma shied away from flashy reporters and camera crews, but Russell discovered that they would talk freely to a tall, bushy-haired guy in jeans who didn't even carry a notepad. His was an ordinary, middle-class kind of face; his manner polite and tactfully incurious. He told people he was a writer and mentioned that he was working on a novel about a man's suicide. Teamed with his nonthreatening appearance, that statement was usually enough to unlock wounded hearts and souls.

Because his penchant for privacy had served him well as he wrote *Darkness*, he guarded it jealously even as success threatened to expose him to a world of readers. Men of science and art should live always at the edge of mystery. He'd seen it happen too many times: Zealous examination by an overcurious public only left the once-adored object wanting in the severe light of scrutiny.

The click of the answering machine stilled the phone's insistent chirping. His own voice filled the small, windowless room he used as an office; then a stranger cut in and took control: "Mr. Russell, we know where you live. We know everything about you. We know about your next book. And we are concerned. It truly would not be in your best interests if your agent sent it out again. I suggest you step out your door and take a deep breath; think it over. And be sure to take in the view while you're out there. I believe you'll find it most . . . illuminating."

The answering machine clicked again; the message light blinked red in the gloom. Russell downed his drink in one stiff, practiced gesture, then walked to the back door. *This has gotta be a prank. No one knows where I live. No one knows anything—I've made sure of that.* Carefully, slowly, he lifted the stiff curtain hanging over the door's windowpanes and peered out. Nothing but velvet blackness. His right hand fumbled with a switch; then a yellow rectangle of light shone onto the wooden deck. From the cage behind him, one of the parrots squawked.

Everything is fine. With a confidence he did not feel, Russell clicked the dead bolt and opened the door. A rush of warm, salty sea air flowed over him; in the distance the gulf rhythmically pushed and pulled at the shore. The wind whispered through the sea grasses, and from far away he heard the hush of cars moving up and down the rural highway that led to this deserted beach house.

Russell took a deep breath. There was no broken glass, no smell of smoke, no warning ax buried in the wall. He managed a crooked smile. *Really fierce, these guys. All bark, no bite. Big deal.*

He turned to go inside and paused by the dark parrot cage. Gigi, the female, blinked unsteadily on her perch, her emerald feathers ruffled. "Hello, Theo," she called. It was the only phrase she had learned before Russell presented her with her mate and, conse-quently, the only phrase she knew.

"Hello, Gigi," he answered, bending down. "Hello, Rambo."

A sudden rise of panic threatened to choke him. The male parrot lay on the floor of the cage, his brilliant plumage flecked with bright spots of blood. He had been decapitated.

"Madison," Russell said, sighing in relief that the man, not his machine, had picked up the phone. At eight o'clock on any given night his agent was usually dining in one of New York's finest restaurants with a delectable blonde on his arm.

"Russell?" Madison Whitlow's cultured voice rang with surprise, then cheerful determination. "Hey, I'm glad you called before I went out. Got a call from the *Oprah* people again, they're really pushing for you. If you'll just come to New York—"

"No," Russell interrupted, moving quickly toward his bedroom. "I want to talk about the new book."

"Hey, the proposal's great! You're really onto something. Contro-versy, man, I can smell it. We're talking the cover of *Time* and *Newsweek*, maybe even *People* if we cut in a personal angle. It's hot stuff, Theo. Top drawer."

"I want you to forget it," Russell answered. He cocked the phone between his shoulder and chin as he pulled a duffel bag from his closet. "Forget all about it. I'll come up with something better, so just trash that proposal, OK?"

"Trash it?" Confused wonder rolled over the telephone line. "But it's *good*. And what a story it will make! I know it goes against popular opinion, but if you dare to swim against the tide, the tide will turn. If you'll just let me—"

"Did you show it to anybody?" Russell threw two pairs of jeans into the bag.

"Show it? Why, I showcased it! Everybody wants your next book. Howarth House is about to eat it up. But if you want me to get some bidding action—"

"Don't. Throw it out." Russell sat on the edge of his bed and caught a glimpse of his wide eyes and pale face in the mirror. He looked like Ichabod Crane—a disaster waiting to happen.

"Listen, Russ, you can't be serious about this. This is a one-in-a-million proposal, one of those high-concept ideas with the potential to take Hollywood—"

"I'm serious, all right. Trash that proposal. Somebody's after me, Madison, and I can't take this. They killed Rambo tonight."

"The bird? Gee, man, no wonder you're upset. But maybe the bird croaked of natural causes."

"They cut his *head* off, Madison."

Silence. Then, "Are you sure?"

Russell held his head in his hand. "No, his head just *fell* off. Of *course* I'm sure! They called me and told me to look outside! I did and I saw what they'd done! They cut his—"

"OK, OK, I get the picture. Listen, don't go ballistic on me, OK? Call the cops if you want, but it's probably just some jerk in your neighborhood with a beef about the birds' squawking. You'll be OK. Now I hate to leave you like this, Russ, but there's a lovely young lady waiting for me. I'll call you tomorrow, and we'll talk."

"I won't be here tomorrow."

"Listen, man, have you been working too hard?" Madison laughed nervously. "Authors don't get to crack up until *after* they've written the great American novel. *Darkness* was good, but you can do better."

"I'm not cracking up. I'm getting out of here, but I need you to do something for me. Call Mrs. Margaret Chambers, she lives down the street from me. Information will have the number—"

"Who?"

"My cleaning lady. I'm leaving; I won't be able to call her, so you do it, OK? Tell her to check on things at the house and take care of the birds. She'll freak out at the mess, but she'll do it—"

"Theo." Exasperation echoed in the agent's voice. "I'm not your house-sitting service. Can't you call this woman?"

"No! I'm outta here, Madison. Maybe even leaving the country. Don't try to find me, and don't worry. I'll check in with you later."

Russell hung up and tossed the phone on the bed, then rummaged in his drawer for balled-up socks and clean underwear. From the closet he extracted several white cotton shirts and a sport coat. Everything went into the duffel bag. He zipped it, picked up the cellular phone, and checked a slip of paper in his pocket before punching in another number.

"Hello?" A woman's voice trilled across the line.

"Anna, this is Theo Russell." He took a deep breath, calming his voice. "Is that invitation to speak at your convention still open?"

"Theo M. Russell, as I live and breathe! Of course it is, darling, even at this late date. When can you come?"

"Tonight. I don't know when I'll be arriving, but if you'll have a room for me in any name but my own—"

She laughed, and Russell closed his eyes, thankful that Anna Burkett, president of the National Authors League, would think his abrupt change of plans merely a charming idiosyncrasy. He and Anna had spoken several times over the phone, and each time Russell had politely but firmly turned down her invitation to speak at the NAL convention. Despite his consistent refusals, she had remained gracious, and Russell had a feeling that netting him had become her personal challenge.

"I'll have a room for you at the Hilton Tower Hotel under the name of Russ Burkett," she said. "Oh, this is wonderful! We're having quite a gathering, you know. People from everywhere, none of those dreary predictable speeches, but a fascinating group of editors, authors, and—"

"Anna, I've got to run. I'll see you in Washington. Probably tomorrow."

"I'll count on it. I'll schedule you to speak Friday night, so you can have an entire day to rest. Everyone will be so thrilled to hear that you're coming!"

"No! Anna, don't tell—" But he was too late. Anna Burkett had already hung up.

THURSDAY
October 17

Chapter 1

THEODORA Ellen Russell pulled the old suitcase from under her bed and ran a disapproving finger through its blanket of dust. "Don't blame me for that," Ann Dawson called from where she leaned in the doorway. "My job description doesn't include dusting under beds."

"Don't worry about it. You do enough," Theo answered. She smiled and moved toward her closet. "You do too much, in fact. If you fix me up with one more loser, Ann, I'm going to stop listening to you altogether. When that last guy found out that I'm a—well, that I'm *trying* to be a writer, he assured me that his life story would make a best-seller. He began with his conception in 1957 and didn't stop talking until he was done with the full account of his third and messiest divorce."

"That bad, huh?" Ann asked. She crossed her arms and studied Theo intently. "You know what I think your problem is? You're *too* together, too self-reliant. You don't need a man, and the men you meet know it." Her blue eyes lit with laughter. "You know, it doesn't hurt to play the damsel in distress every once in a while."

Theo grimaced in good humor. "Puh-leeze."

"Welcome to the wonderful world of dating." Ann chuckled with a dry and cynical sound. "It can be rough out there."

"The dating world can stay out there for all I care. When I was sixteen, dating didn't seem quite so . . . *boring*." Theo moved an armful of clothes from the closet to the bed, and the clatter of plastic hangers woke the little girl sleeping on the pillows. The child took her thumb out of her mouth, mumbled sleepily, then her head fell back onto the pillow, and her deep breathing resumed.

Theo gave Ann a conspiratorial smile. "That was close. If I wake Stacy up now, she'll never go back to sleep." She lowered her voice and began packing clothes into the suitcase. "Ann, I'm really nervous about this weekend. I hate to ask you to look after Stacy overnight—"

"What is there to be nervous about?" Ann asked, shrugging. She left the doorway and perched on the end of the bed. Mindful of the sleeping child, she whispered, "Stacy will be fine with me and Bethany. And if the little darling gets lonely, I'll just move the troops over here so Stacy can sleep in her own room." Ann ran her hand over the soft cashmere sweater on the bed. "Bethany would complain, of course, but spending the night next door won't kill her. It's a law. A fifteen-year-old can't do anything without griping about it first."

The cynical edge of Ann's smile gentled as she looked at the sleeping child. "You're blessed, you know. Stacy will never drive you to Lady Clairol. But Bethany's given me so many gray hairs. . . ."

"I'm sure I'll earn my fair share." Theo stopped packing for a moment and studied the face of her five-year-old daughter. Even in sleep, the flattish skull and almond-shaped eyes of Down's syndrome were evident. But though she and Matt had wept over the news when their daughter was born, through the years Stacy had been nothing but a tender delight, a special gift from God.

"I'm not worried about Stacy," Theo said, picking up a blouse. "I know she'll be fine with you and Bethany. I guess I'm really worried about *me!* This is the National Authors League convention, for heaven's sake! You're not supposed to be there unless you're a *professional* author. And I've never written anything, really. Nothing that counts."

"How can you say that?" Ann said, swiping her bangs out of her eyes. "In my dictionary, a professional is someone who's paid, and those people at the burglar alarm company paid you for the brochure you wrote, right?"

"Well, yes. But that's not the same as being published."

"Well, the church published your column on Down's syndrome kids, didn't they?"

"But they didn't pay me."

Ann shrugged. "Consider it a donation of your time and talent. And it was a good article, Theo. I learned things I didn't know, and I'm here with you and Stacy every day."

"I still feel like an impostor." Theo moved to her bureau and pulled out several articles of lingerie. "I've never written anything major. I'll be surrounded by literary geniuses and as out of place as a milk bucket under a bull. I'll open my mouth and say something stupid—"

"You're an intelligent woman; you couldn't say something stupid if you tried," Ann said, laughing. "You'll be fine. I thought you *wanted* to be surrounded by literary people. Isn't that the idea behind this entire trip?"

"I guess so. But I can still be nervous. Just because I can write a paragraph doesn't mean I can write a book. Could I attempt surgery just because I'm pretty good at carving a turkey? No!"

"But," Ann answered, leaning forward on the bed, "if you can write a good article, you ought to be able to write a book. One's just longer than the other, that's all. So get going, and don't come back until you're rich and famous!"

"Rich and famous?" She managed a choking laugh. "If I don't find an assignment or make a contact at this convention, I'll have no choice but to come home and give up. I've been working at this for three years, Ann, and if God hasn't opened a single window in all that time, it isn't likely he's going to throw open a door in the future. It's more likely," she said, frowning as she zipped the suitcase shut, "that I'm in the wrong room."

Grabbing one of Matt's old handkerchiefs, she smoothed the dust from the suitcase. The rough scar on the vinyl mocked her—had she really thought its haunting memories could fade? Three years ago Matt had taken the suitcase on a business trip, and in the wreck the bag had slid across one hundred feet of sun-baked asphalt. A sympathetic police officer had returned it when he came to tell her that Matt was dead. . . .

Shoving the memories aside, she stood the suitcase upright and looked around for anything she'd forgotten. Her eyes fell upon a photograph on her dresser, and she snapped her fingers and picked up the address book by the phone.

"I nearly forgot," she said, unzipping the suitcase. "I'll need to see how Janette's doing. She was scheduled for a chemotherapy treatment today, and John asked me to call tonight if I could. Sometimes she needs a little cheering up."

"Is there anything I can do?" Ann asked, her voice softening in concern. "I'd be happy to forward a message if John calls here."

"I don't think there's much anyone can do, especially not seven hundred miles away," Theo answered, slipping the address book into the suitcase. "I'm always giving John a hard time for moving my sister to Florida, but since that's where his job is. . . ."

Her voice trailed away with her hopeless thoughts. Janette had been battling cancer for nearly three years. She had been only thirty-seven when she found the first lump in her breast, and by then the cancer had spread to her lymph nodes. Beautiful, vivacious Janette, the world's most perfect big sister, now smiled through her pain and struggled to keep the seriousness of her situation from her two teenage sons.

"Well." Theo looked around one final time. "Time to get down to brass tacks, face the music, take inventory—all those tired old clichés people spout when they run out of options." She gave Ann a smile containing more confidence than she felt. "I guess that's it. Wish me well."

* * *

Theo reluctantly pulled into a parking spot in the hotel garage and grimaced when she realized she'd be paying over twelve dollars a day just to park her car. She could have driven home every night and avoided hotel bills altogether, but her master plan dictated that she totally immerse herself in this convention. How could she impress an important agent or editor with her fabulous ideas if she had to leave after the last session to drive home?

No halfway efforts this weekend, she told herself. *You're going to pay the one hundred and ten bucks a night, plus parking, plus those outrageously expensive meals because this is it. Your last chance. D day. There's only enough insurance money left for three more months, so unless you find something here, you'll have to face the fact that maybe you aren't meant to be a writer. This is your turn up at bat, slugger, so look sharp, be ready.*

The pep talk did nothing to rid her of insecurity, her constant companion. Even her car looked ill at ease in the parking garage. Surrounded by shiny late models and foreign imports, her eight-year-old Ford—littered with Happy Meal boxes and empty cola cans—was clearly out of place. When the uniformed valet approached her car and she reached out to hand him her key, she thought she saw his lip curl downward. She must have reeked of amateurism.

"Ma'am, will you open the trunk, please?"

"What?" Startled, she looked out the window at the valet.

"Pop the trunk. I need to remove your luggage."

"Ah, . . . it's not automatic." He lifted an eyebrow, and Theo pointed to the key she'd just given him. "You'll have to unlock it."

"Fine." He pressed his lips together and moved to the back of the car. Theo sat in silence, her cheeks burning. Since she worked at home, a new car was the last thing she needed. So why was one raised eyebrow from a parking attendant enough to send a wave of embarrassment over her? *Snap out of it!* She grabbed her purse and briefcase and got out of the car.

The valet opened her trunk, pushed aside the rumpled bedsheet with "Call for Help" scrawled on it (one of Ann's ideas), and removed the battered suitcase. Dangling her purse over one shoulder and stashing the briefcase under her arm, Theo extended her hand. The attendant shook his head. "We'll bring it up after you've checked in," he said firmly.

Theo felt another blush creep along her cheeks. Another dollar gone, a tip for this guy when she was perfectly willing to carry the bag herself. "All right," she said smoothly, as if that's what she had planned all along. She turned to go, but the attendant called her back.

"I need to know your name, ma'am," he called, attaching a ticket to her bag.

"Theo Russell," she said, turning toward the escalator that led to the lobby.

* * *

She offered her Visa card at the registration desk and tried to smooth her face into a casually bored expression as the girl behind the counter fretted at her computer keyboard. While Theo waited for her room key, her attention was diverted by two men behind her who slapped each other on the back and embraced as if they'd been apart for ten years. Glancing over her shoulder, Theo felt the chill shock of recognition. Good grief, Ann would faint if she knew George Keeton and Michael Rogers were standing within arm's reach! Keeton's weekly magazine column had just been spun off into a television show, and Theo and Ann had read every one of Michael Rogers's best-selling thrillers.

"George, it's good to see you," Rogers boomed, apparently not caring who heard him. "Saw your book on the *Times* list last month. Four weeks at number two, is that right?"

"Well, it was number two on the *Publishers Weekly* list five weeks in a row," Keeton answered. "But, say—*your* book got some great reviews! What's your secret? Been bribing the critics?"

Rogers laughed and said something else, but the girl at the reception desk had spoken. Theo turned around in time to see her waving a white folder with "Russell, T." neatly laser-printed across the top. "This contains your key for room 2121. You're all set for Thursday through Sunday."

"Thank you," Theo said, taking the folder. She sneaked another careful glance at the two celebrities behind her, aware that everyone else in the lobby seemed to be doing the same thing.

She made her way to the NAL convention table, checked in with a gum-chewing girl who couldn't have been more than a year out of college, and picked up her information packet. She glanced around the lobby for a moment before deciding to take the elevator to her room. She was here to make contacts, but how should she begin? Maybe she'd have a better idea after introductions had been made in the evening's first session.

Theo pressed through the mingling crowd. A hotel signboard had been erected near the elevators, and the weekend's events were posted:

Thursday: 8:00 P.M., NAL, Opening Session, Grand Ballroom

Friday: 9:00 A.M., NAL General Session

7:00 P.M., Special Guest, Theo M. Russell,
Author of *Out of the Darkness, Into the Light*

The elevator opened, and Theo was swept inside with a swarm of other people carrying NAL information packets. She felt a thrill of alarm when she heard her name bandied about, but she smiled quietly when she realized her fellow conventioneers were excited about hearing Theo M. Russell, the novelist.

Maybe, she mused, *I'll have a serendipitous meeting with the*

9

famous Theo M. Russell, and the coincidence of our names will induce him to take me under his wing. Maybe he'll introduce me to an editor or an agent, someone who will listen and recognize my talent and determination.

Maybe. Always maybe. "Maybe" hovered like a bright light over every proposal and query letter Theo mailed to editors and dimmed to the gloom of "not now" with every rejection. *Well,* she told herself as she stepped onto the twenty-first floor, *this time it's now or never. After this weekend there will be no more maybes.*

✳ ✳ ✳

Theo unpacked her suitcase, ordered a burger and a diet cola from room service, and spread the contents of her NAL packet on the bed. Several large publishing houses had sent representatives to the convention, she noticed. She had sent proposals to four of those houses, and two of her best proposals were still out.

She had just circled the names of Howarth House and Double-day in her program when a knock sounded at the door. Glancing through the peephole, she saw the waiter outside with her tray. She mentally debated for a moment whether to take the tray at the door or to allow the waiter to bring it into the room. She knew Ann would scream at the thought of Theo's opening her door to a strange man, but she'd ordered the meal herself, hadn't she?

She was not paranoid and delusional. She was an independent, determined woman, as strong as her sister Janette.

"Just bring it in and set it on the table," she said, opening the door for the young man who stood outside.

He gave her a perfunctory smile and moved past her into the room, returning in a moment with the check. Theo skimmed it, noticed in relief that the gratuity had already been added, and signed the paper with a flourish. "Thanks."

The waiter left, and Theo kicked off her shoes and picked up her convention schedule before moving to the desk to eat. The glass on

10

the tray held a pitifully small amount of ice, so she grabbed her room key and ice bucket, then padded down the hallway in her stocking feet to search for an ice machine.

She had just returned to her door when she heard the phone ring inside her room. Fumbling with the plastic key and the bucket of ice, she inserted the card into the magnetic lock. Nothing. She jiggled the handle in frustration, then pulled the key card from the door, turned it over, and tried again. The light on the lock blinked green, and the handle clicked, but the phone had stopped ringing.

Theo dropped the ice bucket on the desk and immediately dialed Ann's number. Something must have happened if Ann would call so soon. . . .

"Hello?" Bethany answered in her slow drawl.

"Hi, Beth, it's Theo. Did your mom just call me?"

"I dunno, she's in the kitchen. Do you want me to get her?"

"Would you, please?"

Theo felt her heartbeat slow perceptibly when Ann's sunny voice came on the line. "Hi, girl, what's up? Forget your toothbrush?"

"No. My phone was ringing, and I couldn't get the door open with this plastic key card. I thought maybe John had called you."

"Nope, it wasn't me. But you'd better get the hang of that key. What if a mugger was coming after you?"

"Don't be so paranoid, Ann. This is supposed to be a very safe hotel. You'd be proud of me, though. I looked through the peephole before I let the room service waiter in."

"You let him *in?* You're supposed to have him leave the food on the floor!"

"I had to sign the check." Theo couldn't help smiling.

"He can slip it under the door. Remember this, Theo: There are no perfectly safe hotels, especially for women alone. Do you keep the dead bolt on the door at all times?"

"Yes."

"Do you have that Mace I gave you?"

11

"In my purse, right under the brass knuckles."

"Very funny."

Theo laughed. "I promise, I'm being careful. How's Stacy?"

"She woke up in a great mood and seems to be thrilled to spend the night with her Auntie Ann. I don't think she misses you at all."

"Gee, thanks, Ann." Theo smiled wryly. "Tell me she misses me. I'm entitled to a little guilt."

"She does miss you, but she's fine. She and Bethany made cookies. The girls OD'd on the chocolate; I think the cookies are more chip than dough."

"You didn't forget her pink blanket, did you? She can't sleep without it."

"We've got it. And what we don't have, we can get. Now you stop worrying and have fun. Make those contacts! Go be discovered!"

"I'll try."

"Talk to you soon."

"Bye."

As Theo hung up, she noticed that the message light on her phone had begun to blink.

Chapter 2

"THEO, this is Evelyn Fischer of Howarth House. I'm on my way to the first session now, but I'd like to meet you at one o'clock tomorrow to discuss your proposal. Can you meet me outside the Plaza Café for lunch? It's downstairs to the right of the registration desk. I'm looking forward to meeting you."

Theo took a quick breath of utter astonishment, then played the message again. Evelyn Fischer of Howarth House actually wanted to meet and discuss her proposal! Leaning across the bed, she rifled through her thin leather briefcase for the folder containing the proposal for the Down's syndrome book. A handwritten list in the file confirmed that she'd sent the proposal to several publishing houses. Howarth House had received it three months ago.

Theo pressed her hand to her mouth as a strange, warm excitement spread through her. Finally, someone was interested in her work. God was opening a door! Once Evelyn Fischer saw Stacy's sweet picture and realized that this book would help thousands of families, she would offer a contract. Theo would polish up the manuscript, and in about a year, maybe less, she'd be holding her own book in her hands!

All the hard work, time, and sacrifice would pay off. With this contract she'd prove to everyone, including herself, that Theodora Ellen Russell was a *writer*. An author. A professional.

The stack of materials on the bed caught her eye, and she moved

13

toward them, blissfully determined to make full use of her time. *You do belong here,* she assured herself as she began to sort the NAL materials from her own work. *You're meeting an editor for lunch tomorrow.*

Dismissing her plans to attend the evening session in the ballroom, Theo fumbled in her briefcase for a highlighter, then flipped open the NAL program. She needed time to study a description of Howarth House and Evelyn Fischer's biography. Tomorrow would bring what might be the most important meeting of her life, and she was determined to face it well prepared.

* * *

At nine o'clock Theo dialed John and Janette's number. The phone rang twice; then she heard John's breathless answer: "Hello?"

"John, it's Theo," she said, twirling the telephone cord in her hand. "How's our girl?"

"Tired," her brother-in-law answered, his own voice flat with weariness. "And a little nauseous, but not too much. Do you want to talk to her?"

"In a minute," Theo answered, trying to keep the conversation light. "How are the boys?"

"Great. Jared's out playing basketball, and Josh is watching reruns in his room. If you want to talk to them—"

"I just wanted to talk to you for a moment," Theo said, "before I talk to the others. How is Janette, really, John? What is her oncologist saying?"

She could almost see him shrug. "He says she's doing great. The hair will grow back, the nausea will pass, and the CAF course only runs for six months. She goes into the hospital for intravenous administrations twice a month only."

"CAF?" Theo crinkled her nose. "I've never heard of it."

"It's a combination of Cytoxan, Adriamycin, and Fivefluoruracil. Adriamycin is the heavy hitter, the one that makes the hair fall out.

But she picked out a wig, and the boys are used to seeing her in it, so that makes things easier."

"Good," Theo whispered, not understanding how he could even use the word *easy*. She'd visited Janette after her first surgery and the last radiation treatment, and each time she'd come home so tired her nerves throbbed. Part of her weariness was simple exhaustion, part was certainly caused from the emotional strain of seeing a loved one suffer, and part was the lingering fear that somehow *she* might develop breast cancer, for didn't it run in families?

"She's asleep now, but if you want, I'll wake her up," John was saying.

"No, John, let her sleep. Just tell her I called, OK, and that I'll be praying for her. And tell her," Theo couldn't keep a note of excitement from her voice, "tell her that her baby sister may be about to be discovered. I have a meeting with an editor tomorrow. We're going to discuss a book proposal I submitted."

"Hey, Theo, that's great," John said, his voice husky. "Should I tell you to break a leg or something?"

"No, just take care of my sister," Theo answered, closing her eyes. "And tell her I love her."

FRIDAY
October 18

Chapter 3

Too buoyed with hope and energy to rest, Theo tossed and turned for much of the night. She drifted in and out of sleep, dreaming and thinking about signing a huge book contract. When the phone rang with her wake-up call, she sat bolt upright, as wide awake as if she'd just had an intravenous dose of pure caffeine.

Knowing that Ann would be well into her morning routine, Theo called to share the news about Evelyn Fischer and promised to phone after lunch with even more exciting news. She talked briefly to Stacy, then felt a stab of mingled guilt and relief when Ann came back on the line and said Stacy had awakened in the night and cried for her mama.

She showered and put on her makeup, then slipped into her thick, housewifely robe and sat at the desk in the hotel room. Pulling the Down's syndrome book proposal out of her briefcase, she tried to read it from the careful perspective of an editor. She made note of a few possible weaknesses that could be improved and jotted down several suggestions that she might make if Evelyn Fischer seemed reluctant to seal the deal.

The breadth of her own dreams staggered her, but nothing was impossible, was it? An editor had actually called her. Anything could happen now, absolutely anything.

She dressed, checked her hair one final time, smoothed on a fresh coat of lipstick, and tucked her room key into her briefcase. She looked, she hoped, like a casually elegant, confident writer. Evelyn Fischer must never know that under the thin veneer of calm Theo's heart was pounding.

* * *

"Are you Evelyn Fischer? I'm Theo Russell."

The tall, regal woman in a stylish navy jacket and matching skirt blinked in surprise when Theo greeted her outside the café.

"Really?" The word came out amid a throaty laugh. "What a delightful revelation. I suppose I expected a man. Sexist of me, wasn't it?"

Theo forced a casual smile. "My name always catches people off guard. I was named after an uncle Theodore."

"I understand." Obviously not one for small talk, Evelyn Fischer motioned to the hostess. "Excuse me, miss. We're ready to be seated."

Theo followed Evelyn Fischer into the crowded restaurant and noticed that several heads turned to follow them. The editor was a lovely woman with classically handsome features, but the looks directed at them seemed to reflect more than mere admiration. There was clearly respectful attention and more than a little curiosity. Apparently there was a good bit of interest in whom Evelyn Fischer had chosen to interview over lunch.

The hostess seated them at a small table in a quiet corner, and Evelyn pulled her own leather attaché onto her lap. "I must congratulate you," she said, rifling through her case. "This proposal is absolutely brilliant. The medical aspects are well thought out and aptly presented. I wonder that no one has beaten you to the idea."

"I'm sure someone has." Theo took her eyes from Evelyn's for a moment to nod gratefully at a waiter who placed tall glasses of water before them. "But I thought I could bring a fresh approach to the subject."

"Well, you've certainly done that." Though the editor's voice was cool and controlled, Evelyn's eyes glinted in appreciation behind her designer glasses. "I was quite *intrigued* when I read this material. I can't help but wonder what will happen when women in the marketplace read this. I'm certain the repercussions will shake society." She lowered her chin and stared at Theo over the top of her glasses. "Are you confident that you can do this, my dear? That you can carry it off?"

Theo nodded confidently. If there was one topic she knew inside out, it was Down's syndrome. "Absolutely."

Evelyn studied Theo silently for a few moments, then straightened in her chair and smiled. "All right, then, Theo. I base my acquisitions on intuition and insight, and everything tells me this book is going to be the women's book of the year. I'd stake my reputation on it."

"I hope men will read it, too," Theo said, dazed. Though pleased, she was bewildered by the editor's enthusiasm. She nodded again at the waiter who brought a pair of menus to the table. "I don't see this solely as a woman's issue—"

"Of course not. It's an issue for everyone, and we're very intrigued with the project." Evelyn fished a sheaf of papers from her briefcase and dropped them on the table. Leaning over them, she crossed her arms and squinted in some secret amusement as she watched Theo. "I'll come right to the point, my dear. We're open to giving you a contract based upon this proposal. I don't exactly know what sort of money you're looking for, but if this book turns out to be what we think it will be, I'm sure our offer will be more than satisfactory."

Theo didn't know what to say. She sat in stunned silence, searching for the proper, professional response, but nothing came to mind.

Evelyn Fischer frowned slightly. "I assure you, Theo, we will do right by you. Considering the potential of this project, you can be sure that the advance will be quite substantial."

"Quite . . . substantial?" Theo echoed tonelessly, still trying to take it all in.

Mild frustration showed in Evelyn Fischer's eyes; apparently Theo's response wasn't what she had hoped for. With a slight lift of her elegant chin, Evelyn said, "We might be talking mid–six figures."

Six figures.

Six figures! Suddenly apoplectic, Theo's mind went totally blank. Six figures. Goose bumps lifted on her arms. At the very least, six figures would be one hundred thousand dollars. . . . "Mid–six figures" was half a million. . . .

"Six figures," Theo repeated, clenching her hands under the table. She half expected Evelyn Fischer to disappear in a puff of smoke, that it was all a dream, but the editor sat there still, a mollified smile framing her perfect keyboard of teeth.

"Of course, I probably shouldn't even be discussing this without your agent's input," Evelyn went on, leaning back in her chair. "But we'll let the businesspeople work out all the details. What I want from you is a commitment to write this wonderful book for Howarth House."

Theo sat still, a frozen smile on her face. She didn't even have an agent. Something else to take care of this weekend.

With a manicured fingernail, the editor tapped the papers on the table in front of her. "I want you to write this book for us, and I want our written agreement finalized as soon as possible. I'll send the contract to your agent. Once you've had a chance to discuss the details together, have him give me a call. And the sooner, the better."

"All right," Theo whispered, still reeling from the thought of half a million dollars. She felt her cheeks begin to burn. "But no one has been exactly trying to beat my door down, if you know what I mean."

"Of course not," Evelyn answered, a wry smile curling upon her lips. "No one knows where that door is." She slid the pages on the table toward Theo. "This book will set the world on fire. Truly it will. I believe in you. You convoluted the arguments of the euthanasia proponents with *Out of the Darkness,* and you'll upset the entire medical community with this."

Theo felt everything go silent within her as she stared at the proposal on the table. The stack of pages wasn't her outline for a book on Down's syndrome. The cover page was titled *The Savage Breast;* the name at the bottom of the page was Theo M. Russell, represented by Madison Whitlow of New York City.

Theo closed her eyes, fighting the sudden feeling of nausea that washed over her. This meeting wasn't a dream come true—it was a nightmare. Numb with astonishment and disappointment, she leaned back in her chair while her mind struggled to understand how such a mistake could have happened.

The waiter arrived. While Evelyn launched into a detailed query about the restaurant's daily specialties, Theo's mind churned with fear, embarrassment, and grief. It wasn't fair! Ten minutes ago she had been *in the door,* a genuine writer with an eager editor. Now it was all a terrible misunderstanding. She had stumbled into a luncheon appointment meant for Theo M. Russell, the overnight sensation who had probably made more money with his first book than Theo would ever see in a lifetime of articles and ladies' club bulletins.

While Evelyn continued to interrogate the waiter, Theo inched her hand toward the proposal and casually picked it up. Flipping through the pages, she skimmed the facts and outline.

Russell had done extensive research on breast cancer. A bold headline at the top of the second page proclaimed: "An analysis of all reputable studies suggests that women who terminate a pregnancy before their first live birth have a risk of breast cancer 50 percent higher than women who do not."

She was barely able to control her gasp of surprise. Fifty percent higher? Could that be right?

The rest of Russell's proposal contained a synopsis of a novel that would be based on actual research and medical facts.

The exasperated waiter turned from Evelyn to Theo. "And for you?" he asked, his pencil poised above his pad.

"Nothing for me, thanks," she told the waiter. He lifted an eyebrow in surprise.

"Not hungry?" Evelyn Fisher's voice was an elegant drawl.

Theo shook her head. "I'm afraid I can't do this. Ms. Fischer, this proposal—"

"You *can* do this," Evelyn interrupted, leaning forward. "Not enough money? I'll have to run it by my superiors, but we might be able to go higher."

"No, it's not the money. It's this proposal. It's not—"

"You've had second thoughts?" The editor's eyes glowed with determination. "If the proposal isn't exactly what you had in mind, make whatever changes you like, but I must have this topic. Women's health issues are hot right now. Sizzling. I can't afford to let you go elsewhere."

Theo bit her lip and glanced down at the pages again. There was no way she could do Russell's novel. It wouldn't be right. Besides, she wrote nonfiction.

So why not go ahead and write nonfiction?

The idea came suddenly, quietly, as though afraid to make itself known. Theo caught her breath, her pulse racing. She thumbed through the pages once more. "If you really want the topic . . ." She spoke in a low, thoughtful voice. "I can make changes?"

"Of course. Just say you'll do the project, and I'll have the contract overnighted to your agent. If the terms are agreeable, you'll have the advance in less than a month."

Theo's mind blew open to the possibilities. Why not? Why not write a book all her own. A nonfiction treatise of the issue. The medical facts and research weren't Russell's property. They were available to anyone who wanted them. She could write a nonfiction book—one that was her work, her research, her talent—without touching any of Russell's story ideas or characters. Though it was a crazy way to avoid a publisher's slush pile, her work would be read by a genuine editor at Howarth House. And Theo M. Russell, wherever he was, wouldn't be bothered at all. Someone would publish his next great novel, and he'd sell a zillion copies without even trying. No matter what a small-timer like Theo did, she wouldn't hinder his career.

God works in mysterious ways, Theo told herself firmly.

Maybe, a niggling voice responded from within, *but would he work like this?*

Maybe again. Another maybe that meant no. Taking this idea might not be unethical, but allowing Evelyn Fischer to believe that she had snared *the* Theodore Russell definitely was.

"Ms. Fischer," Theo said, picking up the proposal, "I can't—"

An earsplitting beep cut Theo off, and the editor rolled her eyes.

"I can't escape," Evelyn said, her smile flattening to a perfectly straight slash of lipstick. "I'll have to return this call. Listen, Theo, it was really a pleasure to meet you." The editor stood to gather her things. "But I'm expecting to hear from the novelist who just wrote *Paradise Passion.* Have you read it? Quite a major talent and ours for the taking if we're fast enough to snag her."

"Ms. Fisher," Theo said, pushing her chair back from the table. "About this proposal—"

"Based upon your previous success, I don't have a worry in the world," Evelyn said, extending her hand. "Now let me say farewell, and I'll be expecting to hear from you soon. Don't disappoint me, Theo."

"Ms. Fisher—"

"Call me Evelyn."

"Evelyn." Theo shook the editor's hand, then pointed again to the proposal on the table. "You've got to understand something. This proposal isn't—"

The beeper shrilled again, and Evelyn turned, hurrying toward the exit. "Just have your agent call me," she said, moving away.

"But this proposal isn't mine!" Theo finished, lifting her hands in exasperation.

But Evelyn Fischer was waving at a group of diners at another table and was no longer listening.

Chapter 4

BURL Rodenbaugh finished scanning the paper before him, then carefully placed it on the stack of pages and laid them precisely in the center of his polished mahogany desk. He paused for a moment, tented his fingers, and leaned back against the leather of his office chair.

Too bad that young novelist had chosen to travel down this particular story line. Rodenbaugh had enjoyed *Out of the Darkness, Into the Light.* Russell could have had a long, successful career.

With a sigh of regret, Rodenbaugh swiveled his chair to study the white glow of Washington's marble skyline, then turned away from the window and picked up the phone. A moment later a receptionist came on the line, recognized Rodenbaugh's name, and put the call through.

"Yes?" The voice in his ear was gruff.

"I have just finished reading it, Dennison, and I agree. Mr. Russell must be stopped."

"Are you certain?"

"If it were anyone else, I wouldn't bother, but Russell is the current leader of the pack. We're talking a million readers easily, even if the man decides to write comic books. We can't take the risk."

"I thought New York had agreed to handle it."

"They hired someone in Florida to shake him up, but I don't

think they were very . . . effective. According to this morning's paper," Rodenbaugh continued, "Russell's in town to speak to a convention of writers tonight, and I'm a little nervous about his topic. Freedom of speech, freedom from censorship—those are hot buttons and very popular among the literati. I don't think Mr. Russell got the message. And we can't have him mounting a crusade, now can we?"

"We'll handle it."

"Good. We'll make it up to you."

"I know."

The phone clicked in Rodenbaugh's ear.

* * *

Dennison Reyes replaced the receiver, then waved his hand to dismiss his beautiful secretary. "That will be all for now, Daphne," he said, giving her a nod. "But would you mind staying a bit late tonight? I may have some business to discuss over dinner."

"Of course," Daphne answered, untwining her long legs. She stood and walked away slowly, as if she knew he enjoyed watching her go. When the door had closed behind her, Reyes sighed, then picked up the phone again.

The receptionist for BioTech Industries answered the phone, and after a moment, Scotty Salago came on the line. "What's up, boss?" he asked, his New York accent slicing through the hiss of the phone line. Reyes frowned. Scotty had been in Washington for five years, but the practiced polish of most Washington urbanites had managed to elude him.

"We've got a job for you, Scotty. The NCC's run into a potential problem. A Mr. Theo M. Russell."

"Got it. What's this problem look like?"

Reyes pulled a manila envelope from a desk drawer and slid out a grainy black-and-white photograph. "All I have is a bad photo from a surveillance camera, but it'll do, I think. I'll fax it to you."

"OK. Where's the problem now?"

Reyes smiled. "The Hilton Tower."

"I'll get to it."

"Today, Scotty. This morning's paper said Russell is supposed to speak tonight at the hotel. We don't want him talking to anyone, but we don't want him dead. Yet."

"No problem, boss."

"And, Scotty—"

"Yeah?"

Irritated, Reyes rubbed the ridge his glasses had trenched into the bridge of his nose. "Remember, violence is the last refuge of the incompetent. We're not incompetent—so do it quietly."

* * *

Scotty Salago stood up and straightened the lapels on his suit coat. The nameplate on his office door read Head of Security, but Scotty knew his real job was simply to do whatever had to be done. He never failed. He had learned long ago, from his New York *caporegime*, that failure was bad for one's health.

Scotty had taken his lieutenant's lesson to heart and gained a respectable reputation. When the Moreno family had sent him to Washington five years earlier, Scotty had been pleased. The perks were great: a plush apartment overlooking the Potomac, a great salary plus bonuses, and free access to the busy, self-important atmosphere of Washington's business district.

He smiled, remembering his first forays into the city's social circles. The locals—those elegant, refined women who shopped in Georgetown—had taken pains to snub his brilliant opening lines in the bars and clubs. But they couldn't help being impressed by the thick wad of bills he carried. They pretended hard to ignore him, but he'd seen the way even the most blue-blooded of them threw him a curious sidelong glance when he began flashing money around.

He was a New Yorker through and through, but he liked the

flavor of the District. When the family brought him back to New York every Christmas to thank him for representing their interests in the nation's capital, he liked to sigh and pretend he was roughing it among the politicos, but it wasn't really bad. He didn't even mind working for that stuffy lawyer Dennison Reyes or that grim doctor Griffith Dunlap. He'd work for Santa Claus if the family wanted him to.

Scotty left his office and walked to the small lounge where Brennan Connor and Antonio Verde were playing poker. Brennan's lean, attractive face gave away nothing as he studied his cards, while Antonio rearranged his hand, seemingly unhindered by a missing index finger on his left hand.

"Connor, Verde," Scotty said, jerking his head toward his office. "Come in here. We got a job."

Antonio grunted, and Brennan stubbed out his cigarette, then tossed his cards onto the table. The fax machine on Scotty's desk was humming as they entered the room, and through a blur of green light, a fuzzy gray photograph rolled out onto the table.

Scotty ripped the curled paper from the machine as the green light clicked off. He studied the image for a moment. It was a lousy photo, made worse through fax transmission, but Scotty could see that the target was a tall skeleton of a man with dark, bushy hair. The man's face wasn't clear, but it wouldn't be hard to find a human toothpick like that.

Scotty thrust the paper at Brennan. "His name's Theo M. Russell. He's got to be handled today. You'll find him at the Hilton Tower Hotel."

Antonio peered over Brennan's broad shoulder at the photo, his eyes intent. "What do you need?"

"Take him to the little house over in Fairmount Heights," Scotty said. "Get him before six o'clock; then treat him to a good jolt." Scotty sank into his chair and propped his feet on the desk. "Just keep him there until you hear from me."

"Done," Brennan said, folding the photo. With his usual econ-omy of movement, he slid it into his coat pocket, then turned to leave.

"And, guys," Scotty called, rapping the desk with his knuckles. Brennan and Antonio glanced back over their shoulders. "Keep it quiet, you hear?"

* * *

Brennan led Antonio through the kitchen of the Hilton Tower Hotel. The Irishman knew endless ways to find a person in a hotel, but this time extreme measures wouldn't be needed. They usually weren't unless the quarry had been forewarned or was especially clever. That wasn't the case here, so Brennan was investigating the most direct approaches first. He knew the front desk wouldn't give out names and room numbers, but kitchens had computers, too.

He strode confidently toward the small desk where a pretty Asian girl handled room service orders. Her eyes widened in surprise when the pair reached her, but Brennan flashed his most charming smile and put a one-hundred-dollar bill faceup on her desk.

"We'd like to surprise a friend of ours," he said, bending close enough to smell the girl's perfume. "And we'd truly appreciate any help you could give us in locating his room number, lass. I know your helpful computer can tell us. The gentleman's name is Theo M. Russell."

"I-I'm not allowed to do that." The girl's voice was slightly unsteady. "I could lose my job."

"Don't worry," Brennan said, keeping his voice low. His smile was cool as he touched a finger to the girl's upper arm and stroked it casually. "I won't tell. And I really need to know."

Beside him, Antonio shifted his weight and crossed his arms. The girl glanced at him, only to be met with a steady, narrowed gaze. Though neither man did anything openly threatening, the girl swallowed nervously. Her eyes glanced up again to Brennan's face, then downward like a frightened bird's. He smiled humorlessly, trusting the power of his intimidation.

The girl's hands trembled as she typed R-U-S-S-E-L-L on the keyboard. Like a bright beacon, "RUSSELL, THEO—2121" flashed on the screen.

"Twenty-one twenty-one." Brennan glanced back at Antonio, then gave the girl an impenitent grin. "My thanks, lass. And those of our friend. He'll be glad to see us." He scooped up the hundred-dollar bill and pressed it against her palm.

"I don't want your money," she said, her face paling under the fluorescent light. She held the bill between her thumb and index finger as though it repulsed her.

"Of course you do," Brennan answered over his shoulder, moving confidently toward the service elevator.

❋ ❋ ❋

Another hundred-dollar bill convinced a waiter to lend his jacket and surrender a room service tray. As the waiter scurried back to the kitchen, Antonio held the tray as Brennan slipped into the tailored white uniform.

"It's a good thing you're thin," Antonio said as Brennan caught his friend's admiring glance. "I could never fit into that coat."

"Shut up, Tony, and get in."

"How many times I gotta tell you, the name's Antonio!" he muttered as he followed Brennan into the service elevator.

The Irishman chuckled. He could always count on getting a rise out of Antonio when he used the Americanized version of the Italian's name. Calling him Tony was bad enough, but the man nearly went into convulsions when Brennan told him once that Antonio Verde was just a stuck-up version of Tony Green.

Still fuming, Antonio pressed the button for the twenty-first floor and held his tongue as they ascended. When the elevator came to rest, Brennan nodded at his companion. "I'll bring Russell back here, and we'll take off. This guy's obviously no brain surgeon. He's ignored some very clear warnings and hasn't even bothered to make himself hard to find."

"Maybe he doesn't know he's become a . . . high priority."

Brennan rolled his eyes. "He knows. Anyone who's in trouble with the Moreno family knows it. And they know that kind of trouble can be fatal. Just hold the elevator."

All was quiet on the twenty-first floor as the elevator doors opened. Brennan adjusted the tray on his hand and walked casually to room 2121. He cocked his ear toward the door, listening. He heard nothing—no television, no voices, no ringing phone.

Maybe Russell wasn't in the room. Brennan snarled in frustration. They should have had more time to plan this one. He hated rush jobs. Next time, Scotty had better give them the time they needed to do the job right.

He knocked, then drew his lips into a tight smile when he heard movement from behind the door. Someone was peering through the peephole. "Room service," he called, trying hard to keep the adrenaline edge out of his voice.

A woman's voice, faintly muffled, came through the door. "I didn't order room service."

Great. Just great. The guy had a woman in there! Now Brennan would have to leave the food, scope out the situation, and figure out if the woman was likely to be hanging around. They might have to take her out to bring in the bird.

"Complimentary room service," Brennan called again, shifting the tray in his hands. "For Theo Russell."

"Who's it from?" the woman asked.

"They don't give out that information, ma'am, but I assure you I'm legitimate," he replied, his voice coolly confident. "You can call the hotel manager to confirm if you like." Brennan heard the metallic clunk of the doorstop, then the click of the dead bolt, and he smiled. That line always worked. No one ever called to check him out. The door opened a few inches. A good-looking woman with wide green eyes and short brown hair stood in the opening and stared in confusion at the tray. Russell might be mangy-looking, but he had good taste in women.

"As I said, this tray is for Theo Russell. I'm afraid he'll need to sign for it." Brennan tried to peer past the woman into the room.

"I'm Theodora Russell. I might be able to clear up this confusion if you tell me who sent the tray."

Brennan couldn't stop his surprise from showing on his face, and the woman gave him an apologetic smile. What was going on? Somebody had made a mistake, and he'd be the one to pay for it. He'd broken his number one rule: *Never underestimate the opposition.* He had assumed Theo Russell was stupid enough to check in under his own name, but the guy wasn't so careless, after all. If Brennan had been by himself, he would have turned the air blue. As it was, it took all of his finesse to draw a calming breath and look at the woman. There was no reason to involve her in his problem. Not yet, anyway.

"My mistake," he said, bowing slightly. "You, lassie, clearly are not a Theodore. Even so, I suppose this tray is for you."

Before she could protest, he pushed the door open and pressed his way into her room. He heard her sputtering helplessly, but he ignored her and placed the tray on the table near the window. The place smelled of perfume, and for one fleeting moment he wished he could linger. But papers littered the bed, a briefcase lay on the floor, the television sat dark and silent. This pretty woman had business on the brain. He preferred women with much different tastes. Besides, he had a job to finish.

"Could you tell me if I should thank Evelyn Fischer for this?" she asked, fumbling in her purse. She pulled out a dollar bill, and Brennan stared in confusion until he realized she was offering him a tip. *A tip!* If she'd been his target, she'd be unconscious and in the elevator by now. But there she stood, a green-eyed angel, innocently offering him a dollar.

He waved his hand graciously and moved toward the door. "It's on the house," he said, stepping into the hall. "Enjoy whatever it is." He turned to look at her one more time, an engaging smile on his face. "Smells like a hamburger and fries."

"OK. I will enjoy it." The woman smiled back and closed the door. Brennan heard the dead bolt click again. He shook his head and went back to the elevator, wondering how he'd explain this to Antonio.

* * *

It felt good to be out of that uncomfortable monkey suit the waiters had to wear, but a growing sense of frustration sent nervous flutterings through Brennan's chest as he and Antonio sat on a sofa in the hotel lobby pretending to read newspapers. Time was bearing down on them; they had no guarantee they'd snag their prey before Scotty's deadline. What if Russell didn't come out of his room? What if their information was wrong and Russell wasn't even staying at the Hilton?

One thing was certain: It didn't pay to disappoint Scotty Salago. And it was a waste of time to offer reasons or excuses. He accepted neither. Brennan knew they'd better grab Theodore M. Russell by six o'clock or. . . . He grimaced. He didn't even want to think of the consequences.

Antonio stirred restlessly and stood to stretch. Brennan looked up from his paper and scanned the spacious lobby. A kaleidoscope of people surrounded them, constantly changing, shifting positions. The revolving doors propelled people through the lobby; the elevators returned the volley. But neither avenue yielded the thin man in Scotty's photograph.

Among the people flooding through the lobby was the pretty woman from room 2121. She walked to the gift shop, browsed a few minutes, then returned to the elevator with a newspaper under her arm and a yellow bag of peanut candies in her hand. She walked quickly, rarely looking up, and Brennan thought she seemed nervous. Once, she glanced his way as if she'd felt his eyes appraising her, but Brennan raised his newspaper. When he peered out again, she had disappeared.

"Did you see that woman?" Brennan asked Antonio, jerking his head toward the closing elevator doors.

"What woman?"

"The brown-haired one in jeans. Nice looking."

"All the women here are nice looking."

Brennan ignored that comment. "She was the woman in the room."

"The other Theo Russell?"

"Shut up!" Brennan hissed, glancing around to see if anyone nearby had heard. He lowered his voice. "Yeah. That was her."

Antonio grinned and scratched the nub on his freckled hand. "Maybe we surprise Scotty and bring him a companion, huh?"

"We've got to bring him something," Brennan muttered, leaning forward to rest his arms on his knees. He glanced again around the lobby. "Soon."

His watch beeped, and Brennan felt his stomach tighten again. Five o'clock. One hour left. They'd been sitting in the lobby since three, and Brennan had mentally compared everyone who walked by to the grainy black-and-white faxed photo in his coat pocket. Nobody yet had resembled the bushy-headed toothpick man in the picture. Still, Russell was supposed to speak in the ballroom on the ground floor. Unless he was Houdini, he'd have to walk right by them.

At five forty-three all of Brennan's inner warning systems went off at once. A tall man with dark, wet hair stepped off the elevator and hurried toward the gift shop. The Irishman tossed his cigarette into the potted plant next to the couch and snapped his fingers in Antonio's direction. Together they stood and followed.

A row of pay phones hung on the wall outside the gift shop, and

Antonio grinned and lifted a receiver to his ear as Brennan followed the dark-haired man inside the shop. There could be no doubt. The man's hair was slicked back—he was probably fresh from the shower—but he was a clear match. Theodore Russell was all but wrapped up and delivered.

As Brennan pretended to be interested in postcards, the man placed a disposable razor on the counter, then fished a handful of quarters from his pocket and placed them in the palm of an adolescent salesclerk. The clerk joked that toothbrushes and razors were his best-selling items. People always left home and forgot them.

"Right," the tall man said, pocketing his razor. He turned to leave, and Brennan followed him into the hallway.

"Mr. Russell," Brennan called, taking pains to keep his voice level. The tall man stopped in midstep but did not turn around.

Out in the silent hallway, the man's fear was palpable. Brennan injected a smile into his voice. "I understand you're a writer. Being Irish and havin' a way with words, I fancy myself a writer, too. Do you think you'll have time to look at a wee manuscript of mine?"

At the pay phones, Antonio hung up the receiver and blocked the man's way through the hallway. Brennan glanced back at the salesclerk inside the gift shop. The young man had perched on a stool behind the counter and was engrossed in a magazine. Good.

"I don't do manuscript evaluations," Russell said, his voice high pitched and reedy.

"Oh, I think you'll do this one," Brennan said, his tone hard and cold. He stepped up to the thin man's elbow and clasped it firmly as Antonio narrowed the gap, a shadowy sneer hovering about his heavy mouth.

Brennan lowered his voice to a conspiratorial whisper. "You're to come with us, Mr. Russell," he said, his words pitched to reach the author's ear and not a breath beyond. "I'd strongly discourage any resistance on your part. However, we are prepared to compel you should the need arise. And if you do anything to attract attention, I really can't guarantee your safety." He painted on a warm smile. "So, please, no unpleasantness. Just come along for a little talk, and when we're done you'll walk away as free as a bird."

In front of Russell, Antonio smiled and put his hands in his pockets, the careful action pulling his jacket open a bit and exposing the hilt of his .357 Magnum. A small sound gurgled in the writer's throat.

"I don't think you'll want to resist and cause a scene," Brennan said, moving to the author's side. "Antonio's not a very good shot, and he might miss your leg and hit some vital organ. Besides, we're just going to take you on a short ride, Mr. Russell. Remember, in a few hours we'll let you go anywhere you want."

The man still didn't move. Brennan noted how the man's eyes darted quickly to the left and right, as though mentally evaluating the odds of surviving a mad dash for the lobby. Brennan made a tsking sound and nodded to his partner, and Antonio narrowed his dark eyes and pulled the gun from its holster. The unmistakable click of a hammer being cocked broke the stillness.

The writer turned to Brennan, a film of sweat on his pasty face. "I'll be missed. I'm supposed to give a speech tonight."

"Well, we'll have to take care of that," Brennan answered, calmly leading the author toward the escalator that led down to the parking garage. "We can't have your friends worrying about you, can we now? And don't worry, they'll adjust. No one is indispensable, Mr. Russell. Haven't you learned that yet? You'll call the hotel desk and tell them you're not feeling well. Someone else will give your speech, and you'll be perfectly free to spend a little time with us."

Brennan hadn't thought it would be possible, but the author grew a shade paler as the escalator deposited them on the lower floor. He smiled, satisfied. The man was finally getting the message.

Chapter 5

TWO voices played tug-of-war with Theo's brain all afternoon. *Keep the proposal, use it as a basis for your own nonfiction book, and submit it to Evelyn Fischer,* one voice chanted. *She asked for your work, didn't she?*

Call Evelyn Fischer, tell the truth, be up-front and honest, argued the other. *She'll learn the truth anyway when Theodore Russell speaks tonight.*

Sitting at the desk in her hotel room, Theo dithered between the two, feeling a little like Abraham on the mountaintop with his beloved and long-awaited son on the altar. Did she have the courage to surrender her dream? And was God really asking her to do this?

She tried calling Evelyn Fischer's room, but the editor wasn't in, and Theo didn't want to explain the situation through voice mail. She even thought about calling Theodore Russell ("You're going to think this is funny, but guess what my name is"), but then remembered that she was apparently the only Theo Russell registered at the hotel.

So during the afternoon she studied the proposal.

The implications of Russell's theory still dazzled her. If a link between abortion and breast cancer did exist, women needed to know! Her mother had died from breast cancer, and now Janette struggled with the same disease. Whether Theo wrote about Russell's hypothesis from a women's health perspective, a pro-life viewpoint, or simply as a medical breakthrough, the idea was a sure winner. If breast cancer was really aggravated by the physiological changes caused by an abortion, the topic was hot enough to support two books—even a dozen.

So how could she address the topic and still feel good about the way she'd received the material? Evelyn Fischer needed to know that Theodora was not Theodore; that much was certain. And Theodore needed to know that Theodora had seen his material. Perhaps he'd be willing to give his permission for her to use it. After all, she would write a completely different kind of book.

Theo chewed the end of her pencil, thinking. Evelyn Fischer wasn't the type, she decided, to listen to Theo's explanation and then laugh it off as a strange coincidence. She might be angry, even insulted, that a nobody had taken up her time and heard her offer six figures to the wrong person. Better to write Ms. Fischer a letter than to confront her in person. Theo could write the letter first thing Monday morning, Evelyn would receive it within a couple of days, and the editor would save face with her peers. No one else would know about her little mistake.

Except Theodore M. Russell. Theo knew she could leave him out of the confrontation entirely, but she really did want to know more about the abortion–breast cancer link. No one in her family had aborted a baby, but breast cancer ran through their ranks like a crimson thread, binding then separating mothers from daughters, sisters from sisters.

And Theodore Russell was speaking tonight at the NAL convention. Surely Theo could join the crowd of admirers around him after his speech. She'd catch his attention by introducing herself, and the similarity in their names would grant her at least a five-minute audience. She could quietly explain the mix-up of the afternoon and return his proposal. And then she'd ask, even beg if necessary, for his blessing to follow the same research with a totally different kind of book.

He couldn't say no. There was really no ethical, moral, or legal reason why she couldn't investigate the abortion–breast cancer link on her own, but she'd be courteous enough to ask first. And she'd promise to give him credit for the idea in the acknowledgment section of her book when it was published.

"Yeah," Theo whispered, putting the pencil down. A thrill of hope coursed through her as she straightened the edges of the proposal. "This feels right."

* * *

Sitting in the back of the grand ballroom, Theo looked at her watch. Seven-thirty, and still no sign of Theodore Russell. In the crowded seats to Theo's right, men and women talked and gestured enthusiastically as they waited. Several held copies of *Out of the Darkness, Into the Light,* and Theo guessed that they would join her in the crowd around the novelist when he had finished speaking. She tucked a stray strand of hair behind her ear and curled the proposal in her hands.

Just then a trio of women climbed the stairs to the platform. Theo recognized one of them as Anna Burkett, president of NAL and moderator for the convention. Tall and striking in a pale peach suit, Anna was the last woman on the platform. She nodded to the others with a tight smile, then walked to the lectern.

"Ladies and gentlemen," Anna Burkett said, tapping on the microphone for attention. When the room quieted, she leaned forward and gave them a smile that did not quite reach her eyes. "I am sincerely sorry to tell you that Theo Russell will not be able to speak to us tonight. He has taken ill and sends his regrets and apologies."

Stunned, Theo took a quick, sharp breath. How was she supposed to return the proposal if Theodore Russell didn't show up?

The audience groaned audibly, and Anna Burkett gave her audience a slightly frayed smile. "Once again, friends, I've been foiled.

I've been trying for months to snag Theo Russell as a speaker, but that man is more elusive than D. B. Cooper."

The crowd laughed, and Anna smiled again and gestured to the women on the platform. "The two women who allowed me to reschedule their presentations so we could hear from the reclusive Mr. Russell have graciously allowed me to reinstate them on tonight's program. Tonight we will hear from the two top editors at Breckinridge Publications, the newest publishing house in New York. I'm sure you're curious about this company and their plans for the future, and the women behind me are eager to tell you about their vision and the kinds of books they hope to produce."

I have to find him, Theo thought as the crowd politely applauded for the two editors. She didn't want to hear about Breckinridge House; she wanted to return the proposal and get to work. As she turned to look discreetly for the nearest exit, a familiar face caught her eye. Elegant in a pencil-slim jade suit, Evelyn Fischer stood at the door, deep in conversation with the columnist George Keeton. She wore an expression of smug satisfaction, and Theo's blood began to pound in her temples when the editor leaned over to whisper in Keeton's ear.

Theo closed her eyes, imagining what Fischer was saying: "Theo Russell was feeling fine at lunch today. And you'll never believe what I discovered! Theo Russell is a woman!"

Hanging her head, Theo bent low and hurried from the ballroom.

✳ ✳ ✳

Back in room 2121, Theo pulled her clothes from the closet, whisked the toiletries from the bathroom counter, and tossed everything into her suitcase. Her luck had held so far, but she didn't want to bump into Evelyn Fischer in the hall or the elevator. Things were fast becoming complicated.

Rather than risk lingering in the lobby, Theo checked out

through the hotel's video system and applied the charges to her credit card. She gave the room one quick glance, inwardly cringing because she'd paid for a night she wasn't going to stay, then picked up her purse, briefcase, and suitcase and stepped out the door.

"It's still OK," Theo whispered to herself as she struggled to carry her luggage to the elevator. "I can write Evelyn Fischer on Monday and send a letter to Theodore Russell in care of his agent. And while I wait to hear from him, I'll have three months to check out the facts, write my book, and get it ready to submit. It will be fine. My book won't be anything like the novel Russell wants to write, and Evelyn Fischer should appreciate my honesty. I really thought she wanted to see me. I can't help it if my name is Theo Russell too."

Still nervous about meeting Evelyn Fischer in the hotel, she bypassed the lobby, took the elevator down to the parking garage, and stood by the driveway, impatiently tapping her foot until the attendant brought her car around. After the young man had placed her suitcase and briefcase in the trunk, she flung a dollar bill in his direction and sped out of the garage. Not until she turned onto her own street half an hour later did her heart slow to a normal pace.

SATURDAY
October 19

Chapter 6

I DON'T know if this is such a good idea," Ann said the next
morning. She looked up from the copy of Russell's proposal
and gave Theo a troubled smile. "If abortions can cause breast
cancer, why isn't anyone talking about it? This guy writes fiction,
Theo. How do you know he didn't invent all this?"

Theo sighed. Ann didn't seem to realize what she held in her hands.
"His material has the ring of truth," Theo answered, leaning across
the kitchen table toward Ann. "The best fiction is based on fact, Ann.
That's why the guy's first book sold about a million copies. Besides,
in the proposal Russell has quoted two real people, a doctor and a
lawyer here in Washington. If I can confirm what they told him—"

"How are you going to do that?" Ann demanded, dropping the
proposal onto the table. "You can't just call them up and say, 'Excuse
me, but I found your name in this outline I stole, and now I want
to write about you.'"

Theo frowned. "I didn't steal it. Evelyn Fischer practically
dumped it in my lap."

"Only because she thought it belonged to you."

"But I'm not using Russell's novel plot. In fact, I could put that
proposal in an envelope right now and start my research from
scratch. But that would take forever, so I'm going to jot down a few
of his facts before I return his proposal. Facts can't be copyrighted;
they belong to everybody."

"Would you want someone to use facts that were part of your hot new idea?"

Theo bit her lip, then shook her head. "I wouldn't care. If I were as successful as Theodore M. Russell, I wouldn't give two hoots if some minor leaguer got ahold of my facts and used them to break in. I'm no threat to him, Ann. And the book I want to write is nothing like his, could never be like his. But this is a hot topic, and if his research is accurate, this could make a difference for millions of women—*and* be my big break."

Ann moved to the coffeepot and poured herself another cup. "I just think you ought to reconsider. You're almost out of money and time, so you're risking everything on someone else's work. Why not write something of your own?"

"I can make this my own, Ann! Janette, my mom, my aunt Jean—all women in my family, all with breast cancer. And Mom and Aunt Jean are dead."

Ann shook her head as she stirred cream into her coffee. "I don't know, Theo. Have you prayed about this?"

"I think maybe God arranged this. Stranger things have happened, you know."

"But do you really think a big company like Howarth House is going to publish a book that's going to come down hard against abortion? Most of those people won't share your pro-life perspective."

"I've thought about that," Theo said, watching the steam rise from her coffee cup. "A lot. But truth is truth, Ann, no matter what its source. If abortion is causing breast cancer, my personal feelings about unborn life are irrelevant. They aren't going to change the truth. And Evelyn Fischer, and probably a host of other editors, are ready to buy the book based on its relevance to women's health issues."

Ann pulled out a chair and sat across the table from her friend. Warming her hands on her mug, she wrinkled her brow in the thoughtful expression Theo knew well. "If you don't sell this idea," she said finally, "we'll all be stuck. In three months I'll need a job; I really should start looking for one now. I've got to think of Bethany—a teenager is expensive, you know."

Theo's blood thickened with guilt. She'd been so busy thinking about her work, her book, that she'd forgotten that others depended on her, too. "I'm sorry, Ann," she whispered. "But I really think I'm *supposed* to do this. I know I am." She ran her hand through her hair. "I've been doing everything I can to break in, and from out of nowhere this happens. It's like God dropped this project into my lap, with a hungry editor attached. Howarth House will buy my book in a minute if it's any good." She softened her voice. "If you want to look for another job, I'll understand. But this is my last chance. I'm going to set Evelyn Fischer straight, return Russell's proposal, and then write a truthful nonfiction book so good it'll blow Evelyn Fischer right out of her chair. But I've only got three months, Ann, and I could really use your help." She glanced toward Stacy, who had emptied the cupboard and now played happily on the floor with Theo's mismatched collection of Tupperware.

Ann arched her brows into twin triangles, then gave Theo a hesitant smile over her coffee cup. "I guess I should be glad for you. I mean, I'm gainfully employed as long as you're writing, right?"

"Right," Theo answered, rising from the table. "As long as I'm writing, neither of us has to look for a regular job."

"And if for some reason things don't go the way you hope, you'll help me write a resume?"

Theo felt the flicker of a smile rise from the edges of her mouth. "I'll write resumes for both of us. But hopefully, it won't come to that."

SUNDAY
October 20

Chapter 7

THEO forced herself to put her work aside on Sunday. She and Ann took Stacy and Bethany to church, then went out to eat after the morning service.

Church and Sunday dinner out were part of their weekly ritual, and Theo found that the hours of worship and fellowship calmed her nerves and her fears. After spending several hours in the library on Saturday, she'd lain awake most of the night and worried that she wouldn't get the book done on time, that it wouldn't be any good, that Evelyn Fischer wouldn't understand her mistake and would hate the female Theo Russell until her dying day. But the pastor's sermon took her mind off the book, the congregational singing lifted her spirits, and the words of her favorite Scripture kept circling through her mind: "My health may fail, and my spirit may grow weak, but God remains the strength of my heart; he is mine forever."

Please, God, be the strength of my heart, she prayed, watching Stacy and Bethany exchange silly secrets at the table. *Help me get this book done, and whatever challenges lie ahead, help me meet them.*

Usually such a prayer brought her a sense of peace, but this time she felt an odd emptiness. She tried to shake off her melancholy, reminding herself that her enthusiasm for the project had not dimmed in the tedious reality of research. She knew that in this effort she would win or lose it all in this three-year gamble. If she sold the book, she would be a writer. If she failed, God would have dramatically shown her that she'd chosen the wrong field. She'd have no choice but to put Stacy in day care and take a temporary job while she waited to see what else God had in mind for her future.

Maybe she should move to Jacksonville, to be near Janette and John. But Theo had grown up in the District, and every childhood and high school memory centered around some marble national monument. Her parents—and Matt—were buried within ten miles of the hospital where she'd been born. Janette was the one who moved away, and John had a wealth of relatives in Florida. If she and Stacy uprooted and left everything to move to Jacksonville, they might be more a burden than a blessing.

"Wake up, Theo," Ann called from across the table. The corners of her eyes crinkled as she smiled. "Your dinner's getting cold, and seven ninety-five is a lot to pay for a plate of cold spaghetti."

"Eat, Mama," Stacy urged, screwing her precious face into an expression of pained concern.

Theo laughed and picked up her fork. "OK, OK," she said, twirling the spaghetti, "I'm eating."

October 21

Chapter 8

O N Monday morning, after surrendering Stacy to Ann's care, Theo typed a letter to Evelyn Fischer in which she apologized for the misunderstanding. Before sealing the envelope, she enclosed Theodore Russell's proposal. She then typed a letter to Mr. Russell in care of his agent, Madison Whitlow, and briefly explained the mix-up. "I have returned your proposal to Ms. Fischer," Theo wrote, "since she was the one who gave it to me. But I trust that you will not disapprove of my pursuing the study of a link between abortion and breast cancer. If you have strenuous objections, please let me know. If not, be assured that I will thank you publicly and privately, if possible, for your help and insights into this matter. The message is an important one that must not remain hidden."

After walking the letters to her mailbox, Theo returned to her computer and finished entering the pertinent information she had gleaned from the library and Russell's manuscript. She saved the file, then telephoned the offices of Dr. Kenneth Holman and Adam Perry, the doctor and lawyer cited in Russell's proposal.

Dr. Holman's receptionist seemed reluctant to make an appointment for an interview, but when Theo said that she wanted to discuss information the doctor had previously presented to the novelist Theo M. Russell, the woman relented and gave Theo an appointment on Tuesday morning. Adam Perry had no free time until Wednesday, but Theo managed to make an appointment for nine-thirty that morning.

She spent the remainder of her afternoon studying the facts presented in Russell's report and comparing them to information she'd gathered in the library. To her amazement, she discovered that the link between breast cancer and abortion had been documented and discussed for years.

"This must be the most underreported story in America today," columnist Mona Charen had written in one article Theo copied from the newspaper. "We are bombarded almost daily by media attention to breast cancer and its risk factors. We hear stories about the possible risks of birth control pills, alcohol, high-voltage wires and diet . . . but there is almost nothing reported about the greater risk faced by women who . . . elect to have first-trimester abortions."[1]

The basic scientific hypothesis supporting the link between breast cancer and abortion seemed logical enough. "A woman's first pregnancy causes hormonal changes that permanently alter the structure of her breasts," Russell wrote in his proposal. "A premature termination of a first pregnancy interrupts this transition process. Abortion . . . leaves millions of breast cells suspended in transitional states. Studies in animals and human tissue cultures indicate that cells in this state face exceptionally high risks of becoming cancerous."[2]

Theo frowned as she thought about that statement's significance. She had first suspected she was pregnant with Stacy when her breasts had swelled and become unusually tender. No woman could deny that changes of the breasts were one of the first and most noticeable symptoms of pregnancy.

She read on. Russell reported that incidents of breast cancer in the United States were rising at an alarming rate among young black women and poor women in certain states. Genetics and diet were doubtless responsible for a large percentage of the increase, but 60 percent of the rise could not be explained by medical researchers. Could the reason for the rate of increase be abortion?

"Key individuals in the abortion industry have been aware of this link since at least 1982," Russell wrote. "Malcolm Pike explicitly identified abortion as a major risk factor in breast cancer in 1981. In his study, abortion of the first pregnancy was associated with an increased risk of approximately 140 percent. An analysis of all reputable studies done to date suggests that women who have abortions before the first live birth initially have a risk 50 percent higher than women who do not."[3]

Theo fumbled in her desk drawer for a yellow marker and highlighted that last sentence. A 50 percent increase in risk could not be ignored.

"While some might blame the increasing rate of breast cancer on the birth control pill," Russell's proposal continued, "the women of the former Soviet Union have had little access to Western drugs, including the pill. The Soviets, however, have one of the world's highest abortion rates. And, in fact, the incidence of breast cancer among Russian, Estonian, and Soviet Georgian women appears to have tripled between 1960 and 1987. Abortion is one of the few influences that has been linked to breast cancer and has been present on both sides of the Iron Curtain."[4]

Another article from Russell's research supported this hypothesis. Seattle researchers for the National Cancer Institute found that abortion could increase a woman's risk of breast cancer by 50 percent for women under age forty-five. But for women under eighteen, the risk was increased by 150 percent. "The highest risk was among those women under eighteen who waited more than eight weeks to get an abortion." This comment came from Janet Daling, an epidemiologist with the Fred Hutchinson Cancer Research Center. She'd reported that the cancer typically appeared ten to fourteen years after the abortion was performed. "I'm concerned this will be used to alarm people," Daling had said.[5]

"Why shouldn't it?" Theo muttered. "If I'd had an abortion, I'd be scared to death by all of this." She skimmed the rest of the article, highlighted other facts, then pulled out a clean sheet of paper and a pen. She'd need a list of pertinent questions to ask Dr. Kenneth Holman, and this research had given her just the background she needed.

TUESDAY
October 22

Chapter 9

TUESDAY morning dawned bright and clear, unusual for a Washington October. Theo dressed in a wool skirt and a long-sleeved blouse, then threw a light blazer over the outfit. The effect was perfect: lightly feminine, softly businesslike.

Dr. Ken Holman had established his Georgetown practice of obstetrics and gynecology in a handsome brick building on Reservoir Road. An elegant sign proclaimed in gold-toned letters that Theo had found The Women's Center, and as she studied the registry of doctors, she noted with surprise that Ken Holman was apparently the only male doctor on staff. If the names were any indication, The Women's Center offered the services of two female general practitioners, a female gynecologist, and a female family therapist.

Theo walked into the plush lobby and signed in to see Dr. Holman. After she had waited ten minutes, a sturdy, stone-faced nurse opened the door and called Theo's name. The nurse greeted her without a smile, glanced curiously at the briefcase in her hand, and motioned down the hall. "Our first stop is the scale, Ms. Russell," she said sharply. "After that, I have to prick your finger."

Theo stopped in midstride. "You don't understand. I'm here to *talk* to the doctor, not to be examined."

The nurse pointed steadfastly toward the scale in the hallway. "I think you'll find it easier to talk about your problem if you let Doctor examine you."

"I'm not here for an examination." Theo brought her briefcase to the nurse's eye level. "I'm here to interview the doctor for a book I'm writing."

The nurse wasn't impressed but raised her chin in a haughty gesture that told Theo she had better things to do than waste Doctor's time with would-be writers. "All right, then, come with me, and I'll show you to Doctor's office. But I don't know when he'll be able to see you. He's busy this morning with *patients*, people who really need to see him."

The nurse turned and began to storm down another hall, and Theo hurried after her. "I'm supposed to be on his schedule this morning," she puffed. "I have an appointment for nine-thirty."

"Sometimes appointments can't be kept. Babies don't wait, and Doctor has to be there when they come," the nurse answered. She paused by an open door and gestured inside with an open palm. "You just take a seat and be patient. Doctor will see you when he can."

Theo was about to ask if the doctor was out delivering a baby, but before the words could leave her mouth, the nurse had spun on her heel and walked away. Theo sighed and stepped through the doorway.

A faded couch sat against the wall by the door; newspapers littered the sofa, and a Styrofoam cup half-filled with milky coffee sat on the end table. Books and folders covered the hulking desk so thickly that Theo couldn't even see the surface; more books lined the walls in Tower of Pisa stacks. A dime-store bulletin board near the door was plastered with snapshots, and as Theo stepped closer she saw that half of the photos were of sweaty, exhausted-looking, smiling women with babies. The other photos were of a tall, blonde, bearded man in surgical garb who held the babies in his broad hands with pride shining from his eyes. Theo guessed that the bearded man was either Dr. Ken Holman or an extremely prolific father.

"I see you've found my mug shots."

Theo whirled around, embarrassed. The bearded man from the

photographs stood in front of her, a smile on his attractive face. The broad hand that had ushered so many babies into the world stretched toward her. "I'm Ken Holman. What can I do for you?"

Theo shook his hand and struggled to find her voice. "I'm Theo Russell," she said, feeling as awkward as a schoolgirl. He had a good handshake, warm and firm. "I know you're busy, Dr. Holman, but if you could spare a few minutes, I'd like to talk to you about breast cancer and abortion."

"Theo Russell?" He released her hand and moved to the well-worn leather chair behind the desk. "I don't suppose you're related to—but it doesn't work that way, does it?" He smiled and gestured toward the sofa as he sank into his chair. "Please. Just push away whatever you need to. Have a seat."

"Thank you." Theo moved a pile of newspapers onto the floor as she sat down, then pulled one of her business cards from her purse. "And no, I'm not related to Theo M. Russell; I've never even met the man. It's just a coincidence that we're both writers. Here's my card."

He took the card she offered, gave it a quick glance, then tossed it onto the mountain of paperwork on his desk. Stretching his long legs out beneath the desk, he tented his hands. "Sorry about the mess, but I don't usually entertain people in my office. I do my best work in hospitals."

"So I see." Theo nodded toward the pictures on the bulletin board, and the doctor grinned and leaned forward, his blue eyes studying her with mild approval.

"Well, if it's any consolation, I'd much rather look at you than the other Theo Russell," Holman said. "I only met him once, and though he's very talented, you're much prettier."

Theo looked down at her hands as her cheeks burned. Good grief, had she forgotten how to handle a simple compliment? She had to get a grip on herself. Everything depended now on her professionalism.

"Thank you, but I'm not here to be flattered, Doctor," she said, sitting up straighter on the sofa. "I need to discuss the information you gave Theo Russell about the link between abortion and breast cancer. I'm planning to do a nonfiction book on the subject. It's disgraceful that more people aren't talking about this."

He frowned slightly. "If you've never met Russell, how'd you hear about my work?"

"I read his proposal," Theo answered, taking care not to reveal too much. "Evelyn Fischer, an editor at Howarth House, showed it to me. I found Russell's proposal fascinating, as did Evelyn. But, as I'm sure you know, there is not a lot of research to substantiate your claims."

Holman's chair squeaked in protest as he leaned back. "Whose side are you on, Ms. Russell? If I help you, will I regret it tomorrow?"

"I didn't realize we were involved in a battle," Theo said, shifting her weight on the couch to see him better. "Why do I have to be on a certain side? I just want to write the truth."

"I'm always amazed at the way truth is manipulated," Holman answered, his gaze no longer friendly. He seemed to be weighing her motivation. "If I tell you the truth, are you willing to report it?"

"Yes."

"Why?"

She had thought to *ask* the questions, not answer them, and she heard herself stammering. "Well . . . because—because breast cancer is an important women's health issue. Everyone's talking about it—"

"And no one's doing anything," Holman finished. He leaned forward again, and she saw the snap of anger in his eyes. "You probably think I'm terrible, Ms. Russell, but I'm tired of having the results of my research invalidated by reporters who call themselves objective."

"So your results are not truly valid." She felt her heart sink.

"It all depends on who evaluates it. You tell me, Ms. Russell. From what you've read, do you feel a link exists between abortion and breast cancer?"

She studied him silently. Ken Holman had an honest face; his wide forehead gave way to guarded eyes that shone with intensity. His features were classically sculpted, his eyes direct and piercing. He really wanted to know what she thought, but something told her that if she didn't agree with him, she'd soon be on her way out the door.

"I'm not a doctor, but I've read enough to think a link could exist," she said, weighing her words carefully. "If you play fair with me, Doctor, I'll tell that truth in my book."

"Then you need to start playing fair now, Ms. Russell. Before we go any further, I want you to know that I refuse to perform elective abortions. I've come to believe that we can't solve the problems people have simply by eliminating people. Now, according to your personal standard of morality, am I a monster for not allowing women to exercise reproductive control over their own bodies?"

Theo listened with a vague sense of unreality. It was the abortion litmus test. Supreme Court justices, presidents, television reporters were even writers judged by their views on abortion? She knew that she agreed with this doctor, but if she hadn't, what right had he to use her position on abortion to judge her ability and honesty as a writer? She wanted to write a straightforward, fact-based book not predicated on her religious faith. She wanted to give readers an honest look at a troubling social issue that could be appreciated by anyone, regardless of theological or political perspectives. Was she naive to believe that it could be done?

"Is that a fair question?" she whispered, frowning.

"Of course it is," Holman answered, his voice heavy with forced casualness. "If I were hiring you as a receptionist, I'd have the right to ask if you liked people. I'm thinking about sharing my work with you, my confidence, so I have the right to ask what you think of me. Am I a monster, Ms. Russell? A misogynist? A caveman? You needn't spare my feelings. I've been called far worse."

"I believe you have the right to refuse to do anything that contradicts your personal belief system," she said, meeting his gaze squarely. "If our country allows women a choice, we can allow no less for our country's doctors."

Holman pressed his lips together in a thin line, obviously less than happy with her answer, then turned his chair sideways and propped his feet on the edge of his desk. "If I told you I performed thirty abortions a week, would you still be willing to feature my opinions in your book?"

She reflected a moment. "No."

"Now we begin to understand each other," he said, nodding. He gave her a more relaxed smile. "What do you want to know?"

Theo shuffled through her papers and pulled out the questions she had prepared. "In my research, I found a Swedish study indicating that the risk of breast cancer *decreased* significantly with abortion history. The study was—" she shuffled through the papers in her lap—"done in 1989 by Britt-Marie, Lindefors-Harris, and a host of others. Can you explain this?"

Holman smiled and tipped his index finger in her direction. "Very good, Ms. Russell. You've done some homework. Not even Theodore turned up that particular study."

"So," Theo pressed, "doesn't this research refute all you've said?"

"Not if you study it carefully." Holman tented his fingers again. "In Sweden, unlike America, most women who get legal abortions have already had one or more children, and thus most women enjoy the lower risk of breast cancer associated with the protective effect of the first full pregnancy. The Swedish study lumps women who have already had a child in with women who aborted their first pregnancy. The researchers then compared the combined results to the total population rather than to women who have not had abortions."

"What protective effect? I don't understand."

"A woman's first full pregnancy causes hormonal changes that permanently alter the structure of her breasts. The completed process greatly reduces the risk of breast cancer. During a full pregnancy, the breast cells differentiate, mature, and specialize. Once cells have become specialized, they are very unlikely to turn cancerous."

"And that's why women who give birth at a young age have a lower risk of breast cancer?"

"Right. Studies have found that women who give birth before age eighteen have about one-third the risk of women who have their first child after age thirty-five." Holman's expression changed as he continued, "Ironic, don't you think? The entire medical community is warning women about the statistical link between high-fat diets and breast cancer, but they ignore the fact that a woman who has had an abortion is far more likely to develop breast cancer than a woman who eats a diet high in fat. And I have the scientific support to prove it."

Theo paused, thinking. "How did you come to give this information to Theo Russell?"

"I met him at a medical convention. He was gathering material for his book on suicide. I was desperate to get my research published somewhere, and he took my research notes."

"And the lawyer Russell mentions . . . Adam Perry. Was he at the medical convention, too?"

"No, Adam and I play golf at the same club. My wife, you see, had an abortion in her twenties and developed breast cancer ten years later. A classic case. Adam Perry has filed a lawsuit on her behalf."

"She's suing a doctor?"

"No, we're suing the abortion clinic where Linda's abortion was performed. I thought Adam Perry might be able to help Russell, so I arranged for Russell to meet him."

"How can your wife possibly expect to win her case? With so little evidence to support your claims—" She broke off as something dark flitted behind the doctor's blue eyes.

"She can't win, Ms. Russell. She died six years ago. I'm suing on her behalf, and I don't really care about the monetary awards. The real winners, if Adam can pull this off, will be the young women who have swallowed the lie that abortion is simple, painless, and harmless. I want publicity. I want to get the word out. Abortion hurts women. Abortion involves a real death, and some women cannot escape the moral misgivings that are part of the parcel. I've met strong, pro-choice women who tearfully confess that they light a candle every year on the birthday of the baby they never had. And aside from the emotional dangers, women should consider the significant physiological risks. Young women who abort their first pregnancy are playing Russian roulette with their bodies. They have a one-in-six chance of later developing breast cancer. But, like Linda, they may find the cancer too late."

Theo felt her face burning again. How could she ever be an effective interviewer if she kept stumbling onto topics that alienated her subjects? "I'm sorry," she stammered. "Truly sorry if I was tactless. But I understand, truly I do—"

"I don't know if you can," Holman said, standing up behind his desk. He thrust his hands into the pockets of his lab coat. "And I'm sorry, but I have patients waiting. If I can be of any further help, please don't hesitate to call. I'll give you whatever medical information you need, and I'm sure Adam Perry will be happy to help with whatever legal issues you'd like to discuss."

Theo stood, tucked her slim briefcase under her arm, then offered her hand to the doctor. "I know what it's like to lose someone you love," she said, keeping her voice low as he reluctantly shook her hand again. "And I never intended to pry into your personal affairs."

She didn't wait for his reply but turned and walked away.

WEDNESDAY
October 23

Chapter 10

IT usually took Theo forty minutes to drive from her home to
the northern part of the District, but Wednesday-morning
traffic snarled on her way to Adam Perry's office, and she
arrived at his towering complex half an hour late. She was breathless by the time she stepped off the elevator into the suite of offices
reserved for Perry, Johnson, Horwitz, and Malter, and she had to
steady her breathing before she could give her name to the receptionist in the sumptuous lobby.

"I'm sorry, but you have missed your appointment," the silver-
haired woman at the desk said, a faint note of reproach in her nasal
voice. "Mr. Perry is with another client. If the matter is urgent, I
could refer you to one of Mr. Perry's associates."

"I'd like to wait," Theo said, smoothing her skirt. "It's important
that I see Mr. Perry today."

The receptionist murmured noncommittally, "I'll see what I can
do," then turned away to answer the buzzing of a telephone. Alone
in the lobby with the woman, Theo took a seat on the long leather
sofa. She had spent the rest of the previous afternoon and most of
the night reviewing her notes and impressions from her visit to Dr.
Holman's office, and she was eager to question Adam Perry about
the legal ramifications of a link between abortion and breast cancer.

Whenever her mind tired of wrestling with names, facts, and
figures, the image of handsome Dr. Holman rose in her mind.

Perhaps, she reasoned, thoughts of him stayed with her because she regretted leaving his office on such a sour note. She had the feeling she'd hurt him with her blunt questioning, but weren't journalists supposed to pursue the story at all costs?

Come on, Theo, toughen up! she chided herself. *How are you ever going ask the tough questions if you melt into a pool of pity every time you see a handsome man with suffering in his eyes?*

To discipline her thoughts, she reached for a folded *Washington Post* lying on the coffee table. She had been so engrossed in her research that she hadn't even picked up her own paper in two days. She scanned the front page for items of interest, then flipped through the style section to read "Dear Abby" and "Ann Landers." Occasionally she glanced toward the receptionist, but the woman seemed oblivious to everything but the telephone and the silent screen of her word processor. She didn't meet Theo's eye once in twenty minutes.

After half an hour, Theo tossed the front and style sections of the *Post* onto the coffee table and began to read the first page of the metro section. A headline caught her eye:

Novelist Theo M. Russell Missing Four Days

by Pamela Lansky

WASHINGTON—Theodore Marshall Russell, author of the best-selling novel *Out of the Darkness, Into the Light,* apparently disappeared from his hotel room at the Washington Hilton Tower. He was last seen on Friday evening when he purchased a disposable razor in the hotel gift shop. The hotel manager reported Tuesday that his room had not been slept in for several days.

District police are investigating the disappearance and report that any speculation as to the author's whereabouts would be "premature." But Evelyn Fischer, an editor with

Howarth House in New York, says she was first alarmed when a woman calling herself Theodora Russell showed up in Russell's stead for a luncheon appointment on Friday. The woman led Fischer to believe she was the acclaimed novelist and left with a proposal and outline for the author's novel in progress.

"She was as calm and cool as anyone I've ever met," Fischer said Tuesday from her office in New York. "In twenty years of publishing, I've never run across anything like this." Fischer cooperated with the New York Police Department to produce a composite sketch of the mysterious woman.

With terrible suddenness Theo realized that the wide-eyed, black-and-white sketch in the corner of the front page was a startlingly accurate portrait—of herself.

What? She took a wincing little breath. She had explained everything in the letter to Evelyn Fischer—but she had mailed the letter on Monday. The package probably wouldn't arrive in New York until Thursday or Friday.

She stared at the newspaper, too stunned to move, until the buzzing of the receptionist's telephone brought her back to reality. Her heart pounding, she stuffed the newspaper under her arm and walked briskly to the elevator.

Chapter 11

D R. Ken Holman looked at his nurse and gently shook his head as he closed the door of the examining room behind him. Inside, a frightened fifteen-year-old girl lay in tears on the table. She had begun to cry softly when he told her that her venereal warts were caused by the HPV virus that she had been exposed to through sexual activity.

"Is that like VD?" she asked. "What's my mother going to say? Everyone will think I'm a slut."

"Any sexually active young person risks encountering HPV, herpes, chlamydia, and AIDS," he told her. "Anyone."

"Why didn't anyone ever tell me about this?" the girl whispered. Tears rolled from her eyes and dampened the tissue paper on the examining table. "They talk about pregnancy, even AIDS, but no one ever talks about this."

"There are lots of things no one ever talks about," he answered. "And you and I are going to have a long talk later. But now you can step behind the screen and get dressed. My nurse will ask a few questions, and we'll arrange to have those growths removed."

The nurse turned to her patient, and her compassionate "There now, you'll be all right" brought fresh sobs from the frightened girl. Ken pressed his lips together and tried to subdue the anger that threatened to wash over him. Another child's innocence had disappeared, but this girl was lucky. Yesterday, just after his interview with the writer, he had treated a sixteen-year-old for a roaring gonorrheal infection. He'd had to tell her that the infection would probably leave her sterile.

He pulled his microcassette recorder from his pocket and dictated notes to be transcribed later and put on the fifteen-year-old's chart. When he finished, he placed her chart and the tape on his nurse's desk and paused for a moment in the quiet of his office.

The faded photograph of his wife smiled at him from across the desk. Linda would have handled the fifteen-year-old better than he did. She had been fiercely compassionate in her practice, bearing each patient's burdens as her own during the day and shedding them, albeit regretfully, during the short hours she shared with her husband at home. Even through the five years she battled breast cancer, she had kept up an unusually heavy workload, finally surrendering it only when the cancer had spread to her bones. Walking, even standing, became unbearable.

Even though bedridden, Linda had perused the charts of Ken's patients, never failing to offer her insights. In 1989, two weeks before she lapsed into the coma from which she would not awaken, she gave him a folder containing copies of studies linking breast cancer and abortion. Clipped together in the file were copies of substantiating reports she'd gathered from her own patients.

With great difficulty, she told him she had undergone an abortion fifteen years earlier. "I was young, foolish, and proud of my independence," she said, her voice quavering in her weakness. "I never told you because it was so far in the past I didn't think it mattered. But what we do as kids can haunt us forever. Ken, you've got to tell them."

For nearly six years he had continued Linda's study and searched for an abortion–breast cancer link among his own patients. In time he found it but kept silent because he feared being dismissed by his colleagues and described by his rivals as a mouthpiece for the right wing. And yet there was another, deeper reason for his silence—

speaking about breast cancer brought back painful memories of Linda's mastectomy, radiation treatments, and chemotherapy. The lovely woman he had fallen in love with had grown dearer to him with every passing day, and after her death, nothing seemed to empty the secret pool of sorrow within him.

Then, ten months ago, the biopsy of a lump and lymph nodes taken from one of his patients—a thirty-five-year-old mother of four—revealed an invasive malignant cancer. Elisa Jones, a vibrant redhead with a particular zest for living, ate a healthy low-fat diet, avoided caffeine, had no family history of cancer, no exposure to radiation, no history of miscarriage, and would have eaten raw grass before using an artificial sweetener in her tea. The only risk factor he found was a small notation the nurse had made in her chart: an elective abortion at age fifteen. Ken had wanted to tell Elisa that her cancer was probably related to the abortion, but what good would it do? So he hadn't told Elisa about his suspicions but decided to speak out for the sake of other women.

And so six months ago he had given a stack of updated information to Theo Russell, the skeletal man who'd come out of nowhere at the national convention and quietly asked what was new on the medical horizon. Like a recurring nightmare, the same name had appeared on his schedule yesterday, but a different Theo Russell had appeared to ask the same questions.

For better or worse, he was playing his hand with whoever would join the game. And though Holman knew the odds favored the famous novelist, some deep instinct told him to bet on Theodora Russell.

* * *

A few miles away from Ken Holman's medical offices, in the Fairmount Heights section of the District, pedestrians walked the sidewalks, clutching their coats with cold-numbed hands and leaning forward against the wind. Cars maneuvered torturously through the ever-present Washington construction. The houses and sidewalks wore the gray look of a dying autumn afternoon.

One house, a dilapidated brownstone, seemed to squint into the street traffic. Inside, while dried-up wallpaper curled itself from the yellowed plaster, Brennan Connor eased his lean frame into a folding beach chair, and Antonio Verde snorted humorlessly at a sitcom on the portable black-and-white television set. Across the room, Theo M. Russell lay on a bare bed in a dark corner of what had once been a living room. His hands were tied to the narrow wooden posts of the bed frame, his legs drawn up to his chest, his head turned to the side, his eyes closed. Both of the novelist's forearms were scarred and bruised under his wrinkled shirtsleeves.

"Sure, and didn't I tell you our guest would be waking up?" Brennan said, squinting down at the writer as he chomped his cigar. "Do you suppose he's hungry?"

"Nah. Fed 'im yesterday," Antonio grunted, not taking his eyes from the television. "Threw it up. Snacks and smack don't mix."

"Well, watch him. We don't want him coming around enough to start yelling," Brennan said, standing from his chair. He walked over to the bed and hovered over the thin man on the sweat-stained mattress. As if by command, the pale prisoner's eyelids fluttered and opened.

"Hello, laddie." Brennan grinned down at the man. "Hungry, are you?"

The man groaned and closed his eyes. With an effort, he licked his cracked lips. "Water."

"Tony, bring our friend here that bottle."

Antonio grunted and tossed Brennan a squeeze bottle. Brennan nodded in appreciation and put the bottle to his captive's lips, squeezing the bottle until a stream of water jetted forth and dribbled down the novelist's chin.

The weak man ran his swollen tongue over his lips and closed his eyes. He seemed to rest a moment, then lifted his eyelids again and strained gently at the rags holding his wrists. "Could you," he muttered as his body began to tremble, "could you release my hands? I can't go anywhere; I haven't the strength."

"Ah, no, I couldn't be doing that," Brennan said, shaking his head. "You'd be surprised what strength a man has when he needs a fix. But I've got something else for you. Just what the good doctor ordered."

The man on the bed did not protest but closed his eyes in resignation as Brennan moved to the filthy counter where a candle burned and a syringe waited.

* * *

Dr. Griffith Dunlap defiantly pushed the official envelope to the far corner of his desk. Lawsuits were nothing but time-stealing nuisances, like colds, allergies, and ingrown toenails. Though the suit couldn't hurt Dunlap, it would have to be dealt with quietly, decisively, and *legally.* They would bury this annoyance once and for all so no similar suits would rise in the future.

Dunlap rolled his chair away from his desk. *That's why we hired that gold-plated team of know-it-all lawyers. Every doctor is nothing but malpractice bait, no matter what his specialty.*

Standing, he removed his lab coat and tossed it over the back of his chair. In quick, practiced movements, he removed his tie, shirt, and pants, then slipped into the clean surgical scrubs neatly stacked inside a cabinet in his office. He had already finished his morning hospital rounds, and the real work of his Family Services Clinic was about to begin.

He left his office and went to the prep room. After he scrubbed, a surgical nurse snapped latex gloves on his hands and tied his mask about his head. His head nurse read from his first patient's chart. "Tiffany Smith," she said. "Sixteen years old, second pregnancy, negative for AIDS, otherwise healthy. Vitals strong."

"How many weeks?"

"Ten."

Moving quickly into the small room where he did most of his work, Dunlap glanced at the drowsy eyes of the young girl on the table. He winked at her, knowing she couldn't see his smile behind his mask.

"Hello, Tiffany," he said, turning his attention to the surgical instruments on the tray to his left. "Not a thing to worry about, sweetheart. We'll have you out of here in five minutes."

He sat on the stool at the end of the table and motioned for his nurse to adjust the light. "You're going to feel a pinch and a cramp," he told the girl. "The pinch is the anesthesia."

There was no sound but the tinkle of stainless steel instruments, but the girl's legs trembled slightly in the stirrups beside him. He stood and looked past the drape that blocked her view of him. Her eyes were closed, her face emptied of expression and locked. A tear rolled from the corner of her eye and into the mass of golden hair that spilled over the table like a halo.

"Are you in pain?"

"No," she whispered, shaking her head slightly.

"Good. Now you're going to hear the machine."

A low rumble filled the room as the suction machine came on; then it gurgled as the products of conception were vacuumed from the uterus and whisked down a tube that snaked through a hole in the wall. The machine rumbled for less than a minute, then was switched off.

"All done." Dr. Griffith Dunlap nodded to his nurse, who turned off the bright light. He smiled at the young girl. "Nothing to it, was there?"

※ ※ ※

Evelyn Fischer sank into her office chair, consulted her watch, then tapped Madison Whitlow's number into the phone for the tenth time that morning. When the agent's boyish voice came on the line,

Evelyn allowed herself the luxury of fully venting her pent-up anger and indignation.

"Evelyn Fischer here, Madison. If this is some sort of publicity gimmick, I'll never negotiate with you again."

"What are you talking about, Evelyn?" The agent seemed genuinely surprised. "Is there some problem?"

"I'm talking about Theo Russell. You'll never know how humiliated I was this weekend. After talking to that impostor, offering a contract, and swallowing outrageous lies, I discovered that your mysterious Theo Russell is a man! Are you two trying to make fools out of the entire publishing industry, or do you have something personal against me?"

"Evelyn," he soothed, crooning her name like a song. "Back up. Of course Theo Russell's a man. Who said he wasn't?"

"The impostor," she said, biting back an oath. "Don't tell me you don't know about it. At the NAL convention I made an appointment with your author. A *woman* showed up. She said she was Theo Russell and gave me some line about being named after an uncle."

The agent chuckled. "This is great. Hey, I didn't even know Theo was going to the NAL convention. What happened next?"

Evelyn gritted her teeth. "I told her I wanted to buy *The Savage Breast*. She kept giving me the runaround; she didn't even want to talk about the money—"

"Hold on a minute," Madison interrupted, his voice filled with laughter. "That's no client of mine. We always want money."

"It's not funny, Madison."

"Sorry." He paused a moment, and when he spoke again, his voice was properly serious. "I'm sorry someone embarrassed you, Evelyn, but truthfully, I haven't heard from Russ in a week. I don't even think he was at the NAL convention."

"He was there. He was supposed to speak Friday night but backed out at the last minute. He called Anna Burkett and told her he was ill."

"Well, you know how temperamental authors can be. Believe me, Russ is the most temperamental and unpredictable author alive."

"Who was the woman?"

"I have no idea. Unless—was she pretty?"

Evelyn sniffed. "I suppose so."

Madison laughed. "Must have been one of Russ's women. He sent her to do his dirty work as a terrific joke on you."

"It wasn't funny. Very unprofessional, if you ask me."

"Russell isn't the typical professional. He's still new to the business; he still does his own thing his own way. But what talent! I hope you're still interested in the book."

"I don't know, Madison. If this is his idea of a joke—why, I was at the police station for three hours yesterday with a sketch artist and a cop from D.C. The police think that woman might have something to do with Russell's disappearance."

"She probably does. He probably met her at the convention and hasn't come up for air."

Evelyn drummed her nails across her desk. She hated looking foolish, but if Madison was right, she'd been had. And as much as she might like to do so, she couldn't just write Russell off. His proposal was a good one, probably worth twice what she had offered.

"Evelyn? Are you still there? I hope this hasn't caused a permanent rift between us. Howarth House could do great things with a Theo Russell title."

She injected just the right amount of disdain into her voice. "I felt used, Madison. I even told George Keeton that Theo Russell was really a woman. And when your author turned up missing, the police came to me, and I spent ten minutes trying to convince *them* your client was a woman." She felt her temper rise again. "I don't enjoy being made to look foolish."

"You want me to talk to Russ about this? I'll read him the riot act if it will make you feel better."

"We're not kids, Madison. You've got to get this guy to grow up!

His little games aren't funny. Anna Burkett called the police when she checked his room and found that he hadn't slept in his bed on Saturday night."

"The hotel gave her his room number?"

"She said she'd booked the room for him. She left him alone on Saturday, thinking he was sick, but on Saturday night she checked on him. When he didn't answer her knock, she demanded that a maid open the door. When she realized he hadn't slept in the room, she called the police."

"Ooh, bad move. Bad publicity. Why'd she do that?"

"She was frantic. Apparently he'd sounded pretty bad when he called her on Friday night to cancel his speech, and she thought it was serious. The police didn't do anything but look around. The hotel manager wanted to box up all of Russell's things and clear the room out, but Anna stormed around and convinced the police to seal the room off until somebody hears from Russell."

"And I'm sure we'll hear from him soon. He likes his privacy, and the convention probably made him feel a little claustrophobic. I'm sure he just took off to find some space."

"Well, now I really feel like an idiot. I've wasted three days in Washington, spent half a day in the police station, and made a fool of myself in front of the literary world and one of Russell's bimbos. Thank him for me when you talk to him, OK, Madison?"

Madison laughed. "I will, and I'll give him a good scolding. You're a tough negotiator, Evelyn, and Russ probably didn't want to tangle with you. So let me do the talking from now on, OK?"

"I still want the book." She felt better after admitting it. "He may be a total jerk, but his writing is brilliant. We're prepared to make a serious offer if you're prepared to receive it."

There was silence on the line for a moment. "Uh, that's great, Evelyn, but Russ tells me he's working on something better. Something even more stellar, something guaranteed to pull the regulars off the best-seller lists."

"What about *The Savage Breast?*"

"He's changed his mind."

"Changed his mind?" Disappointment and frustration brought a hard frown to her face.

"Yeah. He doesn't want to write the book. Some other idea has come along—"

"It must be a good one," Evelyn said, tapping the eraser end of her pencil on her desk. She paused a moment, thinking. "OK, maybe that's why your demented genius sent the woman to meet me. I did think it strange that the woman didn't want money or mention a contract. I thought you wanted to involve me in a bidding war."

"Nothing of the sort, Evelyn. If you don't get *The Savage Breast,* nobody gets it."

"Well, Madison, I'm not all that impressed by your client or his games."

"But you *are* partial to success, and that's one thing Theo Russell will give you," Madison answered. "I promise, Evelyn. Whenever our missing author shows up here with his next manuscript, you get first peek. That's an ironclad guarantee from me."

Slightly mollified, Evelyn smiled and said good-bye.

✳ ✳ ✳

Not willing to give last rites to a story until it had been dead for three days, Pamela Lansky played one of her famous hunches and drove to the Hilton Tower to check out the last known whereabouts of the reclusive novelist. After nosing around for an hour with no luck, she spied Detective Howard Datsko in the lobby of the hotel. Wearing a ten-year-old suit and his signature pout, Datsko was sitting on a couch, scrawling something in his pocket-size notepad. "Hey, Datsko," she yelled, ignoring the startled looks from well-heeled guests lounging in the hotel lobby. "What's the latest on the missing author?"

She could almost hear him groan when his eyes met hers. Instinctively on guard, like a pit bull in the ring, Datsko flipped the cover of his notepad closed, an action Pamela found rich with meaning. He didn't intend to share his information with her unless she worked for it. She met his stubborn gaze with her own. She hadn't earned a top spot at the *Post* on free handouts from the police department.

The detective grinned at her from behind his glasses. "Lansky, you're a little late on this one, aren't you?" he quipped, slipping the notebook into the pocket of his overcoat. "I thought the *Post* had finished with this story."

"As long as you're here, I'm here," Pamela returned, lifting her chin. "We know the author's missing, and we've printed that sketch the New York editor gave your man. Anyone in the hotel recognize the woman?"

Datsko shook his head. "The hotel was full of literary types, and apparently they all look alike. Last week this place was a sea of black turtlenecks and tweed sport coats."

"What about the novelist's room?"

"Nothing's been touched, and the hotel manager's mad as a beaver with a toothache about that. It's a suite, and they're losing big bucks while it sits empty. But it looks like the missing person walked out of it and fully intended to come back. Sport coat on the bed, melted ice in the ice bucket. The notes for a speech he was to make were out on the table."

Pamela frowned. This was coming too easily. What was he hiding?

"Can I see the room?"

Datsko's faded blue eyes narrowed to slits. "Not unless you've joined the police force lately. The room is off limits for at least a week."

"Why'd it take the hotel so long to call the police?"

Datsko shrugged his hefty shoulders. "They didn't call; some lady named Anna Burkett did."

"The president of the National Authors League?"

"Yeah. She freaked out when she couldn't find the guy in his room, and she called in a missing persons report. We waited twenty-four hours, then came down to check things out."

"Why'd you wait?"

"Required to. The guy's an adult, and I'm still not convinced he's not holed up in a hotel room with some woman."

Pamela looked around the wide lobby. "The guy was famous, Datsko. Any idea who'd want to kidnap him?"

"Kidnap a novelist? Some crazed fan, maybe? But this ain't exactly the setting for *Misery*. Besides, we've found no ransom note, gotten no phone calls."

Pamela bit her lip. "Any John Does turn up in the Potomac?"

"Not this weekend." Datsko's voice was dry. "It's been a slow season for jumpers down on the waterfront."

She ignored his black humor. "Anything else you can tell me?"

"I shouldn't have told you this much," Datsko growled, but his eyes were bright behind his glasses. "But what can I say? I'm a pushover for blondes. So I'll tell you this: We knew the guy was Theo Russell because his name's all over his luggage and among his personal effects. But the room was registered to Russ Burkett. We thought for a moment that he and this Anna Burkett woman had something going on, but it turns out that she's never actually seen the man in the flesh. They've talked on the phone a few times, that's all."

Pamela looked the detective straight in the eye. "It's not unusual for famous people to check in under fake names, is it? He wanted to avoid the autograph hounds."

"Did he?" Datsko asked. He lowered his voice. "Then why was another room registered to Theo Russell and also vacated suddenly on Friday night?"

"What?" Pamela stepped closer, certain she had misunderstood.

"You heard me," Datsko said, grinning at her, and suddenly Pamela knew why he'd been so free with his information. Datsko the great detective had run into a puzzle—and he was hoping she could solve it. Apparently there was still a lot of life in the Theo Russell story.

"Another room, you say?" she asked, looking toward the registration desk. "Which one?"

Chapter 12

THEO, is that you? How'd things go with the lawyer?"
Theo heard Ann's cheery greeting through a vague sense of unreality. She leaned against the front door and let her purse fall to the floor. The purloined *Post* fluttered from beneath her arm and draped itself across her handbag.

Ann appeared in the kitchen doorway. "Good grief, girl, you look as if you've seen a ghost!" she said, her eyes widening. "What happened? Were you in a wreck?"

"I'm a wanted woman," Theo murmured, stiffly bending to pick up the newspaper and her purse. She walked toward the kitchen, her head still swimming.

Ann gave her a lopsided smile. "That's not very funny."

"I'm not joking."

Ann stepped back to let her pass, and Stacy looked up from where she sat at the kitchen table with a flour-filled mixing bowl in front of her. She gave Theo a wide smile, then continued stirring the flour with a wooden spoon. "Look, Mama," she said.

"That's great, sweetheart." Theo ran her hand through Stacy's golden hair, then glanced at Ann. "Have you read today's paper?"

Ann shook her head and gestured with floured hands toward the folded newspaper on the kitchen table. "Stacy and I were mixing up a batch of cookies. I was going to take a look at the paper while they were baking."

Theo pulled the metro section from beneath her arm and spread it on the table. "There," she said, pointing to the article by Pamela Lansky.

A look of disbelief crossed Ann's face as she looked at the police sketch. "That's you, Theo."

"Read the article."

Ann yanked a chair from beneath the table and sat down, concentrating on the paper in her hands. Relief washed over Theo like an ocean wave as she pulled out a chair and sat next to Stacy. Ann would know how to handle things. Ann's picture hadn't appeared in four million newspapers that morning. She, at least, could think clearly.

"This article implies that you had something to do with this guy's disappearance," she finally said, looking up. "You've got to call the police and tell them what happened."

"But I don't know anything about what happened to him," Theo protested, her eyes watering. Stacy looked up, startled at the sound of fear in her mother's voice, and Theo forced herself to smile at her daughter. "It's all right, sweetie. What kind of cookies are we baking?"

"Chips," Stacy answered, her pudgy fingers wiping a trail of flour across her nose as she rubbed it.

"Chocolate chip," Theo replied automatically. "My favorite."

"Theo, you've got to do something," Ann said, wiping her flour-encrusted hands on a dish towel. "Just call the Washington police and tell them you don't know anything. Then you'll be done with it and out of it. No more sketches of your face on the front page."

"But Evelyn Fischer's saying I deliberately stole his proposal," Theo protested. "What if the police ask about that? What can I say?"

"Tell them the truth," Ann said firmly.

"What if they don't believe me? It's my word against Evelyn Fischer's, and she's a big-time editor. I'm nobody, just a wanna-be writer." She propped her elbow on the table and rested her head on her fist. "I've been thinking. I used my own name and address when

I checked into that hotel. And I paid for everything with a credit card. The police could trace me in a minute if they wanted to, couldn't they? I called home several times, too. They keep a record of things like that. If they really wanted to talk to me, they'd be on my doorstep right now."

"OK, maybe. But if the police don't want to talk to you, why is your picture in the paper?"

"Because I'm cute?" Theo tried to smile, then decided it was a bad idea. "I don't know, Ann; maybe somebody's on a wild goose chase. But this thing has rattled me. I've never even had a traffic ticket in my entire life, and when I opened the paper and saw that sketch . . . well, it threw me completely. I ran out of Adam Perry's office like a scared rabbit. He's met Theodore Russell, you see. If he read the paper and thinks that I'm trying to steal Theodore Russell's work or something . . ."

"What about the doctor you saw yesterday?" Ann asked quietly. "Are you going to call him and explain everything? He's probably read the paper, too."

Theo paused while the image of Dr. Ken Holman flitted across her mind. He had been cautious and careful, but he had believed her. Why wouldn't he? She hadn't lied to him.

"I didn't tell him anything but the truth," she finally answered. "And if he sees the article and wants to call me, he can. But I can't be worrying about all this stuff, Ann. I've got to get started on my book. If I can get an outline and a few sample chapters together within three months, I can get a contract. We can live on the Visa card until the book advance comes through."

"You're talking crazy, Theo. First, I wouldn't even *touch* that guy's proposal after all this. And second, if you're still dead set on writing that book, you should clear the waters you've helped to muddy. If this guy is really in some kind of trouble, you could save the police some time by calling them. You don't want them to get sidetracked from finding him because they're trying to check you out, do you?"

Pressing her palm to her forehead, Theo stood stiffly to her feet. "OK," she said, making her way toward the extra bedroom that she used as an office. "I'll call. Right now. So I can get out of this and get on with my life."

✳ ✳ ✳

The phone buzzed on Howard Datsko's desk. "Datsko," he said, picking it up. He stuffed a corner of his salami sandwich into his mouth while he waited for a response.

"Hello, I'd like to speak to someone about Theo Russell, the novelist who's missing." The woman spoke in the low voice reserved for dreaded things, and Datsko's inner antennae centered on the sound.

"Speak." Howard paused to swallow. "Go ahead, lady. I'm listening."

"I read the article about the woman who met Evelyn Fischer. Well, I think I'm the woman."

"You *think* you are?"

"I know I am. But I didn't lie to Ms. Fischer. My name really is Theo Russell, and I thought she wanted to see me. I'm a writer, too, you see, and Howarth House has one of my proposals. But I don't know anything about the guy who's missing. I've never even met him."

Datsko switched the receiver from his right ear to his left, then reached for a pencil on his desk. "So you were at the hotel under your own name?"

"Right. I wasn't pretending to be the novelist. I really do have the same name. Except I'm Theodora, not Theodore."

"Were you on the twenty-first floor?" He searched his notes. Theo Russell had been assigned room 2121; the novelist had been in 3018 under the name of Russ Burkett.

"I think so."

"Why'd you take the guy's outline?"

94

"His proposal."

"Whatever. This Fischer woman thinks you were out to deliberately steal Russell's work."

"No, I wasn't. By the time I realized she thought I was the famous Theo Russell, I'd seen the proposal. I kept trying to explain that I wasn't who she thought I was, and I tried to give the proposal back. But someone beeped her, and she left in a hurry."

"Are you trying to tell me," Datsko drawled, "that you couldn't say, 'Hey, lady, you've got the wrong writer'?"

The woman on the phone sighed. "Have you ever had a conversation with Ms. Fischer? It's hard to get a word in edgewise."

Datsko grinned. Yeah, this lady had talked to Ms. Fischer, all right. "OK, so you got stuck with the writer's proposal. So what'd you do with it?"

"I mailed it back to Ms. Fischer on Monday. She should have it by Thursday or Friday, whenever snail mail gets it there. I'll admit that I read Russell's paper—and I want to write about the same topic—but I could never steal his outline. If I had published a novel like his, he could have sued me for plagiarism or copyright infringement. I'm only interested in his facts, and you can't copyright facts."

"Hey, lady, I'm not trying to judge you." Datsko wrote *seems honest* on his notepad. "So you never met the guy, and you don't know where he is."

"Right. Since my picture's in the paper, I figured I should call you."

The woman ended this last statement with a sigh of relief, and Datsko drew a question mark and thumped the page with his pencil. "Sorry about the picture, lady. That was the reporter's idea, not mine. We're just trying to beat the bushes, see what might crawl out. OK. Will you give me your address and phone number in case we have other questions?"

"Is that necessary?" Her voice was hesitant. "I don't know anything else."

"It might be helpful."

"OK. I live at 2035 Pineview Lane in the Adams Morgan area. The number here is 202-555-3947."

"Thanks." He heard the phone click before he had even finished saying the word.

* * *

Her work went slowly that afternoon. A medical research database she accessed on her computer yielded some information on abortion and breast cancer, but Theo had to read through summaries of fifty-eight articles to cull out the few that were pertinent to her work. She read for three hours, the printed articles under her left hand and a medical dictionary under her right.

A database comprised of newspaper articles brought her more usable material. One article featured the compassionate work of Dr. Griffith Dunlap, a gynecologist in Washington, D.C., who offered low- or no-cost abortions for inner-city women who could not otherwise afford them.

"These women should not be denied the opportunities afforded wealthier women in this country," the doctor was quoted in the *Post.* "Should a woman who struggles to feed three children be forced to feed four? No. I feel it's my duty to do what I can to help these women better their lives. Society's attitude seems to be, 'You've had your pleasure, now pay the price.' Which is more immoral, granting an abortion or forcing young girls, some of whom are as young as twelve or thirteen, to assume the responsibility of a baby? In this pampered nation where Barbie dolls get more love and attention than human beings, it's hard for me to take the antiabortion debate seriously."

Dunlap went on to say that safe abortions were a medical necessity in this country and that it was ultimately healthier for a woman to have an abortion than to bear a child. But the doctor said absolutely nothing about breast cancer.

* * *

"Ann, I'm begging. *Please* do this for me." Theo leaned against the kitchen counter while Ann rolled out an industrial-size pizza crust. Bethany was at the kitchen table, an open geometry book in front of her, and Stacy sat in her little rocking chair, a worn baby doll in her arms. Behind Ann, Theo heard the preheated oven begin to beep on a perfect B-flat.

"No way." Ann shook her head as she worked the dough with her fingers. "I'll do anything I can to help you, Theo, but I'm not the private eye type. You want to play investigative reporter, you go right ahead."

Theo tried to ignore the electronic beeping. "He knows my name, Ann! The secretary will recognize me! I can't go back to Adam Perry's office, but I've got to have these facts verified."

"You should have thought of that before you shot out of that place." Ann frowned and looked over her shoulder at Bethany. "Isn't anybody going to shut off that oven? My hands are covered in flour."

"I'll do it if you'll let me go to the lawyer's office," Bethany said, grinning. "It will get me out of school early tomorrow."

Ann ignored her while Theo walked over to the oven and pressed the timer switch. "That pitch drives me nuts! Matt's alarm clock was a B-flat. Woke me up every morning."

"You know, there are lots of folks who'd give their eyeteeth to have your perfect pitch," Ann remarked, jamming a can of pizza sauce under the electric can opener. "Just like there are lots of people who'd be happy to never again set foot in a lawyer's office. I'm one of them."

"*Please*, Ann." Theo paused. "It's only this one time, I promise. And you don't have to lie. Just ask the questions I'll give you and say you're gathering the information for a friend. Adam Perry's answers will be simple, and you can just drive home and tell me what he said."

"Why can't you do this on the phone?" Ann asked, her irritation evident in the way she slapped sauce on the pizza crust.

"He'll ask too many questions if I tell him my name, and I don't want to get into the Theo Russell thing. I'll stay home with Stacy while you swing by his office. You'll be home before you know it. Please, Ann, will you do just this one thing for me?"

Ann lifted her eyebrows. "Is this guy single? Good looking?"

Theo grinned. "Could be."

"If you get me an appointment, I'll go," Ann answered, reaching for the can of Parmesan cheese on the counter. "But after this, I'm not visiting any more lawyers. The last one I saw took me to the cleaners."

"This one won't cost you a cent, I promise," Theo said, giving her friend a quick hug. "I'll take care of everything."

THURSDAY
October 24

Chapter 13

ANN fidgeted uncomfortably in the upholstered chair in front of Adam Perry's desk. This was worse than getting audited by the IRS. She found herself tugging too often on the hem of her skirt and was painfully aware that her slip-on canvas shoes were out of place in this environment. She should be back at her house, busy with the affairs of hearth and home. This white-collar atmosphere left her feeling awkward.

"Well, what can I do for you, Ms. Dawson?" Adam Perry asked. He leaned back in his chair with the competent air of an individual who is at home in many worlds.

Ann cleared her throat, then rested her chin on her fingertips in what she hoped was a casually elegant gesture. "I'm here on behalf of a friend. She's run across some material that she thinks may be useful for a book she's writing, but she needs to have the details verified. Research has proven, she says, that abortion may be linked to breast cancer. She thinks the information may be a legal threat to the abortion industry. Could women who have had abortions sue the doctors who performed them?"

"Whoa, wait a minute," the lawyer interrupted, holding up a manicured hand. "We're talking theory here, unproven research. I'm familiar with the study, but I don't know if I'd say that the abortion industry is liable. That might be overstating the case."

"Why?" Ann persisted, glancing down at the notes Theo had given her. "People are suing tobacco companies for the cancer they've developed as a result of smoking."

"That's an alleged result, and that's true. But they're not winning their cases. At least, not yet." The lawyer drew in his breath and leaned back in his chair, folding his hands neatly at his waist. "It's an interesting idea, Ms. Dawson, but it's hardly new. I have filed a suit similar to the one you're proposing for another client, but I'm not at liberty to discuss the case at this point."

Ann felt her pulse quicken. He had to be referring to Ken Holman's case. "Do you think you'll win?" she asked.

"I don't know. This is a new area of law, and, unfortunately, public opinion isn't as set against abortion as it is against smoking. To date, no legal precedents have been set regarding breast cancer and abortion."

"But you took the case." She tilted her head, studying the lawyer. "Why'd you take such a risk, Mr. Perry, if things really look so hopeless?"

"My client is a friend," the lawyer said, standing up. "And maybe I like championing lost causes." He gave her a crooked smile that she found surprisingly charming. "Or maybe I'm just vain enough to think that my gilded reputation will survive association with the so-called right-wing fringe."

He held out his hand, and Ann took the hint. The interview was over. "Thank you for your time," she said, standing. She shook his hand and smiled, glad that she'd come. "I think what you're doing is very . . . *noble*, Mr. Perry. I wish you well on your lawsuit."

His brow cocked in surprise. "Well, thank you, Ms. Dawson. Best of luck to you and your friend. If I can be of any service in the future, please don't hesitate to let me know."

Ann smiled, a blush of pleasure warming her cheeks. "I'll keep that in mind."

* * *

After listening to Ann's report, Theo drove to Georgetown and read magazines in Ken Holman's waiting room until the head nurse walked through the lobby and locked the front door. "Is the doctor free now?" Theo asked, standing. "I've been waiting three hours."

The nurse drew her mouth into a disapproving knot. "Doctor's patients come first, miss. He's with his last patient now."

Theo sighed and sank back into the upholstered couch in the lobby. "Don't forget me," she called as the woman walked away.

Theo flipped through the only magazine she hadn't read, a copy of *Sports Illustrated,* for another fifteen minutes, then decided to take matters into her own hands. Opening the door from the waiting room, she padded quickly down the carpeted hall toward Dr. Holman's cluttered office. She cleared a space on the couch, then pulled her notebook from her briefcase.

Five minutes later, Ken Holman entered. Intent on the file in his hand, he didn't even look up until she said, "Hello, Doctor."

Holman actually jumped. "How did you—," he began, but then he broke off and shrugged slightly. "How can I help you, Ms. Russell?" he asked, his voice calm and professional. "I'm sorry. Did we have an appointment?"

"No," Theo said, pulling a copy of the newspaper article from her notebook as he made his way to his chair. "Did you read this story about our friend Theo Russell?"

"My friend, don't you mean?" Holman asked. "You said you never met him."

"I feel like I know him now," Theo answered. "It's a long story, Dr. Holman, but I'll fill you in because I need your help. It all began last weekend when an editor at the National Authors League convention mistook me for the novelist Theo Russell. Fool that I am, I was naive enough to think she was interested in a proposal *I'd* submitted. Before I knew the truth, I had a copy of Russell's proposal in front of me. I tried to give it back, but the editor took off before I could. Then I began to study it. The premise was so fascinating, even though it was a novel—"

"And you write nonfiction," Holman interrupted, his voice dull with exhaustion. "I remember."

"Yes." The doctor was obviously tired, so Theo decided to dispense with the rest of her explanations. "I've been investigating the facts. This morning my friend talked to Adam Perry."

"So what did Adam say?"

Theo shrugged. "Not much. It's a risk; there are no legal precedents. Everything hinges on your case, Dr. Holman. If you and Perry win, the earth will shake. Lots of women will sue. But if you lose . . ."

"I lose big," Holman muttered. "I know." He looked at her with chilling intentness for a long moment. "So you've thoroughly checked out Russell's proposal. My congratulations. But why are you here now?"

Theo glanced down at her empty hands and turned them over. "I've reached a dead end. I need help. I've accessed the best databases I can, and aside from a couple of studies the experts routinely debunk, there's not much to link abortion and breast cancer. Some of the more statistical studies are so technical I can't understand them. I need information. I need someone who can explain it. And I need a medical doctor who will go on record and state that the link and risk exist."

Dr. Holman picked up a pencil and swiveled his chair to face her. "You've exhausted all your resources?"

"Yes." Theo felt her cheeks burn. Did he think she was too lazy to do her homework? "I've looked up everything I could find, but for every study that suggests a link, some so-called expert refutes it. No one has been willing to flatly state that abortion can cause breast cancer. And I can't figure out why."

"There are lots of reasons," Dr. Holman answered, "including the possible repercussions. If women know that abortion can cause breast cancer, odds are that they won't be so quick to have a so-called safe and harmless abortion. And what if women with the disease sue the family-planning clinics and the hospitals where they terminated their pregnancies? Will doctors be able to perform fifty abortions a day knowing that there's a great chance their patients will develop breast cancer within fifteen years? And most important, will our Supreme Court, which has stated that we can regulate abortion only as it pertains to the life and health of the mother, consider breast cancer a risk great enough to curtail our nation's liberal abortion laws? They don't see it, but the lives and health of millions of women are at stake."

He paused, and Theo sat for a moment in the silence as his questions echoed in the office. Stunned, she realized that she hadn't even begun to consider the full range of consequences and implications involved in the issue she'd adopted.

"You might say there's been a quiet conspiracy," Holman went on, staring at the pile of paperwork on his desk. "Nothing anyone will admit and probably well intentioned. But people who set out to investigate this link usually change their minds. Or, like Theo Russell, they disappear."

Despite the warmth of the room, Theo shivered. "Has anyone else disappeared?" she whispered.

Holman nodded his head. "One of my colleagues was excited about the research and was set to publish in a medical journal last year, but he died in a car accident before the final draft of his report could be submitted. Another doctor in New York was delving into the topic but suddenly withdrew his research and declared his results flawed." He brushed back a hank of sandy hair that had fallen across his brow. "I don't know, . . . maybe I'm seeing things that aren't there. It's hard to face the denunciation and ridicule of one's colleagues." He looked over at her suddenly. "Have you had dinner?"

"Um . . . n-no," Theo stammered.

"Have it with me," he said, planting his hands on his desk. He gave her a steady look. "Unless you'd rather not."

Theo thought of a dozen reasons why she shouldn't—Ann and Stacy waiting at home, the risk involved in having dinner with a man she hardly knew, the long drive home—and then she surprised herself by accepting the doctor's invitation. It was work, after all. Ann would understand.

FRIDAY

October 25

Chapter 14

T HEO clung to the soft darkness as hard as she could, burying her face in her pillow, but Stacy's giggle pulled her from the sea of sleep. "Morning, sweetheart," she said at last, reaching out to catch her daughter's hands. "Climb into bed and cuddle with me a few minutes, OK?"

"OK," Stacy answered, climbing over Theo. She pressed her soft cheek against Theo's in a fierce caress, then bounded to the foot of the bed and reached for the television's remote control. As was her habit, Stacy pressed the red button, then waited for *Sesame Street* to come on. Theo yawned, stretched, and pulled herself out of bed.

She rumpled her daughter's hair as she stumbled to the bathroom for her robe. Seven o'clock. She had two hours to fix breakfast, do laundry, and watch the morning news before Ann came over. Two hours to think about the work that lay ahead . . . and Ken Holman.

Dinner had been wonderful. Ken had taken her to Hogates, a popular seafood restaurant on the water's edge. While they ate, Ken asked about Theo's husband, her writing career, and her ambitions. She told him honestly that this project was important to her because she was up against a self-directed deadline.

"I wondered," he said, sipping his iced tea. "You seemed awfully determined that first day."

"I still am," she said, methodically pulling the tail from a fried shrimp. "I'm not convinced the conspiracy you suggested exists, but this is such a relevant topic I can't believe no one else has written about it."

"The enlightened elite don't want to write about it," Ken answered. "Abortion is a sacred cow; to deny it is to deny an individual's 'reproductive freedom.'"

"What about those who say they want abortion to be safe . . . and rare? I read that a leader of Planned Parenthood once said that both the pro-life and pro-choice sides favor the elimination of all abortions."

"The 'permit but discourage' myth," Holman answered. "Those folks say we should attack the root causes that drive women to abortion while not diminishing the legal rights of women, but that's just another name for choice. And choice permits no compromise. The choicers are intractable. If they really want to eliminate all abortions, why not do it now? But they want full rights and no restrictions."

"They would allow abortion until the moment of birth?"

"Technically, yes." Something flickered far back in his eyes as he looked at her. "What are your feelings, Ms. Russell? You know that I'm on the pro-life side of the question."

"I'm a Christian," Theo said, wiping her hands on her napkin. "I've always been against abortion, even though I never really thought much about why I'm pro-life until last week. It was the cancer angle of Russell's story that first caught my attention. My mom died of breast cancer at age fifty, and my sister, who's forty, is in chemotherapy right now."

She looked down at the food on her plate, not nearly as hungry as a moment before. "I know what they say about breast cancer running in families. I'm thirty-two, I have a daughter, and I don't have a husband or parents anymore. My only sister has cancer. Sometimes I think about going to the hospital and demanding a double mastectomy. I don't care what they cut off; I just want to live . . . for my daughter. I'm all she has left."

"So—the abortion issue is secondary to you?"

"No." Theo took a deep breath. "It's just that whenever I read the words *breast cancer,* the hairs lift on my arms. But I feel strongly about the pro-life issue, too. I'm a mother, so I know what it's like to feel life stir within you. I know women haven't always been fairly treated, and I would march myself into blisters to defend a woman's right to equal treatment in the marketplace. But after feeling my baby kick, I could never deny that life exists before birth."

Holman stirred his iced tea. "It exists. When Dr. Bernard Nathanson came out with the film *The Silent Scream,* the choicers said the fetus was pulling away from the probing needle reflexively, not as a reaction to pain. And yet British researchers have noticed a dramatic rise in fetal stress hormones when they insert a needle into fetuses for blood transfusions. It's pain, pure and simple, but the choicers don't want to admit that. Too much guilt involved."

"I can understand that." Theo put down her fork and rested her chin on her hand, studying the doctor. Away from the office, he seemed more alive, more relaxed. For the first time it felt right to call him by his first name, and she tried it out just to see how it would sound: "I understand, Ken."

"I dare you to try a little test," he said, leaning forward over the table. His eyes gleamed with mischief. "Write a press release about my research results and give it to the press—to a reporter, for instance. Then sit back and see what happens."

The challenge echoed in her ears again as she stared at her reflection in the bathroom mirror and ran her hand through her mussed hair. She had resisted the idea last night at dinner, but in the light of a new morning it sounded logical. Why shouldn't she call a reporter and conduct her own experiment? Any reporter should be thrilled to jump on a story like this, especially since it concerned women's health and a missing novelist. And if nothing happened, "The Silence of the Press" would make a great chapter in Theo's book.

A name dropped into her consciousness as she brushed her teeth, and she smiled. She wouldn't call just any reporter; she'd go to the top. She'd call Pamela Lansky, the writer from the *Post* who had covered the story about Theo and the missing novelist.

Humming the refrain to *Sesame Street,* Theo wiped her face with a towel and hurried to get breakfast.

* * *

Two hours and three phone calls later, Theo finally had the reporter on the phone. Pamela Lansky listened without comment as Theo identified herself as the woman who had spoken with Evelyn Fischer and obtained the copy of Theo Russell's proposal.

"So why did you steal his proposal?" Pamela asked when Theo paused.

"I didn't steal it. Evelyn Fischer gave it to me, and I couldn't return it before she abruptly departed," Theo insisted. "Then, when I read it, I was fascinated. And now that I know the facts behind his proposal, I think you'll be interested, too."

"Keep talking. I'm listening."

"Essentially, Russell's proposal contains the results of a medical study strongly suggesting that abortion can lead to breast cancer. The study indicated that women who abort their first pregnancy have a one-in-six chance of later developing the disease. For young women, the odds are even higher."

"Really." It was a statement, not a question.

"Yes." Theo paused. "Anyway, I thought the information would make a great article for the *Post.* And the study quoted in Russell's proposal isn't the only one to confirm this theory. I can fax you copies of other medical reports—"

"What's your opinion?"

"Mine?"

Pamela Lansky sounded exasperated. "Yes. Are you anti-choice?"

Theo paused. "I prefer to think of myself as pro-life. You see, my daughter has Down's syndrome, and I've learned that all life is precious. But that has nothing to do with my wanting to get this information to the public. It's a health issue that concerns all women. Can I fax you an abbreviated synopsis of the research?"

"Sure." Pamela Lansky recited the fax number, thanked Theo politely, and hung up.

* * *

Theo worked the rest of the afternoon compiling her research into a brief report, then faxed the information to the newsroom of the *Post*. She settled back in her chair as the fax machine hummed. It was a good day's work. Her report was thorough and compelling; Pamela Lansky would certainly use it. When the abortion–breast cancer link became public knowledge, not only would Theo have the pleasure of telling Ken Holman that there was no conspiracy to hide the facts, but she'd also profit from a groundswell of interest that might prove helpful in marketing her book.

"Thanks, Ken," she murmured sleepily as the machine clicked off. She lifted an imaginary glass. "I couldn't have done it without you."

October 26

Chapter 15

SATURDAY morning's *Post* proved Theo wrong.

Second Theo Russell Steals Slice of Author's Success
by Pamela Lansky

WASHINGTON—A woman identifying herself as Theodora Russell claimed to be the mysterious impostor who took a copy of Theo M. Russell's book proposal from New York editor Evelyn Fischer. Theodora Russell, an aspiring author, said she honestly believed that the renowned editor was interested in meeting with a beginner. After she skimmed the novelist's proposal, though, she saw in the work an opportunity to write a nonfiction book that would point out, as she said, the "dangers" inherent in abortion. "I'm pro-life," Theodora Russell said, explaining her actions. "I've learned that all life is precious."

Washington police still have no information on the whereabouts of the missing novelist, nor has Mr. Russell spoken to his agent in New York, Madison Whitlow. Russell disappeared from the Hilton Tower eight days ago, leaving his personal effects behind. Police have not said whether Theodora Russell is a suspect in his disappearance.

Theo felt the blood drain from her face as she lowered the paper. Ann stopped stirring her cup of coffee. "What's wrong?"

Theo struggled to find her voice. "Pamela Lansky did nothing with the information I put together for her. This article makes me sound like some kind of lunatic. She even implies that I'm a suspect in Theo Russell's disappearance."

"Let me see that." Ann leaned over the table and scanned the article, then pushed the paper back across the table. "Stop worrying about the book," she said, lifting an eyebrow. "Your biggest problem now is the novelist. Find out where he's hiding, tell him what happened, and get his OK to keep working. Then everything will be out in the open, and you'll feel better."

Theo rested her chin on her hands and studied her friend. "You know," she said, a slow smile spreading across her face, "I think I know why God sent you to me. You see right to the heart of things. You're right. I'll be the 'mysterious woman' who stole Theo Russell's work as long as he is in hiding. But if I find him—"

"You'll be able to clear your own conscience," Ann volunteered, looking at Theo across the rim of her coffee cup. "And don't say you haven't felt guilty. I know you have."

Theo didn't answer but smiled at her friend and folded the newspaper into a neat bundle. "OK," she said, pushing her chair away from the kitchen table. She reached for a dish towel to wipe a dribble of milk from Stacy's chin. "So how do I go about finding someone who doesn't want to be found?"

"Don't ask me; I haven't read a Nancy Drew in years," Ann said. "But Jessica what's-her-name on *Murder, She Wrote* always returns to the scene of the crime."

"So do V. I. Warshawski and Adam Dalgliesh," Theo murmured.

"Who?"

"Never mind." Theo tossed the dish towel into the kitchen sink.

"If Russell left his stuff at the hotel, he'll have to come back and get it." She paused to kiss the top of Stacy's head and then waved as she left the kitchen. "Yesterday a researcher, today a private eye. It's not a job. It's an adventure."

Chapter 16

VICTORIA Elliott, city editor at the *Post,* carefully sipped her steaming coffee while she read the information Theodora Russell had faxed late Friday afternoon. Pam Lansky had barely glanced at the pages before submitting her story, remarking only that the anti-choice side had come up with a new angle. But Victoria, her coffee cup steady in her hand, read the information from a different perspective. Under her wool blazer lay a silk blouse, under the blouse, a camisole. Under the camisole ran a vivid mastectomy scar, a reality Pam Lansky had yet to face.

If she had known, Pamela would undoubtedly say that Victoria's judgment was clouded by personal fears and interests, but Victoria knew that breast cancer haunted the waking and sleeping hours of thousands of women in Washington alone. She had seen their pale faces in her oncologist's office, heard their trembling voices in her support group, shared their hopeful smiles in the halls of the building where she received her outpatient chemotherapy. Women with cancer did not have the luxury of choosing sides in politics. Women with cancer abandoned all things trivial to continue the all-important fight for life.

Victoria's brow furrowed as she read the facts in the report. At one point, she slammed the Styrofoam cup to her desk so suddenly that coffee spilled onto a stack of computer printouts, but she scarcely noticed. According to a study conducted at the New York

State Department of Health, she read, women who had an abortion almost doubled their chances of developing breast cancer later. The statistics were indisputable, in part because every abortion in New York had to be recorded in a "fetal death registry." There was no possibility of underreporting abortions.

She drew in a quick breath. In May 1965 she had graduated from Bethune Cookman College as a journalism major, determined to make her mark in the world. In June of that year she discovered she was pregnant, but a friend had hastily arranged an illegal abortion. She'd been scared to death but willing to endure what she had to. The pregnancy was aborted, saving Victoria's career. She married Gresham Elliott two years later and promised herself that she'd take time off to rear their children. But because she'd been internally damaged somehow by the abortion, the children never came. Eventually, as their careers pulled them in two different directions, she and Gresham separated and finally divorced.

Now nearly at the top of her profession, she was a lonely survivor. A pioneer in the battle for women's rights and choice—one who'd been scarred from the battle.

She could almost feel the scalpel slicing across her chest again as she folded the report and put it aside.

* * *

The cheap plastic phone on the laminate kitchen counter chirped, and Brennan motioned for Antonio to turn down the television as he picked it up. Nothing on but stupid Saturday cartoons, but Antonio watched them like they were as great as God.

"Yeah?" Brennan mumbled into the phone.

"It's Scotty. How's our friend?"

Brennan glanced over at the novelist, who lay curled into a fetal position on the bed. The man's dark hair stood out from his head like a Brillo pad; a week's growth of scraggly beard lay on his face. Even in sleep, the man's teeth chattered.

"Well, naturally, he's been better. What's up?"

"Just got a call. We're not finished with this thing. Some woman has been asking questions. The order's come down. We're to shut her up."

"A woman?"

"Yeah. Some stupid lady in this morning's paper. You're not gonna believe this, but her name's Theo Russell. Same as the guy you're baby-sitting."

Brennan swallowed slowly, caught up in déjà vu. "Ah, no, not a woman with the same name? Unbelievable. What are the odds?"

Antonio looked up from the television, and Brennan rolled his eyes. At least Scotty hadn't found out they'd visited the woman's hotel room by mistake.

"Get to her and fast. I can get you her address."

Brennan frowned at the receiver. "Come on, Scotty. You know how much I hate doing women."

"Relax. They want her quiet, not dead. Now wake up our friend and pump him full of coffee or uppers. He's got to make a call this morning."

Brennan glanced again at the writer. The man hadn't uttered an intelligible word in four days. When he was awake, he merely stared at the ceiling; when he was stoned, he curled into a ball and shivered.

"We'll try to get him up."

"Good. Now this is what you've got to do. . . ."

✳ ✳ ✳

An hour later Theodore Russell sat on the bed, huddled under a blanket. His eyes were watery and blurry, his nose pinched. For the first time in days he felt alive, but his hands trembled as they pressed the familiar number into the cellular phone.

"Remember how we told you," Antonio said, smiling amiably at his prisoner. "Nothing suspicious. Just like you're on the beach someplace, havin' the time of your life."

"Sure, and you *are* having the time of your life, aren't you?" Brennan whispered. He sat at the writer's right hand and leaned close to speak directly into the man's ear. "Just one wrong word, mind you, and we'll give you a hot shot. Then you won't have to worry about anything. Ever."

Determined not to show his fear, Russell closed his eyes and brought the phone to his ear. Carefully, intimately, Brennan leaned closer so he could hear, too.

One ring. Two. A third. Then the click of a telephone answering machine. Russell felt the spark of hope within him die as the agent's cheery greeting mocked his pain.

"Hello, you've reached Madison Whitlow. I'm either on another line or out right now, but your call is important, so you know what to do at the beep. I'll talk to you soon."

"Remember, laddie," Brennan whispered.

A shrill beep pierced the silence, and Russell forced a bright tone into his voice. "Madison, this is Russ. I heard about all the fuss down in Washington. Don't worry. I'm all right. I'm working on something new. I'll be back soon. Give your wife my love and—"

Another shrill beep cut off his message. Brennan glared at him. "I don't recall telling you to say anything about his wife. Why did you say that?"

Russell raised his chin. "His wife and I are friends. He'd think it strange if I didn't say hi to her."

Brennan took the phone and seemed to weigh it in his hand. "OK," he said finally, replacing the phone on the filthy counter. A cockroach scurried past, its antennae waving frantically. *A week ago,* Russell thought, *I would have jumped at the sight of a cockroach. Now I don't care.*

"Now," Antonio said, rising from his chair, "will you take your medicine easy, or do I have to hold you down again?"

The vague, half-sleep of the drug was better than sitting in this stifling room with these two cretins. "Do I have a choice?" Russell asked, thrusting his needle-scarred arm toward Antonio as Brennan prepared another syringe.

The spoon passed over the flame, the syringe was filled. Within a moment the needle bit into his vein. Russell had the feeling that death was bearing down on him with a slow and steady deliberateness, but he could not move to stop it.

He was barely aware when Antonio unfastened the belt that served as a tourniquet on his upper arm. As the television droned on, Russell leaned back against the rough plaster of the wall and felt the room spin about him. His breathing slowed; the room seemed to glow in pleasant colors as though some beneficent presence warmed the place. He shook off the matted blanket that lay across his shoulders. Smiling as a pleasant drowsiness replaced his fears, he slipped over and lay down on the bed to sleep.

* * *

An hour later, in New York, Madison Whitlow punched the button on his answering machine and listened to Russell's message.

"Madison, this is Russ. I heard about all the fuss down in Washington. Don't worry. I'm all right. I'm working on something new. I'll be back soon. Give your wife my love and—"

How unlike Russell. Short, dull sentences without a spark of imagination. And what was that business about a wife? Russell knew Madison wasn't married.

He replayed the message again. Something was definitely wrong. He dialed Russell's home on the Gulf and let the phone ring ten times before hanging up.

His next call was to his travel agent. Glancing nervously at his watch, Madison arranged a weekend flight to Washington. It was time to find his missing author.

Chapter 17

As Theo drove through Washington toward the Hilton Tower Hotel, she realized Ann was right. Theo's conscience was heavy with the knowledge that she was using someone else's idea, and making this small effort was the least she could do. If the man had left his things at the hotel, he would come back, so she'd leave a note for him at the front desk. And maybe, if God smiled on her, the novelist had simply caught a flight to New York or Paris with a lady friend and would come back to the hotel soon to pick up his things. If he'd gone overseas, he probably had no idea the police were searching for him. Russell was known to be reclusive and eccentric. Anything was possible.

She pulled into the parking garage and gave her car key to the attendant, grimacing at the thought of paying an outrageous parking fee just to ease her guilty conscience. *But forgiveness comes at a price, doesn't it?* she thought, pulling her purse from the car. *In this case, twelve bucks a day or four and a quarter an hour.*

Riding the escalator up to the lobby, she looked carefully around. The hotel looked the same—did it ever change? She hesitated when she reached the lobby. She knew she ought to just write a note and leave, but it was Saturday, a transition day at the hotel. If the writer had taken a week off for a jaunt somewhere, he might come back this weekend to gather his things and officially check out. And even if he didn't show up, she could ask around to see if anyone had seen him. But whom should she ask?

Taking a moment to arrange her thoughts, she took a seat on a sofa and pulled a steno notebook from her purse. "Dear Mr. Russell," she wrote, "this is an incredible coincidence, and I'm sure you'll hear all about it from Evelyn Fischer and your agent. I've sent both of them letters to explain everything. But just in case you've been reading the papers and haven't heard from your agent, I wanted you to know that I obtained a copy of your proposal by mistake and have returned it to Ms. Fischer. But I was intrigued to hear of your work with abortion and breast cancer and would love to follow up on the idea, unless you object, of course. In any case, I wish you the best of success in your work."

She signed the note with her name and phone number, then ripped the paper from her notebook and folded it neatly. The clerks behind the hotel desk were busy with guests, and Theo paused, thinking. Theo M. Russell had stayed in this hotel but had registered under a different name because the hotel switchboard connected Evelyn Fischer to her room, not his. The paper had said he was last seen late Friday afternoon in the gift shop, shortly before he was to speak at the convention.

Why couldn't she ask around on her own? If she was going to investigate Russell's topic, she might as well begin by investigating Russell himself. If she got lucky and found him, he might even be willing to give her more information than he had written in his proposal.

Gathering her courage, Theo wandered into the gift shop, paused before a display of candy, then walked over to a fresh-faced boy working behind the cash register. "I wonder if you can help me," she asked, opening her notebook. She gave the clerk a friendly smile. "I'm a freelance writer looking for information about the novelist Theo Russell. I understand he was staying at this hotel before he disappeared."

The boy's face lit up at Russell's name. He straightened his shoulders and slapped the counter with his right hand. "Another one! You guys just keep coming, don't you?"

"You've talked to someone else?"

"Yeah." He tossed his blond hair and counted the list on his fingers. "Another reporter, the police, and an insurance investigator."

"Well then," Theo said, clicking her pen. "You won't mind talking to one more, will you?"

"No." The boy leaned his elbows on the counter and launched into the routine he'd obviously performed before. "I talked to Theo Russell Friday afternoon, sometime between five and six. Tall, skinny guy, with slicked-back hair, like he'd just gotten out of the shower. I remember the time because I get my dinner break at six. He came in, bought a disposable razor, and left. That was the only time I saw him."

"He was alone?"

"Yeah."

"Anyone else around, out in the hall, maybe? A woman?"

His mouth tipped in a faint smile. "No. I'd have remembered if he had a woman waiting. He was alone."

"Was he carrying anything? A suitcase?"

"No." The boy shrugged. "Nothing."

Theo poised her pen over her notebook. "And your name is?"

"Jacob Benson," the boy said, leaning forward to watch her write. "B-e-n-s-o-n."

Theo wrote his name in bold, block letters. "Have you worked at the hotel long, Jacob?"

"Two years. I started working here as part of a high school jobs program. When I graduate from high school, I'm going to enter management training."

"Excellent." Theo forced a smile. "Do you know many of the hotel staff?"

"Oh yeah, everybody," he waved his hand. "We eat meals together down in the kitchen."

"The maids, the reservations people?"

"Everybody. This place is real good about making sure everybody mixes. Even Mr. Cox, the manager, eats in the kitchen with us every once in a while."

"That's nice." Theo paused and looked over her shoulder through the plate-glass doors. "I suppose everybody's talking about your missing guest."

"Only the people who work here." The boy ran his hands through his hair and lowered his voice. "Mr. Cox's plenty mad. The woman paying for the room stopped payment when the guy disappeared. Mr. Cox wants to open that suite, but the police said they won't release it until their investigation is completed. But every day it sits empty the hotel loses a ton of money."

"A suite?"

"Yeah, the Ambassador Suite."

"Is that the one on the twenty-fifth floor?"

Jacob frowned. "No, it's on the thirtieth. There are no suites on the twenty-fifth."

"Right." Theo sighed as if he were telling her nothing new. "I suppose the police talked to everyone last week, huh?"

"Yeah. The police even asked the operator for records of the guy's phone calls—"

"Is that unusual?"

"No. But it was weird because the guy didn't make any calls, at least not from his room. That's the first famous guy I've ever heard of who didn't call anyone."

"Wait a minute." Theo snapped her fingers. "I thought he called one woman to tell her he couldn't speak at the convention Friday night. Wouldn't there be a record of that call?"

"Not if it was made room-to-room," Jacob answered. "We only keep records of calls that go outside the hotel."

"Oh." Theo scribbled a note. "What else did the police ask about?"

He shrugged. "Nothing, really. There wasn't much to go on. No one saw him come in except the girl working at the front desk that night, and no one saw him leave. He just disappeared. Only Kathy—she's the front desk girl—and I saw him at all."

"Luggage? Didn't one of the bellhops help him carry his suitcase to his room?"

"No." Jacob shrugged. "They say he only had one bag. It's still upstairs in the suite."

"I don't suppose he had a car in the garage."

"No. They checked that, too."

Theo closed her notebook. "Well, Jacob," she said, giving him a sincere smile, "I really appreciate your help. Are you sure you can't think of anything else about Mr. Russell?"

The boy shook his head. "Same as I told the police. I don't know anything else."

"Thanks, then," Theo said, lifting her purse onto her shoulder. "Good luck in management training."

＊ ＊ ＊

She'd learned one thing, at least. Theo Russell had stayed on the thirtieth floor, and that room was still just as he left it. She rode the elevator to the thirtieth floor, then stepped off and looked around. An elegant gold sign pointed left toward the Ambassador Suite, and Theo followed the curving hallway until she reached the suite's double doors. A Do Not Disturb sign hung from one of the brass door handles.

Theo paused to consider her options. She'd left her own hotel key card in her room when she checked out, so she couldn't even hope that the same card code would permit access to this room. As she stood thinking, the sound of footsteps caught her ear, and she glanced nervously about, uncertain of what she should do. As a

131

room service waiter came around the gentle curve of the hall, she made a quick decision and walked toward him, giving him a polite smile of acknowledgment. *Be natural, Theo. Look like you belong here.*

Her mind racing, she kept walking through the circular hall, knowing it would bring her back to the Ambassador Suite. Could she get into that room? She had a credit card in her purse—could she try to jimmy the lock? But if she did manage to get into the room, what did she possibly hope to find?

The pleasant hum of voices drifted through the corridor, and Theo continued along the hall until she found a housekeeper working from a towel-laden cart. A soap opera blared from a television inside one of the open rooms. "Excuse me," Theo said, when the maid appeared in the doorway. "Can you help me?"

The housekeeper tossed a mound of wet towels into the hamper at the end of the cart and turned bored eyes upon Theo. A big mound of sternly coiffed beige hair tilted her head backward, and two red slashes marked her thin lips. "What?" she answered, working a piece of chewing gum for all it was worth.

"I, um . . ." The housekeeper had the humorless look of someone who'd heard everything and believed nothing, so Theo decided to give her the unvarnished truth. "I need to get into the Ambassador Suite for a few minutes," she stammered. "I'm not going to steal anything; you can watch me the entire time. I just want to look around."

The woman grunted as she closed the door of the room she'd just finished, but she grabbed her cart and lugged it toward the Ambassador Suite. "I don't know if that's a good idea," she said, jerking her head toward the sign on the door. "The manager doesn't want anything messed up in there."

"Oh, I know what Mr. Cox said," Theo answered, shrugging as if she'd talked to the manager herself. "But I won't touch or disturb anything."

The woman pinched her lower lip with her teeth. "Are you with the police?"

"No. But I need to get in touch with the guy who disappeared from here." Hesitantly, Theo fumbled in her purse and pulled out the twenty-dollar bill she'd planned on using to fill her car for the next two weeks. "I just need a couple of minutes, OK?"

The woman grunted at the sight of the money, then cracked her gum. "Well, since the police haven't found 'im, I guess it won't hurt for you to look around," she said, taking the bill. She pulled a key card from her apron pocket and slid it into the lock. "Just don't touch nothin', OK?"

* * *

Downstairs in the hotel kitchen, Amy Chang lowered her eyes when Steven Winston stepped off the elevator and turned her way. He carried a room service bill in his hand, so this was probably a legitimate visit, but lately her stomach tightened every time he looked in her direction.

Steve casually laid the bill on her desk, then placed his hand over hers and leaned to whisper in her ear: "Remember those two guys last week who paid us for Theo Russell's room number?"

Despite the sudden bands of tightness in her chest, Amy took a deep breath. "I thought we agreed to forget that ever happened."

The waiter gave her a saucy grin. "You can forget it if you want to. But one of the guys came back about an hour ago and gave me a twenty to call him if I ever saw this woman." He pulled a folded sheet of newsprint from his pocket and unfolded it. Amy recognized the sketch; it had been in the paper along with a story about the missing novelist.

"So?"

"So—" Steve grinned and leaned back, pocketing his hands— "the woman's here! I just saw her upstairs outside the Ambassador

Suite." He pulled a scrap of paper from his pocket and dropped it on Amy's desk. "Dial the number for me, sweetheart."

"No. It's all too weird, Steve; I'm not going to do it. Especially after that guy Theo Russell disappeared—"

A buzz from the phone interrupted her, and Amy turned away to answer a room service call. When she had taken the order and relayed it to the kitchen, Steve pulled the headset from her ear.

"Steven! Let go! You'll get us both fired."

"Dial the number," he said, grinning as if he enjoyed her dismay. "If you don't, I'll tell Mr. Cox the truth about that hundred-dollar tip you got last week right before that guy disappeared." He turned the paper and read it: "555-3047."

Her fingers trembling, Amy tapped in the number.

✳ ✳ ✳

In the neglected Fairmount Heights house, Antonio answered the phone, mumbled "OK," and hung up. He looked at Brennan. "We don't have to go to the woman's house," he said. "She's at the hotel. Our boy spotted her upstairs."

"You want to take care of it?" Brennan asked.

Antonio jerked a thumb toward the man on the dingy mattress. "One of us has to stay with Sleeping Beauty."

"Then I'll go. I know what she looks like." Brennan swung on his overcoat, patted the pocket for assurance, and hurried to his car. A sudden draft of chilly air knifed through the room as the door slammed shut, but the sleeping novelist lay as still as stone.

✳ ✳ ✳

Theo held her breath as the green light on the electronic lock blinked and the housekeeper swung the door open. "Better hurry," the woman called as Theo moved inside. "I can't wait here all day."

The heavy room-darkening curtains had been pulled back, and

134

bright morning light flooded the room. "Was the suite just like this when he left?" Theo called over her shoulder.

"I don't know about *exactly*," the housekeeper said. "The guy left on Friday, and the maid cleaned Saturday morning, I think. The police were upset about that—said she shouldn't have emptied the trash cans. But how were we supposed to know the guy had disappeared? We thought he was just staying somewhere else. You'd be surprised what people do in a hotel."

"Nothing surprises me anymore," Theo answered, moving farther into the room. The outer room contained two small sofas with a coffee table between them. Absolutely nothing was out of place, and none of the author's personal effects had been left there. In the bedroom, however, Theo saw a tweed sport coat laid out on the bed and shiny brown loafers on the floor. A duffel bag lay open on the floor. *Theo Russell liked to travel light.* She shuddered when she realized she'd just thought of him in the past tense. *Come on, get a grip,* she told herself sternly as she moved toward the bathroom. *The guy's just been jet setting to Paris or someplace, remember?*

The bathroom was clean and tidy. The tub was spotless, the towels still neatly arranged. A comb, a can of shaving cream, a toothbrush and toothpaste lined the counter with military precision. "No razor," Theo murmured. "He was ready to shave, but he forgot his razor."

"Lady, you'd better hurry." The housekeeper's nasal voice cut through Theo's musings. "I just heard the elevator ding. Someone will be coming around the corner."

Theo left the bathroom and moved to the desk. If she were invited to a convention, she'd prepare for a speech at the desk. She opened the drawer. A phone book, a Gideon Bible, a tablet of Hilton stationery. But a masculine hand had scribbled on the paper. Theo squinted, barely able to decipher the handwriting. "Rambo?" she whispered, crinkling her nose. "BioTech Industries?"

"Hurry, lady!" Theo tossed the stationery back in the drawer, took a last look around, and committed the names on the notepad to memory. Rambo—whatever could that mean? Was Theodore Russell a Sylvester Stallone fan? Was he working on a screenplay? And BioTech Industries? She'd look up the company name on her computer when she got home.

Theo came out of the bedroom and smiled her thanks at the nervous housekeeper. "Thanks very much," she said, holding her hands up for inspection. "See? I didn't take anything."

The housekeeper rolled her eyes and snapped her gum in appreciation.

✳ ✳ ✳

Howard Datsko felt his stomach churn as he stepped off the elevator. *Too much coffee on an empty stomach,* he told himself. *Better have the cinnamon rolls tomorrow.*

He wasn't happy about being sent to the Hilton Tower on a Saturday afternoon. He wasn't happy about being assigned to the Theo M. Russell case at all. He worked in Robbery Special Section, and as far as he knew, no robbery had been committed at this hotel. But if a guy disappeared *with* his wallet in D.C., robbery was the first department the chief called. There was, of course, always a dim chance that the guy might turn up dead with his wallet. Then the case would be transferred to Homicide. But nine different stiffs had moved through the coroner's office last week, and none of them had been Theodore Marshall Russell.

Datsko's job today was to make a final sweep of the hotel room and verify once and for all that no clues remained behind. After that, he'd watch that plump polyp of a hotel manager box up the man's belongings and stash them someplace in case Theo M. Russell ever showed up to claim his stuff.

The hotel manager was supposed to meet Datsko in the novelist's suite, and Datsko frowned when he saw no sign of the man in the hallway. But a maid's cart stood outside the open door, so Datsko cooled his temper. Maybe the guy was inside.

"Cox?" Datsko pressed past the cart into the suite. A maid with enormous blonde hair stood there, the corner of a folded bill peeking from the neckline of her uniform. Another woman in jeans and a sweater stood in front of the maid, her hands raised like a kid trying to convince her mom that she really did wash her hands.

Datsko narrowed his eyes, confused. The second woman looked familiar. Did he know her?

"I'm looking for the manager, ladies," he said, offering regulation police politeness. The second woman lowered her hands and blushed, so he kept his gaze steady upon her. "You wouldn't happen to know where I could find Mr. Cox, would you?"

"No." She shook her head and took a side step as if she wanted to move toward the doorway, but Datsko and the cart blocked her path.

Datsko didn't budge but pinned her with his eyes. "Excuse me, ma'am, if I seem impolite, but do I know you? You look kind of familiar."

She glanced up at him quickly, then lowered her eyes to the floor. "Sorry. But if you'll excuse me, I'm in a bit of a rush."

Where had he seen that face? And the hair was wrong; it wasn't supposed to be smooth like that, but curlier, more upswept.

He snapped his fingers and leaned on the cart, effectively sending the message that she wasn't going anywhere until she answered his questions. "You're Theodora Russell," he said, pointing at her. "You called me. Howard Datsko, Metropolitan Police."

She blinked, then looked up at him with something very fragile in her wide green eyes. "Yes. I suppose I did."

"You told me you had nothing to do with Theo Russell."

She tensed like a cat and backed away from him. "I don't."

"Well then, would you mind explaining why you're here in his hotel room? For that matter, since you seem to have a great deal of interest in Theo Russell, maybe you should come with me down to the station."

She took another step back. "I can't."

"Why not?"

She cast about for words, then stammered, "Because I'm trying to find him myself!"

Datsko threw his head back and laughed. Taking advantage of the shift in his mood, the housekeeper yanked her cart away and scurried down the hall. "I tell you what, Ms. Russell," Datsko said, reaching for her arm, "let's have a nice long talk on our way to the station."

"I haven't done anything wrong." Her eyebrows rose in alarm. "I just wanted to leave Mr. Russell a note. And then I got curious and thought it wouldn't hurt to look around."

"Oh?" Datsko gave her a disbelieving smile. "Didn't I see a bill tucked into that maid's dress? What did you pay her to break in on a crime scene, Ms. Russell? Ten bucks? Twenty? Or maybe you don't mess with less than a hundred when you set out to bribe someone."

"Bribery?" Her face fell, and Datsko's conscience rose up to shake a warning finger in his face. The lady hadn't disturbed the hotel room, and for all he knew it wasn't even a crime scene. But something wasn't right. He'd bet his pension plan that this woman was somehow connected with Theodore Russell's disappearance.

He shook his head and made gentle *tsk*ing noises, determined to play out his bluff. "Bribery is serious business."

He moved to touch her, but just as his fingers were about to close around her upper arm, she stepped back and blazed up at him. "Casting blame on innocent people is worse than bribery," she said, yanking her arm up and out of his reach. "I gave the maid a tip, that's all. And I don't know anything about Theo Russell that you didn't know last week!"

Datsko pressed his lips together and moved toward the door. "Now, Ms. Russell, we need to talk, and I'd rather do it at the station than here. So since Mr. Cox has stood me up, I think we can be on our way. Shall we go?" He held out his hand, gesturing toward the door. The woman glared at him for a moment, then moved past him with spirited quickness and headed toward the elevator. He followed her, relaxed and confident—then wondered for a moment if she would consider bolting for the stairs. Thirty flights? She wasn't that desperate.

The light outside the elevator blinked and a bell rang. The doors slid open, and she stepped inside with vigor and grace as Datsko followed. One other passenger was aboard, a lean, broad-shouldered man who seemed engrossed in the sports section of *USA Today*. The paper rattled slightly as Datsko and the woman boarded; then the doors closed.

Datsko folded his hands and glanced at the buttons on the control panel. None were lit, but the other passenger blocked Datsko's reach. "Lobby, please," he said. The newspaper lowered; the man's finger pressed *L*. Datsko cut a look from the control panel to the man. He wore an overcoat, not unusual for late October, but his sunglasses were out of place in a dim elevator. Obeying the sixth sense he had developed after twenty years on the force, Datsko casually crossed his arms against his chest so his right hand would be nearer the holster under his left arm. Reflexively, he shifted his weight so that his body blocked the woman's. Over his shoulder, he heard her sigh. She probably thought he had moved to block her escape.

The elevator began its gradual descent. From behind him, the woman whispered with a false smile in her voice: "You really are making a mistake." Datsko had the feeling she'd be very pretty when she smiled honestly, but he couldn't turn to check out his theory.

"Nice day," Datsko ventured, looking toward the other man. The guy in the overcoat didn't move but kept his hands in front of him, the newspaper folded across the opening of his coat. Why had the guy been on the elevator in the first place? The thirtieth was the uppermost floor, so why had the guy been riding *up* if he wanted to go *down?*

Twenty-five, twenty-four.

The stranger tucked his newspaper under his arm, then folded his hands. Though the sunglasses veiled the expression in the man's eyes, Datsko relaxed slightly and leaned against the wall. Theodora Russell nudged his shoulder. "Just let me go," she whispered. "I haven't done anything! I have a little girl waiting at home. Let's forget about this, OK?"

Nineteen, eighteen, seventeen.

The other man hadn't moved. Maybe he was a joyrider hoping to sneak a peek at the skyline out of a window and was embarrassed he'd been caught in the elevator when he wasn't a paying customer. Datsko grinned. The guy probably thought he was hotel security, especially since he was obviously escorting a woman off the thirtieth floor.

More at ease, Datsko turned to glance at Theodora Russell. Her wide eyes were soft and vulnerable, so different from the hardened eyes of the women he routinely arrested. By heaven, how had this innocent stumbled into his line of work?

He was about to put her fears to rest by saying that he only wanted to ask her a few questions when he felt, no *sensed,* movement from the man in the overcoat. Before Datsko could turn his head, he heard the muffled *thwack* of a bullet whizzing through a Smith & Wesson silencer and felt something hit his chest. The impact tossed him against the elevator wall like a rag doll; colors exploded in his brain. As he crumbled to the floor, stunned beyond movement, he smelled the acrid scent of gunfire and heard the woman scream.

The man in the overcoat moved toward Theodora, his rough hand clapping over her mouth until her scream became a muffled gurgle. The elevator came to an abrupt stop when the man hit the hold button with his other hand. Datsko tried to reach for his gun, but his limbs would not obey his frenzied thoughts. For one terrifying moment he had the impression that he was sitting helpless in a darkened movie theater watching a horror flick.

The woman struggled, the villain cursed, then the screen went black.

Chapter 18

As Datsko's eyes closed in deathly stillness, Theo tasted the man's hand across her mouth and closed her eyes as if she could block the scene from her mind.

"Listen to me, lassie," the man who held her whispered, a ruthless edge to his voice.

He's going to kill me, she thought, struggling to remain on her feet as waves of grayness passed over her. *If he shot a cop, he won't think twice about shooting me.*

"We're going to get off in the lobby. We'll just let the doors open, then you and I will step out, ever so casually, and go down the escalator to the garage. You're not going to scream or struggle or do anything stupid because I have a gun pointed right at your back. You mentioned a wee girl waiting for you. If you're wanting to see her again, please, lass, mind your manners."

He paused, apparently waiting for some sort of response, so Theo nodded slowly. The man's hard hand slid from her mouth to her neck, then over her shoulder and down to her back. With an almost graceful ease he moved to stand directly behind her, and Theo thought she could feel the cold metal of the gun against her sweater. She shivered through fleeting nausea. Satisfied with the results of his threat, the man applied a slight pressure to the gun at her back. "Would you be so good as to release the elevator hold button?"

Her hand shaking, she stepped forward and did as she was told. He moved with her, stepping over the detective's sprawling legs. The elevator resumed its smooth downward movement and chimed softly as the doors slid open.

A handful of people stood at the elevator opening in the lobby, and their polite expressions melted swiftly to horror when they saw Datsko's body on the floor. "Heart attack," the shooter yelled as he pushed Theo from the car. "Call a doctor!"

Theo sprang into movement as the gun at her back prodded her forward. Her teeth began to chatter as pandemonium broke out behind her. The man hurried her toward the escalator with firm persistence. Disjointed thoughts flew through her mind—in the purse under her arm she carried a can of pepper spray; in the trunk of her car, a Call for Help banner. What good was either of those things now?

Her hand trembled as she reached for the rail of the escalator. The man was still behind her, so close that she could smell his cologne. She had yet to get a good look at his face.

The bottom of the escalator loomed beneath her. A dim ripple ran across her mind, the dark memory of how escalators had always frightened her as a child. Her mother had always told her to be careful; your shoelace could get caught in the stairs, your leg could be ripped to bits before anyone arrived to help. . . .

She looked past the escalator's grinding teeth. A small circle of Asian men in dark suits bowed to each other in the garage lobby. This man would have to push through the crowd, then put her in his car and drive only God knew where—

She couldn't let him take her. She wouldn't.

As the final step of the escalator approached, she felt the pressure of his gun leave her back for an instant. Knowing that he would look down to gauge the timing of his final step, Theo took advantage of his hesitation and whirled away from his grasp.

"What the—!" he yelled; then she heard nothing but the pounding of her own footsteps.

Please, God! she prayed as she sprinted toward the rising escalator. *Please, please help me run!*

She ran doubled over in case he began to shoot, and all but flew up the escalator stairs. He was still behind her, his heavy feet pounding the metal steps, but she was lighter and faster on her feet. Reaching the lobby, she glanced for a moment at the crowd gathered at the elevator, then dashed for the double entrance doors guarded by two uniformed doormen.

She was too frightened to scream. The stranger's footsteps had merged with the frightened pounding of her own blood in her ears, and Theo thought of nothing but those double doors and freedom. She was dimly aware that no one even seemed to notice her as she raced by; every bystander's attention was glued to the open elevator and the fallen policeman.

Every bystander but one. As Theo skirted the sofas and flew toward the doors, a small girl in a red bathing suit and towel stepped directly into her path. "Move, please!" Theo yelled, swerving, and the misstep brought a stab of blinding pain to her right ankle. Gritting her teeth, she continued to run. A bellman saw her coming and held the door open as if guests routinely ran marathons through the lobby, but the valet at the curb gaped at her as she staggered toward him. "Taxi," she whispered hoarsely, turning in front of him to hide behind his broad shoulders. She looked past the valet into the lobby. The man was there, his dark glasses turned toward the crowd at the elevator. In a moment he would realize she had gone out the front door.

"Certainly, miss." The valet signaled a cab waiting in the circular drive, and the taxi's engine snarled to life. As soon as the car pulled up to the curb, Theo yanked the door open and jumped into the back. Without giving the driver time to greet her, she pounded on the back of his seat. "Drive! Drive, now! Please!"

"Yes, ma'am," the driver said, grinning. He hit the clock and shifted gears; the taxi shot out of the drive. Theo turned to look out the back window and saw her would-be abductor grinning at her from the curb, her purse in his hands.

* * *

"Lady, are you ready to tell me where we're going?" Theo lifted her face from her hands and stared at the cabbie. They had been driving for five minutes, and Theo had no idea where she was or where she could go. She didn't even know how she was going to pay for the cab. The man from the elevator had her purse with her wallet, her credit cards, her checkbook, Stacy's picture—*her address and house keys!*

"I need a phone," she gasped. "I have to call home."

"Do you want me to stop and find one?"

"Yes. Right now. The first phone you see."

The man threw her a curious grin, then gunned the cab toward the curb. Theo leapt out, landing in a burst of pain on her sprained ankle, and gasped as she turned to bend through the cab's open window. "Please don't think I'm a cheat, but can I borrow change for a call? You can add it to the bill."

The driver shook his head but fished some coins from his jeans pocket and handed them to her through the window. As though the devil himself were still on her heels, Theo hobbled to the phone and punched in her number.

"Hello." Ann's cheery voice sounded blessedly normal.

"Ann, it's me. Something's happened, and I've lost my purse. Take the girls and go to your house now. Don't stop for anything. Lock my house up tight and just wait for me at your place."

"Theo, is this a joke?" A trace of laughter echoed in Ann's voice, then died out. "What's happened?"

For the first time, Theo felt the sting of tears in her eyes. But she couldn't stop to cry now. "I'll tell you later, OK?" she whispered, her voice breaking. "Just get out of my house. Keep Stacy with you, please? I'm OK, and I plan to stay that way."

"Can I come get you?"

"No, it's too far, and I don't want to upset the girls. I'm in a cab. Don't worry about me."

"Does this have anything to do with Ken Holman? He called for you earlier."

For a moment Theo's mind went blank. *Ken who?* But then her adrenaline surged. "What did he want? Has he discovered something?"

"No, I think it was a social call. He sounded very pleasant and said he'd be at his office today if I heard from you."

"OK." Theo's mind raced. Holman's office was safe, quiet. "I'll be there, Ann, if you need me. But get out of my house now, OK? I'll call you when I can."

Something in her voice must have convinced Ann, for she agreed and hung up. Dashing the wetness from her eyes, Theo went back to the cab and climbed in. "How far are we from Reservoir Road?"

"Lady, I can get you anywhere. Just tell me where you want to go."

"The Women's Center on Reservoir Road. I don't know the number, but I'll know it when I see it."

"I know the place," the driver answered, studying her in the rearview mirror. "It's a doctor's office, right?"

Theo nodded and shut the car door, clamping her mouth closed. Unspent fear and emotion swelled within her like a tidal wave. She felt the muscles in her face quiver and knew she was on the edge of a crying jag.

The taxi driver must have noticed. "Just sit back and relax, lady, and I'll get you there." His gentle voice soothed her nerves, and Theo leaned back and stretched her leg across the seat to ease the pressure on her ankle. The thug hadn't followed her, but she'd known from that last smile on his face that he wouldn't. Why should he? He had her purse, even her notebook with her compiled information about Theo Russell. He would know everything.

But who was he? And why had he come after her? Why did he shoot Datsko? She closed her eyes and tried to remember any detail that might give her a clue but recalled nothing. What had he looked like? In the final seconds as she drove away she'd seen little of his face because her eyes were fastened on the purse in his hands. She had an impression of black hair and dark eyes, or had her mind superimposed on him the features of the typical television bad guy? Underneath her fear and confusion was an overwhelming conviction that she *knew* the guy, that she'd seen him before, even talked to him. . . .

Unwillingly, she relived her flight through the lobby. The crowd of Asian men at the bottom of the escalator. The scent of her abductor's cologne. The crowd of gawkers around the cop in the elevator. The vile taste of a hand over her mouth. The startled doorman. The little girl in a red bathing suit. The stranger's accent—Scottish? Irish?

The cab stopped. "The Women's Center," the cabbie said, turning to her with a smile. "And in a hurry. I sure hope they're open on Saturday."

"Me, too," Theo said, lifting the door handle. She paused. "I, uh, have no money with me. But my friend works here, and he'll give me a loan. If you'll wait, I'll be back."

"If you don't mind, I'll come with you," the driver answered, suddenly serious. "My trusting nature has lost me too many fares."

"I understand," Theo answered. She waited for him to park the car, then let herself out. Grimacing in pain as she hobbled toward the door, she led the way into the medical center.

Ken Holman paid Theo's cab fare without complaint or question. The driver thanked him, smiled broadly, and left the building. During the entire transaction, Theo felt the doctor's nurse frowning at her.

"Of course, I'll want to know what has brought you here and in this state," Ken said, pulling her into an empty examining room. He looked pointedly at Theo's swelling ankle. "But I'm afraid one of my patients is miscarrying. I was just about to meet her at the hospital."

"I'm sorry to bother you, but when Ann said you called, I thought this would be a good place to go. I know I ought to be able to take care of myself, and I hate to ask it of you, but I really need someplace where I can . . . be safe." Theo shifted her weight for an instant, and a spasm of pain crossed her face.

"It's bad, isn't it?"

"It's nothing. Just a sprain."

"I mean, whatever's brought you here. You looked like a deer caught in a hunter's light when you came in."

Theo forced a laugh. "This afternoon I saw a man shoot a cop in an elevator; then he dragged me out with him. I sprained my ankle getting away but dropped my purse when I took off. He knows my name, my address, he has all my credit cards—" Theo felt her chin begin to quiver, and when she put her hands to her cheeks, she discovered she was crying. "I don't know what I'm doing, Ken, or why I'm doing it." A sudden sob broke from her; then Ken's strong and comforting arm slipped around her shoulders.

"Nurse, bring me some aspirin and an ice pack," he called out the door. He turned to face Theo, pressing his hands to her cheeks and bending to look into her eyes. "Theo, I'm going to look at that ankle, and then you're going to rest on the couch in my office. Have you had dinner?"

She struggled to speak around the lump in her throat. "No."

"We'll bring you something. Now I want you to rest."

Placing one of her arms on his shoulder, he helped her limp to the faded but comfortable-looking couch in his office. He shoved a stack of books and newspapers onto the floor, and she sat down while he fumbled for a pillow to put under her foot. "I've got to get to the hospital, but I'm going to send my nurse in. You do what she says, Theo; then lie down and take it easy. We'll talk when I get back."

"OK."

He turned out the light, and before the nurse arrived, Theo was asleep.

* * *

A few hours later she opened her eyes. Boxes of Chinese takeout lay on a cleared portion of the doctor's desk, and Ken Holman knelt on the floor near her feet. He had slipped the shoe from her foot and was examining her swollen ankle.

"You should take lessons from Cinderella," he quipped as she blushed. "She ran in one shoe, didn't she, and didn't turn her ankle once. But you haven't done too much damage." He began to gently wind a length of Ace bandage around her ankle. "I think a few hours of ice and rest will do the trick if you stay off the foot."

His hands felt wonderfully competent, and Theo fought the urge to close her eyes and revel in the feeling of pampered care. It had been so long since a man treated her like this! But this was not her husband. This man was barely a friend.

"I'm sorry to trouble you with this," she said, sitting up. "I know you were hoping to work today, but I didn't know where else to go. I didn't want to go home because I thought that man might follow me. At least I managed to call home and warn Ann. My daughter will be fine; she'll stay at Ann's house."

She told Ken the entire story as they shared boxes of kung pao shrimp. When she had finished, he put down his chopsticks and looked at her steadily. "You need to drop this entire thing," he said, crossing his arms. "If you were a patient, I'd tell you to go back to what you were doing last month. You were happier then. You were safer."

"Last month I wanted to be a writer," Theo mumbled, stretching her foot out on the sofa. "Last month I would have done practically *anything* for a big break."

"And now you realize that big breaks don't just happen," Ken answered. "And because you've involved yourself with Theo Russell, your life's been threatened, you've practically been slandered in the paper, and a police officer has been shot. Why can't you forget about him and that book? Write something nonthreatening, like stories for children."

"I'd love to write stories for children," Theo wailed, her frustration brimming over. "But I can't *sell* them! I don't know what it takes, Ken, but I just don't have it. Nonfiction is the one thing I think I do well. The material in the Russell proposal is the best chance I'll ever have. But you're right. Right now I'd be thrilled to drop everything and forget I ever heard of Theo Russell. I'd even change my name if it'd help, but it's too late. I'm caught in this maze, and I don't have any idea how to get out. I've got to find answers, fast, because somebody out there has my name and address. He knows who I am, and I don't know anything!"

"Have you talked to the police about what happened this afternoon? Maybe they can give you some answers."

Theo shook her head. "Thanks to a policeman, I almost got kidnapped. They think *I* have answers. Isn't that crazy?"

Ken sighed, then rapped his hands on the desk in a short rhythm. "OK, you can't do anything now." His blue eyes seemed almost tender. "Your daughter is OK for the night?"

"Yes."

"Tomorrow we'll call a locksmith. We'll have the locks on your house changed, and you can cancel your credit cards. Forget this entire book idea; go back to what you were doing before last week. And you will need to call the police, just to give your version of what happened to the cop in the elevator."

"They'll hate me. That detective was shot because of me—"

"You don't know that."

"Don't I?"

He stood up and came out from behind the desk to stand beside her. "I'm going to give you something to relax you and ease the pain in your ankle. You can sleep here tonight; we have a comfortable cot in an examination room." He gave her a crooked grin. "It's not the Hilton, but you'll be safe. I'm on call at the hospital tonight, so if you need me, you can have me paged."

She closed her eyes in gratitude. "I really hate to be a bother to you, but that'd be great." It would be a blessed relief to let go of everything, to forget that she'd ever met Evelyn Fischer or heard of Theo M. Russell. Someone else could write the definitive book on breast cancer and abortion. Someone else was bound to after Russell's novel came out and exposed the link.

Ken left the room and returned a few moments later with a cup of water and a couple aspirin. She swallowed the pills, then obediently followed him to a small room in the back of the office. A neat cot, a table, a cabinet, and a stool were the only furnishings.

"Our fathers' fainting room," Ken said, laughing. "You'd be surprised how many times we've bedded people down in here. I think you'll be comfortable."

"I won't stay long," Theo said. "I want to go to church tomorrow with Stacy."

"That's fine." He looked steadily into her eyes. "I'll be back early in the morning and take you to breakfast. We'll see things more clearly in the light of a new day, I'm sure."

"Yes, sir," Theo said.

Ken smiled at her as he left and closed the door behind him.

SUNDAY

October 27

Chapter 19

THEO was awake and dressed when someone rapped on the door of the fathers' fainting room early Sunday morning.

"Come in," she called, hoping to see Ken. But the nurse stood behind the door, her face as starched as the uniform she wore.

"Doctor asked me to come in and tell you he's delivering a baby," she said, her eyes as hard as dried peas. "I'm to send you home. And see if you need anything."

She added the last comment as an afterthought, and Theo decided to ignore the nurse's thinly veiled hostility. She hadn't done anything to the woman, for heaven's sake, so maybe the lady was a chronic grouch.

"I'm ready to go," she said, easing her weight from the chair onto her good ankle. "I just want to freshen up a bit." She held up the gown she'd worn the night before. "I don't know where your laundry basket is."

Wordlessly, the woman pointed toward a canvas hamper at the end of the hall. Theo walked toward it, carefully favoring her injured foot. "I know you must think this is all a little strange, Nurse," she called over her shoulder, "but Dr. Holman thought I'd be better off here last night."

"The doctor—!" the nurse stammered, the soft sag beneath her chin quivering in indignation. "He didn't stay here, too, did he?"

"No." Theo tossed the gown into the hamper and turned to face the woman she'd come to see as only slightly less malevolent than Nurse Ratched from *One Flew over the Cuckoo's Nest*. "He was on call at the hospital."

Without another word, the nurse clapped her mouth shut and stalked toward the cubicle where the patient files and computers were kept. Theo stepped into the small restroom in the hall, splashed water on her face, and groaned when she realized that not only did her attacker have her purse but he also had her hairbrush and emergency makeup kit. *And I doubt Nurse Ratched has an extra tube of mascara and lipstick,* she thought. *I'll just have to look like a wreck until I get to Ann's house.*

She dried her face, finger-combed her hair, and grinned as she sprayed her wrists with a can of air freshener she found on the toilet. Without her makeup she had the sleepy, lashless look of a rabbit, but at least she looked clean enough to take a cab to the hotel garage, get her car, and drive home.

The deep sleep of the last night had calmed her nerves and left her feeling almost cheerful. *I will have the locks at the house changed,* she told herself as she stared into the mirror. *I'll cancel my credit cards and get another purse. I didn't have much cash in my wallet, so that's no loss. And the valet at the hotel garage has my spare car key, so that's no problem either. I can handle this. Life goes on, and I can forget what happened yesterday. . . . I can forget all of it—except Ken.*

She paused in the open doorway to the office area where the nurse was pretending to be busy. "I'm leaving now to hail a cab," she told the sour-faced woman. "If you'd be kind enough to loan me ten dollars and thank Dr. Holman for me—"

"I'm not Doctor's personal message service," the nurse answered, primly turning toward a drawer in the desk. She pulled a key from her pocket, unlocked it, and slapped a ten-dollar bill on the counter. "And I don't know what you think you're doing with Dr. Holman. Lots of women have tried to get his attention, but you're the first who's come in screaming about murderers and kidnappers." The nurse turned to face Theo, an expression of disapproval calcified into her face. "I can smell a gold digger from a mile away, and I think it's truly indecent of you to be chasing the doctor right in front of his dead wife's picture!"

Theo stepped back, stunned, as the nurse turned on her heel and went out another door. She stood in silent shock for a moment, then sighed. The nurse thought she had invented yesterday's entire story just to seduce Dr. Holman!

If only she had.

* * *

Madison Whitlow stepped through the impressive doors of the *Post* offices and stopped at an information desk to inquire where he might find Pamela Lansky. "Third floor, if she's in," the young man behind the desk said, pointing to the elevator. "I don't think she's usually around on Sundays."

"She'll be around today," Madison answered, moving toward the elevator.

The third floor was a calm sea of beige desks and computer terminals. The only sound was the electric hum of the fluorescent lights overhead. Madison slowly zigzagged between the desks, scanning nameplates. The last desk in a row near a wall of windowed offices bore Pamela Lansky's name, but the reporter was nowhere in sight.

"Can I help you?" a woman asked. Madison looked behind him. A stately looking black woman, her hair pulled softly into a chignon, stood in the doorway of a private office.

"This is Pamela Lansky's desk, right?" Madison asked, feeling foolish and out of place in the graveyard environment.

"That's what it says," the woman answered dryly. She took a sip from her coffee cup, thoughtfully surveyed the sea of empty desks before her, then stepped back into the privacy of her office.

Madison took a seat in the beige plastic chair by the side of

Lansky's desk and waited. Five minutes later, a blonde woman of about thirty-five swept down the hall, a pencil clenched between her teeth. She took one look at Madison and raised an eyebrow.

"Pam Lansky?" he asked, standing.

She took the pencil from her mouth and abruptly gestured for him to sit. "Yes. You're Madison Whitlow?"

"I am." Madison extended his hand. "Thanks for agreeing to meet me on your day off."

"Good reporters don't take days off," she quipped, slipping out of her heavy denim jacket. She tossed it over her chair and sat down, tucking one leg beneath her. Looking up, she regarded him with shrewd eyes like little chips of quartz. "What brings you to see me, Mr. Whitlow?"

"Russell does."

"Well, I have nothing new to tell you. Unless you have something for me, the story's dead."

Madison leaned forward, resting his hand on her desk. "I don't know if I can help you, Ms. Lansky, but I'm here because Russell called me."

The reporter's eyes widened. "You've heard from him?"

"Yes. He left a message on my answering machine. He said he was all right and he was working on something new. He said I shouldn't worry about him."

"Did he say where he was?" she asked, her voice edged with impatience.

"No."

"Well," she said and shrugged a slender shoulder, "end of story. Apparently he's fine. I've wasted nearly a week on this while he's been off somewhere writing his next book—"

"He's not fine."

"How do you know?"

"Because he told me to give my wife his love—and I don't have a wife."

The pencil in Pamela Lansky's hand fell to her desk. "Could he have been confusing you with someone else? Is he absentminded? Alcoholic?"

"Not Russ." Madison leaned back in his chair and smiled. "He knows I date a lot; he's always teasing me about my women. No way would he marry me off unless he was trying to tell me something."

He watched Lansky's face carefully and repressed a smile. She smelled a story; he could tell by the way she hunched lower and leaned toward him across the desk. "Could he really be in trouble?" she asked, softening her voice. "I have to tell you, the police have given up. Yesterday they allowed the hotel to clear out his room. And the detective working the case has been sidelined, shot in an episode of random violence."

Whitlow tapped the folded newspaper on his lap. "In this morning's article you said that the wounded police officer was working on Russ's case. That's why I came to you, Ms. Lansky. I thought maybe we could help each other."

"You want to know what I've learned that I haven't printed. Well, not much, Mr. Whitlow. Sorry to disappoint you."

"Then maybe I can help you. Did you know that Russell was scared to death before he disappeared? He wanted me to pull a great proposal that he'd submitted. The story line of the novel revolved around a supposed link between breast cancer and abortion."

Pamela made a face. "I know all about that stuff. Theodora Russell faxed a synopsis to me."

"The woman who talked to Evelyn Fischer?"

"Yeah. She's a flaming anti-choice zealot."

"Well? Did you see anything dangerous in that synopsis? Russ was convinced someone wanted him to shut up."

She shook her head impatiently. "That research was and is nothing but smoke and mirrors. The entire idea is preposterous. I wouldn't even waste my time writing about it."

"From what I've read, Theodora Russell thought there was something to it. She thought it was good enough to use herself."

"She's a rank amateur who happened on a pro's stuff and wouldn't let it go. She's also a closed-minded fundamentalist who couldn't care less about reason and scientific inquiry. Getting her hands on that copy of Russell's proposal must have been her dream come true."

"So you don't think this woman had anything to do with Russ's disappearance? Your articles seem to imply that you do."

Pamela leaned forward and looked steadily into Madison's eyes. "What I think doesn't matter. My job is to report the facts, and if those facts stir things up, well—" she shrugged—"that's the nature of the game, Mr. Whitlow."

* * *

Dennison Reyes slammed his coffee cup to his breakfast tray, then pulled the folded newspaper closer to him. The muscles in his face tightened into a mask of rage as he skimmed the article again; then he threw the paper down onto the massive oak table and furiously punched Scotty Salago's number into his cellular phone.

"What's this I'm reading about a cop being shot yesterday at the Hilton Tower?" he snapped, taking pains to keep his voice level, though he gripped the phone so tightly that his knuckles were white. "Tell me your men had nothing to do with it, Scotty."

A heavy silence lay on the line for a moment. "Well, Mr. Reyes, the woman you sent us to pick up was with the cop. We did good to get there before she went downtown with him. Brennan did what he thought he had to do."

"So we've got the woman?"

"Uh, no, Mr. Reyes. She got away, and she didn't go home last night. But Brennan got her purse. The police will think some hanger banger just got a little sloppy and took out a cop while trying to get the bag on some woman's arm."

"My people don't like sloppy, Mr. Salago. They like clean. Neat. No loose ends."

"Yes, sir, I know that."

"Good. I'll confer with my colleagues, and then I'll be in touch later today. But in the meantime, Scotty, take care of your sloppy hanger banger."

"Will do, Mr. Reyes. He knows the rules."

"And wake Mr. Russell up again. In light of this article, he needs to place another call, this time to someone at the *Post*. Call today, right away; speak to a janitor if you have to, but don't let this go on. Tell him to say that he's fine, he's sorry a cop was hurt, but he's working in a quiet place for a while."

"Got it, boss."

"And, Scotty?"

"Yeah, boss?"

Reyes's jaw clenched. "Call me boss again and you'll regret it."

Reyes clicked the phone, then tapped in another number. Blasted fools. A conference call was the last thing he wanted to deal with on a Sunday morning.

✴ ✴ ✴

Pam Lansky jumped when the phone on her desk buzzed. She held up a quieting finger to interrupt Madison, then picked up the phone. "Lansky." Taking a quick breath of surprise, her eyes darted toward Madison. "Why, yes, Mr. Russell," she said, her eyes open and slightly accusing as she stared at the agent. "I understand that it's a mistake. So why don't you tell us where you are?"

Madison felt a chill shock when he heard Russ's name; then he automatically reached for the phone. "Let me talk to him," he whispered, and Pamela shook her head as she scrambled to reach for her pencil. "OK," she said, scribbling in shorthand on a notepad. "Got it. By the way, your agent's sitting right here next to me. Would you like to speak to him?"

Madison grabbed the phone she offered. "Russ?"

"Hey, Madison, big guy! What are you doing in Washington?" It was Russell's voice, no doubt, but the words were slightly slurred, and the bright cheerfulness wasn't natural. Russell was melancholy, thoughtful, sometimes cynically humorous. But never had Madison known him to be this casually lighthearted.

"Russ, it's good to hear your voice," Madison answered. "But you've got us all worried. I'm here in Washington checking up on you." Madison turned slightly in his chair because Pamela Lansky was staring at him the way a scientist studies a specimen under glass. "What's wrong, Russ? You sound tired."

"I just woke up," Russell answered. Inexplicably, he laughed. "Woke up," he echoed, still laughing.

"So where are you, Russ?"

"Not to worry. I'm writing. Sorry about the cop. Read it in the paper, and I had to call and set things right."

"So you're in Washington?"

"Am I?" The question seemed to confuse Russell, and through the phone Madison heard sounds of movement for a few seconds. Finally Russ spoke again. "Hey, Madison, the *Post* travels. Did you give your wife a kiss for me?"

"I tried to," Madison answered, a hard fist of fear growing in his stomach. "I'm still trying to, man, but I can't seem to catch up with her these days. Do you know where she might be?"

"I don't think she could be far away," Russell answered, his voice a thin whisper. "Keep trying to reach her, OK? I gotta go, man. Take care of my work."

There was a click, then nothing. Madison glumly handed the phone back to Pamela Lansky.

"He was saying good-bye," Madison muttered, more to himself than to the reporter. He slouched in the plastic chair and rested his head on his hand. "Something's wrong, and he was telling me good-bye."

"He's perfectly fine," Pamela argued. "He sounded great when he talked to me. He was lucid, bright—"

"You don't know him at all," Madison answered, glaring over at her. "And you probably never will."

Chapter 20

JUST before noon, Scotty Salago pulled his black Mercedes to the curb outside the house in Fairmount Heights. He got out of the car and scanned the street. An elderly woman, her hair knotted in pink sponge curlers, peered curiously at him from a window of the house next door but let the curtain fall when he caught her eye. Grinning, Scotty walked up the broken sidewalk and rapped on the door.

"This place smells like a locker room," he muttered when Antonio let him in. He kicked a stack of old pizza boxes out of his way. "Or a brewery." To his right, the grimy kitchen sink overflowed with empty beer cans, the counter littered with fast-food trash. The dull hum of a television echoed from the front room, and Scotty followed Antonio's broad back into the darkened space.

Brennan sat in a sprained beach chair, the Sunday edition of the *Wall Street Journal* spread across his lap. Across the room in a corner, Theo Russell sat on the bed, his back against the wall and his knees drawn up under his chin. His thin body shook, and his hands trembled as they picked at the thin blanket around his shoulders. The pale skin under his beard looked like snow under a fresh layer of dirt.

"Sheesh, he looks like a prisoner of war," Scotty said, brushing the sleeves of his sport coat as if the grime of the house had somehow contaminated him. "Is he going to make it outta here?"

The author lifted his head at the words, and a spark of life flashed from his bloodshot eyes. "That's right, Mr. Russell," Scotty said, rocking back on his heels as he slipped his hands into his pockets. "You done good. You did what we asked, you been quiet, and today you get your reward."

A slow smile crawled across Russell's face.

"But first," Scotty said, turning to face Brennan. "There was a mess-up at the hotel. The cop. The boss says we gotta take care of it."

Brennan looked up from the *Journal,* his eyes narrowing.

"Brennan, it was you who went to the hotel, right?"

The Irishman lifted his chin. "Yes. Antonio stayed here to watch our guest."

"Did you have to shoot the cop? The boss didn't like that."

Brennan held his silence, his gaze locked with Scotty's. After a moment, he nodded slowly. "Yes. I barely had time to get to the hotel, mind you. The woman was with the cop by the time I caught up with her—"

"But you lost her," Scotty broke in.

Another pause. "Well, naturally she ran into the crowd. I couldn't exactly start shooting up the lobby."

"Smart thinking. But losing the woman wasn't good." Scotty took a deep breath. "I guess you know what's next."

Brennan's eyes hardened. "I'll be wanting to get a second opinion before we decide on that."

A gun appeared, as though out of nowhere, and came level with Brennan's face. "No second opinions, but you've got two choices," Scotty said, his voice low and reasonable. "You knew about *omerta* when you joined the family, Brennan. The code of silence is simple. You mess up, you pay or you die. It's the only way we can trust you. Now, I'd hate to lose you 'cause you're good at what you do. Usually." Brennan's eyes flickered, and Scotty smiled as he went on, "But the choice is entirely up to you."

The Irishman studied him in silence, then rose to his feet in a quick, spare motion. Without a word he moved toward the kitchen.

Scotty nodded. "Good choice. I'll make it quick."

Brennan entered the kitchen and spread his left hand on the stained countertop. Scotty followed him, slipping his gun back into its holster and pulling a glistening knife from its leather sheath beneath his shirt. He stilled for a moment, admiring the gleam of the blade that completed and made him whole. Let Brennan and Antonio rely on their guns. To Scotty Salago, guns were little more than a necessary evil, a tool to be used when brute force was called for. Personally, Scotty was more of a craftsman, more drawn to finesse than brawn. He smiled. He had done some of his finest work with a blade.

He approached the silent man, noting with admiration the way Brennan's unwavering gaze followed him. *The man's a pro, I'll give him that,* Scotty thought. "Do you want a shot of vodka or something? I got some out in the car."

"No. Just do it." Brennan's words were clipped, almost impatient.

A soft, strangled sound came from the corner of the living room, and Scotty glanced back at the man on the bed. The novelist looked like a living skeleton, his staring eyes little more than black holes in the center of his face. On the other side of the room, Antonio had respectfully turned his head.

"Anytime you're ready." Brennan's voice was cool, infinitely controlled.

Scotty laid his blade over the third joint of the little finger on the Irishman's hand, then pressed down in a sharp, deliberate motion.

Theodore Russell felt the thin, cold blade of foreboding slice into his heart as the knife severed Brennan's knuckle. They weren't going to let him go. Men who went around snipping off their friends' fingers weren't about to let him walk away. But they were finished with him, of that he was certain. There was a resoluteness in the new man's step, an authority in his voice. Russell knew the time had come.

It was over. Madison had come to Washington but not in time. That reporter hadn't picked up on the urgency in his voice, and the detective who'd been working his case was out of commission, probably dying. It was over.

While Antonio bandaged Brennan's hand, the new guy, Scotty, fished a couple of white pills out of his pocket and dropped them onto the kitchen counter. "Take those," he told Brennan, moving to the corner where the kitchen met the living room. With his good hand, Brennan tossed the pills back without comment.

Russell lifted his watery eyes as Scotty came into the room and smiled at him. "We wouldn't want to send you out on the street with nothing in your system," he said simply, "and you haven't had much of an appetite, have you? We're going to fix you up one more time before you go."

"Please—" Russell closed his eyes, his throat constricting. A fountain of words wanted to pour from his heart, pleas for his life, for his future, for the books he wanted to write and the family he wanted to raise. But this man wouldn't understand a word of it. Thirty-seven years of life had come down to a few dark moments in a filthy house with three brawny, brainless thugs. But though they couldn't know what he felt in his heart, they did understand the fire pouring through his veins.

He needed the heroin, needed it like he needed air to breathe. His arms and legs were quivering in anticipation of the rush to come; his heart pounded sluggishly, awaiting the buzz only the drug could bring.

Scotty smiled, recognizing the signs of heroin dependence. "Haven't had a fix lately, huh?" he asked, his voice heavy with compassion. "Too bad. Brennan and Antonio should have taken better care of you." He leaned against the wall of the living room and crossed his arms. "Hey guys, you two get the car ready to take our friend home. I'll get his fix."

For a moment, Russell dared to hope that he'd been wrong. Brennan and Antonio left the house, and Scotty turned to the counter where the drug paraphernalia had been scattered about. He measured a generous dose of heroin into the spoon, heated it, then vacuumed it up into the tiny needle of the syringe.

While Russell watched and waited, Scotty held the syringe up to the light, pressed the plunger until the air was gone from the tube, and reached for Russell's trembling arm. There were more than half a dozen bruises and clear needle marks on this arm alone, and Scotty *tsk*ed in quiet pity as he strapped the tourniquet around Russell's upper arm. Scotty didn't even look for a vein. He simply slid the needle into a fresh bruise, pressed the plunger, and fastened his eyes to Russell's face.

The needle stung, but Russell sighed in contentment. Brennan and Antonio came back into the room, a heavy duffel bag in their hands, and Russ knew that was how he'd leave the house.

Too bad. He felt a sharp pang of sorrow for the life he had meant to live but hadn't; then his heart lurched in his chest, and Theodore Russell closed his eyes.

* * *

With the confidence of a man who knows the power of his charm, Dennison Reyes prowled easily through the crowd outside the ballroom of the Washington Converse Hotel. Completely aware that he was the "friend in high places" to whom many of the tuxedoed men and sequined women owed their invitations, he moved through the gathering with the hard grace of one who has total control of himself. In a holding pen cordoned off by velvet ropes, a small pack of reporters yelped for his attention. In an hour or two he would give it to them.

Dr. Burl Rodenbaugh, executive director of the National Committee for Choice, shouldered his way through a knot of silver-haired women. Reyes stopped to shake his hand, mindful that their greeting was being recorded by the photographers.

"Mr. Reyes! Dr. Rodenbaugh!" one of the paparazzi shouted. "This way, please."

The two men paused in their handshake to smile for the cameras. Blinking away the effects of the flash, the men turned to follow the surge of the crowd into the ballroom.

"Everything all right with you, Burl?" Reyes asked, extending a hand so the doctor could precede him through the doorway.

"Business is as firm as the Rock of Gibraltar," Rodenbaugh answered. "How's the lawyering?"

"Same as always," Reyes quipped, following him into the room.

Senator Lauren Scott had already been seated at her place at the head table. Reyes and Rodenbaugh shared a few polite jokes as they snaked their way through the crowd to find their places on the platform.

The meal was typical, the introductions predictable, but Lauren Scott could not give a bad speech. Reyes studied the faces of the audience as the senator spoke; the crowd sat in rapt attention, absorbing every word.

"Where would we be without the National Committee for Choice?" she asked, her elegant hand sweeping the air. "Fifty years in the past, ladies and gentlemen. If America is to move forward, we must move in the direction granted by the freedom of choice. We cannot listen to those who are nay-saying the victories recently won in the areas of research, and we cannot return to the days when women were forced to carry the products of rape, incest, and abuse."

She paused dramatically as the audience applauded.

"Each new day brings incredible developments in science," Senator Scott continued. She leaned over the platform, her hands gripping the lectern for emphasis. "Juvenile-onset diabetes, Huntington's disease, Alzheimer's, sickle-cell anemia, immune deficiencies—cures for these and other diseases are only a few months away due to the research funded in part by our government. But without the NCC, my friends, none of this would be happening. Without the support of the NCC, safe, legal abortion would be impossible, and women would be forced to return to the butcher shops and clothes-hanger abortionists of a more primitive society."

The crowd murmured in united approval, and Senator Scott held up a hand for silence. "America cannot go back; we must go forward. We're asking tonight that you contribute to the movement that will ensure America's future and America's health for America's people. Support the NCC, my friends, because by doing so, you are supporting our country. You are supporting the child with diabetes, the elderly woman with Alzheimer's, the man who suffers from Huntington's disease. You are supporting the helpless people of our nation who cannot speak for themselves."

Senator Scott sat down; the audience leapt to its feet in thunderous applause. As Dr. Rodenbaugh stepped to the lectern for his follow-up appeal, Reyes took a slim telephone from an inner pocket in his tuxedo and touched a number. "Salago?" he whispered, turning his head from the audience. "Get that *Post* reporter and her photographer past the security guard *now*."

He had just disconnected from the call when he heard his name. Burl Rodenbaugh was introducing him as "the finest lawyer in Washington. Always working, you'll see he's on the phone as I speak. And that, my friends, is why the NCC hired him."

The crowd laughed; Reyes stood and bowed in a dignified gesture. Senator Scott stood to her feet in appreciation, and the audience roared in approval.

It was a grand night for abortion rights.

A few miles away, under cover of darkness, Brennan and Antonio moved in the shadows of the Family Services Clinic owned and operated by Dr. Griffith Dunlap. Brennan gritted his teeth as he followed Antonio. The medication had worn off; his hand throbbed in pain.

Pressing his lips together, he reached up and tapped Antonio on the shoulder.

Reflexively, Antonio's fist swung wide, and Brennan stepped back. "Man, Brennan, don't scare me like that!"

"Then move along there; I want to get this done. My hand's killing me."

"We're almost done. Just two or three more containers to load."

"The driver's trustworthy? I don't want to mess up again, if you take my meaning."

"The driver works for BioTech. He don't know nothing."

"Good."

Brennan helped Antonio heave a few more metal containers onto the truck; then he stood back while Antonio locked the doors and pounded on the side of the cab. The driver waved, then cranked the engine and pulled slowly away from the back of the building.

Brennan and Antonio turned and walked briskly through the clinic. The last employee had clocked out hours ago, the lights were out, the front doors locked, the parking lot clear. No one happening by would think this night different from any other at the Family Services Clinic.

Moving to a corner of the clinic's waiting room, Antonio found the shopping bag he'd brought earlier. Wiring was his specialty, and this job was simple and straightforward. Pushing a dusty silk plant out of the way, he wired a mound of plastique into a timer, set the timer, set the device in the corner, and then pulled the cheap-looking plant back into place. He picked up the shopping bag and looked around.

Brennan held up the index finger of his bandaged hand. "Don't forget the final touch," he called, and Antonio nodded. From the bag he pulled out Theodora Russell's purse, then casually drop-kicked it under a padded metal chair in the waiting room.

Gritting his teeth against the throbbing agony of his hand, Brennan activated the building's alarm system, then jerked his head toward the back door. Taking the now empty shopping bag, the two men slipped out and walked away.

October 28

THROUGH the embracing folds of sleep, Theo felt something fall on the blanket that covered her. She forced her eyes open. She was on the couch in Ann's living room, and her hostess had just dropped a section of the *Post* on Theo's chest.

"Time to get up and see what God hath wrought," Ann said, her voice unusually sharp. "Look at that front page."

"Give me a minute. I'm not a morning person, remember?"

Theo sat up and waited for her sleepy eyes to focus. Yesterday she'd tied the frazzled ends of her life back together, and the effort had left her more than a little drained. The locksmith wouldn't come on a Sunday, but he promised to come first thing Monday morning. She'd called the police, who sent a pair of officers out to record her statement about the shooting in the elevator. After reporting her stolen credit cards, she had settled on the couch with Stacy to watch *Pocahontas* for the fiftieth time. Theodore Russell, abortion, and breast cancer were the last things she wanted to think about.

"Mama!" Stacy popped up at the end of the couch and reached for Theo with sticky hands.

"Good morning, sweetheart," Theo said, sitting up. She blew her daughter a kiss. "Are you having fun?"

"Mommy's foot better?" Stacy asked, her hands probing the blanket for Theo's foot.

Theo nodded and slid her foot closer to Stacy's little hands. "Look and see for yourself, honey. It's much better." She picked up the newspaper and unfolded it. The headline and article midway down the page jumped out at her. Fully awake now, Theo pulled the paper closer.

Brilliant Author Found Dead among Homeless

by Pamela Lansky

WASHINGTON—Police identified a dead body found outside a homeless shelter Sunday night as Theodore Marshall Russell, the enigmatic and brilliant novelist whose first book, *Out of the Darkness, Into the Light,* spent fifty-one weeks on the best-seller lists last year. The author, who had been missing for nine days, was identified by his agent, Madison Whitlow. Whitlow, who had come to Washington to find Russell, spoke to the novelist by telephone a few hours before the body was found.

A cursory examination of the body indicated that Russell had been using heroin, but prior to an official autopsy, the coroner would not speculate as to the cause of death. Other informed sources have stated that if Russell was an addict, it is likely he died from an overdose or another complication of his drug use.

Anna Burkett, president of the National Authors League, first reported the author's disappearance. Burkett said that to her knowledge Russell had never used drugs, then later admitted that she had never actually met the author. She spoke to him just before the NAL convention from which he disappeared. Burkett has claimed throughout the investigation that Russell was a victim of a random robbery attempt.

Russell's agent, Madison Whitlow, told police that Theo Russell definitely did not use drugs. According to Whitlow,

Russell was "an artist, a professional, and an eccentric, but he was no junkie. The man would hardly take an aspirin unless absolutely necessary." Whitlow insists that despite a reassuring phone call the author made Sunday morning, Theo Russell's death is suspicious and should be investigated.

Police Sergeant Howard Datsko, recently released from the hospital for an injury he suffered in the line of duty two days ago, has said the police department will hold a press conference when its investigation is complete.

The horror Theo felt the first time she read the article faded to a mingling of sorrow and relief during her second reading. She felt terrible that the man had died, but if Theodore Russell had overdosed on heroin, no one could seriously consider her a suspect in the man's disappearance. She, after all, knew absolutely nothing of the seamy side of crime and drug dealers in the District.

But how tragic the novelist's death was! Had he begun to use drugs because of his success or in spite of it? She had heard hundreds of stories about alcoholic writers who felt they wrote better while slightly drunk. Had Theo Russell relied on a drug-induced euphoria to aid his writing? Surely not! The work she had seen in the proposal was crisp, clear, and insightful. That kind of thinking didn't come from a whiskey bottle or a chemical compound.

Shaking her head, she swung her legs off the couch. Her ankle was still slightly swollen and a greenish bruise colored the side of her foot, but it would bear her weight. She crossed the living room and went to join Ann in the kitchen for breakfast.

Ann was grim-faced at the breakfast table, but she said nothing until Bethany had gathered her books and slammed out the front door on her way to school. When Stacy had eaten her breakfast and parked in front of *Sesame Street*, Ann finally opened up.

"Well?" she said, pausing in midstep as she carried breakfast bowls to the sink. "What are you going to do now?"

"Keep on researching," Theo answered, grimly picking up scattered Cheerios from Stacy's place at the table. "Theo Russell is dead, and that's a tragedy, but apparently he was an addict."

"Theo." Ann crossed in front of Theo and blocked her way to the sink. "Wake up, dear heart. You're blind as Mister MaGoo. A man in an elevator tried to kidnap you. No one believes Theodore Russell used drugs, and yet he ends up on the street pumped full of heroin. A nice cop who just wants to talk to you ends up in the hospital—"

"The elevator thing was a purse snatching," Theo argued, her voice beginning to tremble.

"When's the last time you heard about a purse snatcher shooting a cop in broad daylight? In the *Hilton Tower Hotel*, for heaven's sake? Purse snatchers take purses; they don't grab women out of classy hotels."

Theo closed her eyes. "I'm going home today, Ann. I'm going to put all of this behind me and get on with writing the book. A purse snatcher stole my purse. He took my credit cards, which I've canceled, and threw the rest of my junk into a garbage can somewhere. That's all there is to it. The crimefest is over. I feel sorry for Theo Russell, but my life has to go on. I have to think of Stacy."

"Yes, you do," Ann said, her voice tight with mutiny. "I'm giving you an order, Theo. As your friend and someone who cares about Stacy, you can't ignore the possible danger. That goon had a gun! What will you do if he comes to your house?"

"Stop it!" Theo covered her ears with her hands and whirled away from Ann's brilliant eyes. "You weren't there! You didn't smell the smoke and see the flash. You didn't hear that policeman's head hit the wall and watch him crumple onto your feet. That guy had his hand over my mouth, Ann! I was helpless! I never want to feel that way again."

"Honey, that's what I'm trying to say! You don't have to." Ann sighed and nodded with a taut jerk of her head. "OK. I didn't want to do this, but you give me no choice." She turned and walked into the living room. Perplexed, Theo followed.

Ann stood at the antique writing desk near the window. Moving smoothly, she opened a small drawer, pulled out an old skeleton key, then inserted it into a locked drawer. From under a false leather surface at the bottom of the drawer she pulled out a gun.

Speechless, Theo only stared.

"I bought it right after my divorce," Ann explained. "I was scared, Theo, living alone with a child. Every single noise in the night nearly sent me through the wall. After reading the horrible stuff in the papers, I couldn't even walk outside without being afraid that a rapist or murderer hid behind every tree. I couldn't relax in my own home, in my own bedroom, so I bought this gun and hid it here. Bethany's never found it. And Stacy's not allowed to play near this desk, so don't worry."

Theo felt a shiver pass down her spine. "Is it loaded?"

Ann gave her a blank look, then shook her head. "No. But it looks seriously scary, doesn't it? I want you to keep it at your house for a while."

Theo sank down on the couch, her eyes still riveted on the black object in Ann's hand. "No thanks. I don't want to see another gun for as long as I live."

Ann dropped the pistol back into the drawer and locked it; then she crossed swiftly to Theo's side. "You've been through a lot, but you've got to realize that we're living in a rough time. Washington is the murder capital of the country. We live in a violent age, and someone tried to hurt you. You've got to think about yourself, Theo."

Theo stood up, cast a subdued glance toward the desk, and moved toward the small den where Stacy was watching TV. "Just let me gather our things, and we'll be out of your way," she said quietly.

"Are you upset with me?" Ann called, her voice choked with emotion.

"No." Theo stopped and shook her head. "I'll think about what you said. Maybe you're right—you usually are. Maybe I should drop the book, but right now I just want to go home and get life back to normal. I just need to be alone, to think and pray and . . . wait."

"For what?" Ann whispered.

Theo shook her head. "I don't know. A road map for the future, I guess."

* * *

For a few hours the ordinary routine of life in her own home kept Theo's thoughts occupied. There was laundry to do and rancid leftovers in the fridge begging to be tossed out. Theo moved through the blessed comfort of housework but realized how jittery she was when the telephone rang and she jumped as if a shot had been fired. Her hand shook when she picked up the phone.

"Hello?"

"Hi, little sister." Janette could hardly lift her voice above a whisper, and a wave of guilt immediately slapped at Theo. She'd been so busy with her own affairs that she hadn't taken the time to call. . . .

"Hi, yourself," Theo answered, sinking into a chair at the kitchen table. "How are you feeling? I've been meaning to call you—"

"Sure you have," Janette interrupted, but there was a trace of humor in her voice. "I know you've been out partying all night. John tried all day yesterday to reach you, and all we ever got was that goofy answering machine of yours."

"Sorry," Theo answered, feeling a twinge of remorse as she looked at the blinking red light on her answering machine. She hadn't checked it. "But tell me about you. How are you feeling?"

"I'm like fine wine; I just keep getting stronger and better," Janette answered calmly. "I lie in bed, I read, I watch *I Love Lucy* reruns. Someone said that laughter does good like medicine, so I'm laughing as much as I can. But I didn't call to talk about me—I'm tired of the subject. How's your love life? Who's the man keeping you out at all hours?"

Theo managed a choking laugh. "Funny you should ask. I've just endured the worst week of my life, but in the midst of it, I did meet a man. A really nice one. A doctor."

"Do tell," Janette purred.

"It's a long story," Theo said, making herself comfortable in the kitchen chair. "And it all began with a phone call." And so Theo told her about Theodore Russell, Evelyn Fischer, and the details of the proposal. She even worked up enough courage to talk about the terrifying encounter in the hotel elevator. And somehow, sitting in her cozy kitchen with her sister's concerned voice in her ear, the episode lost its power to frighten her. She actually found herself laughing as she described Nurse Ratched and the woman's crazy conviction that Theo had staged the entire situation to snag the handsome and eligible Dr. Holman.

Janette laughed, too, but halfheartedly.

"Are you really OK, Janette?" Theo whispered. "Tell me the truth."

She heard a deep sigh on the other end of the line. "I think you need to keep going," Janette whispered, her voice fragile and shaking. "You need to write that book. Now that the novelist is dead, no one's going to tell the truth about breast cancer. But you can."

"Lots of people are talking about breast cancer," Theo said, shrugging. "In fact, I told Ken that I was ready to have a mastectomy because it's often hereditary, and he told me about this new genetic study they're doing. Apparently there's one gene that predicts breast cancer, and if I don't have that gene, I don't have to worry."

"I don't think you have to worry about your genes," Janette answered with quiet emphasis.

"But Mom's cancer started in the breast. And so did yours."

"Maybe." A tense silence hummed over the telephone line. "But we never told you, Theo. You were only a kid, and there were things we didn't want you to know."

"What?" Theo asked, searching anxiously for the meaning behind Janette's words. Everything went silent within her as she waited.

"I was sixteen. You must have been ten or eleven. I guess our family never thought it would happen to us, and we never dreamed we'd do what we did. But when it happens—well, sometimes you don't think clearly." She paused, as if to gather her strength. "I got pregnant, Theo. And I had an abortion."

A thunderbolt jagged through Theo; she stared at the swinging pendulum of her kitchen clock in hypnotized horror.

"Mom and Dad let you spend that night with a friend, and no one ever said anything." Janette paused, obviously finding it difficult to confess something that had happened so long ago. "So you see, Theo, you probably don't have to worry about breast cancer. But you can't quit working now. God sent this information your way, and women are dying because they don't know the truth."

Her voice, as she finished, was fainter than air. "You've got to write this book. No matter what."

* * *

Theo moved through the rest of the morning in a daze, thinking and rethinking her family's history. Her sister had been a pregnant teenager! That in itself was inconceivable. Janette had been a perky, pretty, popular cheerleader, her boyfriends all outstanding student government types. Janette had been an honor student; she had wanted college and a career and had known that a baby would ruin her dreams.

And so she'd had an abortion. And her parents, God bless them, had been blind enough to value their dreams more than wisdom. As active Christians they had condemned the Supreme Court's decision allowing abortion; as frantic parents they had quietly gone out and arranged one for their eldest daughter. Of course, it would have been humiliating for them to have a visibly pregnant daughter in school, in church, in the youth choir. . . .

Why? Theo's eyes welled with tears of frustration. It was all such a waste, such a tragedy. What must have seemed like a simple, private decision had resulted in endless grief. After marrying John, Janette had given birth to two healthy sons, but she'd also endured three miscarriages, and now breast cancer was devouring her body and the happiness she had managed to find.

The phone rang again, interrupting her dismal train of thought.

"Theo, hi. It's Ken Holman. We missed our breakfast date, and I haven't been able to reach you. I wanted to see how you were doing."

The soothing sound of his voice sent a flood of relief coursing through her. "I'm fine, Ken. Thanks for asking," she said, grateful for his concern. "The ankle's much better. Still a bit green, but I'm getting around."

"I wasn't asking about the ankle. I was asking about *you*. How are you doing? And why'd you run off so soon? I know I'm not the perfect host—"

"You were great," Theo said, smiling. "I couldn't have asked for more, except maybe for a hot shower. But I had the feeling your nurse wanted me out from under her feet, and Stacy and I had a church-and-Sunday-dinner date. I meant to call and thank you yesterday, but I spent the night at Ann's house and was a little . . . distracted. But it was very kind of you to take me in. I know I was a hysterical wreck when I wandered into your office."

"Anyone would have been. So, have you talked to the police and called a locksmith?"

"Yes, sir," Theo answered, smiling. "I've been good. I even talked to my sister." The smile left her face, and her voice flattened out. "Ken, I just finished talking to Janette. She told me—well, she said she had an abortion when she was sixteen. And she's had active

185

breast cancer for three years. I was almost ready to let this book go, but I can't now."

"I'm sorry." His voice was filled with compassion.

"Sorry that I'm still going to do the book?"

"No, I'm sorry that you're upset. But if you really want to keep up the work, I'll try to help."

"Good." She felt herself smiling again. "There's a lot to be done. I've got to come up with an outline and a few sample chapters. And by the way," she said, recalling a detail that had nagged her subconscious for two days, "have you ever heard of BioTech Industries?"

She heard the frown in his voice. "Yes. How'd you hear of them?"

"A note I saw in Theodore Russell's hotel room. The name was scrawled on a paper along with the word *Rambo*. Does that ring a bell?"

"Only if you're talking about the movie. But BioTech I know. A noxious business."

"Why?"

She heard him sigh. "It's a long story, Theo, and since I'm personally opposed to abortion I have no dealings with them. But BioTech takes fetal materials from aborted babies and delivers them to a handful of research labs in the United States."

Theo crinkled her nose in disgust. "Is that legal?"

"Yes. But there are a lot of ethical gray areas as far as I'm concerned. Fetal research has a horrible history, and I wish it were banned altogether."

Theo frowned, disturbed by a sudden elusive thought she could not quite fathom. "Ken, can you meet me for lunch? I want to hear more about this. I have a hunch Theo Russell was investigating BioTech Industries before he disappeared."

"I thought you were going to work on your book."

"This may be part of it! Please, Ken, I need to know more."

She held her breath as he considered. "OK. I've only got an hour

186

today for lunch, so can you meet me at the office? I hate to make you drive all the way to Georgetown."

"Spoken like a true gentleman."

"And I'm helping you on one condition. Since it could have been this topic that got Theodore Russell into trouble, I want you to find out what the police know about Russell's case. If they're absolutely sure there's no connection between the attack on you and the novelist, I'll feel a lot better about this."

Flattered by his concern, Theo smiled. She'd get no rest from either Ken or Ann until she agreed to check things out. "OK. I promise. But I'm sure there is no grand conspiracy here."

"Just be careful. I'll look forward to seeing you at lunch."

As she hung up the phone, Theo wondered why she was blushing.

❋ ❋ ❋

At lunchtime, Theo and Ken left his office under the watchful eyes of Nurse Ratched (Mrs. Wilson was her name, Ken explained, but Theo couldn't adjust to it) and walked to a small Italian restaurant a block away. After they had ordered light pasta dishes, Theo leaned across the checkered tablecloth and folded her hands. "So tell me about BioTech Industries and fetal research. Why would Theo Russell be interested in them?"

Ken turned his long frame sideways in the booth and shrugged. "As I said, there are a lot of gray areas involved. I can only guess that Russell was investigating BioTech because of his inquiries into various aspects of abortion. But the history of fetal research is grisly."

"How grisly?"

He gave her a look that mingled both compassion and a warning. "In 1973, a team of Finnish and American scientists aborted a dozen live human fetuses through hysterotomy."

"Hysterotomy?"

He nodded. "Removed from the womb as a baby is removed in a

cesarean section." Ken paused and slowly stirred the straw in his iced tea. "The babies were decapitated, and the heads kept alive for study. The experiment, funded in part by the National Institutes of Health, was designed to measure fetal metabolism."[6]

Theo felt her eyes stinging. Surely he was mistaken. Such things just didn't happen in the twentieth century.

"At about the same time," Ken went on, "another research team kept a batch of aborted babies alive in saline solution to find out if they could absorb oxygen. One child survived for nearly a day."[7]

"Saline . . ." Theo's voice wavered.

"A salt solution," Ken answered. "The salt acts as a poison. In medical school I saw fetuses that had been expelled after saline abortions. The babies' skin appeared to have been soaked in acid." The muscles in his face tensed. "Medical journals explain that hypertonic saline solution causes women 'exquisite and severe pain' if, by accident, it enters the body of a woman having an abortion. Other experts have deduced that unborn babies suffer the most severe and longest-lasting pain in a saline abortion. Can you imagine what those babies felt as they were forced to endure this experimentation?"

Theo closed her eyes. "You have seen babies like these?"

Ken nodded. "One of the vagaries of medical school, I'm afraid. The fetuses I saw had the agonized faces of children forced to die too soon. I will never forget them. And I can never accept abortion, no matter how fervently some of my colleagues insist upon its necessity. You don't have to be a Roman Catholic or a right-wing Republican to reject the claim that life begins at some distant point after conception. Every doctor knows that an embryo in the womb is genetically complete at conception. There is no obvious reason to think a preborn human is any less alive than you or me. Whether in the womb or out, we all must eat, breathe, and be sheltered."

Theo pulled a notebook from her leather briefcase. "Does BioTech Industries perform these kinds of experiments?" She scribbled a note in her steno pad.

Ken shook his head and seemed to force himself out of another line of thought. "Not that I know of. The public outcry in the seventies was so great that the NIH halted all federally funded research except that which directly benefited the fetus. Those rules still hold, but at the present time NIH is free to fund research using aborted human tissue for transplantation."

"So BioTech gets money from the National Institutes of Health?"

Ken shrugged again. "I don't know, Theo. I suppose what they do is similar to the program at the University of Washington. For nearly thirty years they have collected fetuses through private clinics and distributed them to research labs nationwide."[8]

"But I thought that research was illegal—"

"It was. In '88 President Reagan banned the use of fetal tissue from *elective* abortions. But fetuses from miscarriages or from therapeutic abortions were allowed to be used in research, so the work went on. Researchers used private money for transplants and over forty-five million dollars from the National Institutes of Health to continue. When President Clinton did away with the ban during his first week in office, the lid came off. Researchers are now having a field day."

The waiter arrived with their meals, and Theo found that the dish of pasta and tomato sauce did not seem in the least appealing. She pushed the plate aside and flipped a page in her notebook. "Tell me more," she said, writing NIH at the top of the page. "What's the big deal about fetal cells?"

Ken stirred his linguine with his fork. "Fetal cells grow quickly and are more likely to insinuate themselves into a patient's existing tissue," he explained. "They lack the surface markers that a recipient's immune system will recognize as foreign, so they're unlikely to be rejected. Most important, though, fetal cells are 'plastic.' A very young fetal cell has the potential to become a kidney, brain, or blood cell. They can grow to be anything; they can fit anywhere."

"So these cells are given to people with diseases—"

"Serious diseases," Ken said. "Incurable conditions. I can't deny that miracles have occurred. I read about one couple whose unborn baby suffered from bare lymphocyte syndrome. The baby would surely have died without a fetal-cell transplant. The parents faced three options: abort the baby, try a white-blood-cell transplant after birth, or receive fetal cells while the baby was still in the womb. The parents' first child had been born with the same condition, and the white-blood-cell transplant had failed. So they elected the third option."

"And the baby?"

"He was injected with immune cells from the liver and thymus of two aborted fetuses. After birth, he was given another injection of fetal cells. So far, the child is doing well and developing the immune system he would not have had otherwise."

Theo stopped writing and covered her mouth with her hand, thinking. If Stacy had been born without an immune system, would she have accepted cells from an aborted child to save her daughter? Would she have accepted fetal cells if doing so would somehow have eradicated Stacy's Down's syndrome? Those questions made her pause, but there was another side to the coin. What if someone had told her that Stacy, with Down's syndrome, would not have "quality of life" and should therefore be used as "spare parts" for someone else?

Fury almost choked her.

Ken fixed her in a blue-eyed vise, studying her reaction to her thoughts. She lowered her hand and looked down at her notepad. "So even though abortion is abhorrent," she whispered, her voice simmering with barely checked passion, "how do we answer people who insist that good can come out of it?"

"Good?" He laughed humorlessly. "This generation is literally consuming its offspring. We are harvesting the next generation for spare parts, taking tissues for the elderly from the youngest and most innocent lives. We have gone as far as we can go, Theo. We have reduced life to nothing more than matter for manipulation. Death has become a solution for social problems."

Staring past her notebook into her own thoughts, Theo could not argue.

Chapter 22

THE quarrel began before their dishes had been cleared away. After Ken's pessimistic summation of current medical research, Theo tried to change the subject. "This book is going to be harder to write than I thought," she said, dumping a fresh packet of sugar into her refilled iced tea. "I've heard that nobody ever committed suicide while reading a good book but many have while trying to write one."

"Theo," Ken leaned back in the booth and draped his arm across the seat. "I've got to admit that I answered your questions about BioTech in the hope that you'd reconsider pursuing this. Who do you think will buy it? After the publicity and Russell's death, that editor you talked to won't read your manuscript. Russell is dead. Why don't you let that proposal die with him?"

"Don't you think he'd want his work to continue?" she asked, her voice tight. She forced a smile, trying not to let him see how his words had lacerated her hopes. "It was you who gave him the information on abortion and breast cancer, remember? This was originally *your* dream, Ken. *You* wanted to see this information made public. Maybe I'm not as good as Theodore M. Russell—"

"I didn't know Theo Russell very well," Ken answered, his eyes darkening. He leaned forward, and his hand inched across the table as if it would grasp hers but stopped short. "But I've come to know you, and I'd like to keep you around awhile. Please, Theo, drop the book."

A tumble of confused thoughts and feelings assailed her; she struggled for control of her voice. "You're talking like Russell was murdered or something. The police say it was a drug overdose."

"There's more than one way to die from an overdose. Please, if you won't drop it completely, just give it up for a while. Write something else. Just leave this alone."

"I don't have the luxury of time. I'm living on dreams and a dwindling bank account."

"So postpone your dreams. I can take care of the bank account; I'll get you a job in my office."

Theo grinned and shook her head. "No way. Nurse Ratched hates me."

"Nurse Wilson. OK, then, I'll find you a job with one of my colleagues. And later, if you still want to write, you can write about something that won't inflame anyone."

"What's wrong with inflaming people in the name of a just cause? Where would we be without *Uncle Tom's Cabin?* Or *Silent Spring?* The truth is, women like my sister are dying because they weren't aware of the hard facts. And I'm getting smarter, Ken. I'm not carrying a purse anymore, you'll notice. I hide my money in my shoe and my car key in my briefcase."

His smile was strained. "Theo, I'm not joking. Please stop working on this book."

"You're asking too much. I don't think you have any right to ask me to stop."

"I thought I might." A look of clear, intense light poured through his eyes, and Theo felt her face grow hot. Exactly how deep did his interest run? She had instinctively liked this man from their first meeting, and she couldn't deny that awareness radiated from the blue depths of his eyes when he looked at her.

Hold on, girl. You don't have the time or the energy for an emotional involvement right now. He doesn't even know about Stacy; you've never told him about Matt. You've eaten three meals with him, and he's already asking you to give up your career. This isn't the way to go. Shut down your heart; stifle those feelings of confusion. Cut it. Now.

Looking away from the pull of his gaze, she stirred her tea. "I don't think I'm ready for . . . whatever this is."

"Then why are you here with me? Why did you come to me when you were hurt and afraid?"

"Because . . . I had no one else to turn to." Sudden tears stung her eyes, and she realized with dismay how pitiful she sounded. *Some strong, independent woman you are!*

"So I was a last resort." A wall came up behind his blue eyes, and he straightened himself and slapped his hands on the table. "Well, I have patients. And you have work to do."

"Yes," she whispered, trying to control her rebellious emotions. "I do."

He reached automatically for the check on the table, but Theo caught it and slipped it from his grasp. "I interviewed you, so lunch is on me," she said lightly, sliding out of the booth. "Writers have expense accounts, too, you know."

"I didn't know." He nodded smoothly and stood up behind her. "I'll walk you to your car."

"Don't bother. Your patients are waiting," she said, moving to the cashier. "Nurse Ratched will be wondering where you are."

Stiffly, he nodded again and walked out the door.

❋ ❋ ❋

Three blocks away, a nurse dismissed the last of Dr. Griffith Dunlap's young patients from the recovery room and locked the double doors of the Family Services Clinic. She checked the premises, tidied up the individual procedure rooms, and at 1:23 she left the building by a back door. The other nurses and Dr. Dunlap had left before lunch, their work done.

At precisely 2:00 P.M. the mechanism of a timer clicked into place, and a solid mound of plastique blew the clinic's waiting room apart, shattering the glass doors. The fire alarm sounded in an earsplitting wail as flames roared along the broken walls and paused to lick at a woman's purse tucked behind a twist of mangled metal.

Chapter 23

THEO felt the blast before she actually heard it. The parking lot seemed to shudder beneath her feet; then a roar echoed along the street. A man walking nearby crouched low as if gunfire had suddenly erupted. The explosion had come from the north, and as Theo turned toward the source of the sound, smoke towered into the gray heaven and turned the peaceful sky into a mass of dark, boiling clouds.

She ran to her car, her pulse quickening. Had someone bombed one of the government buildings? Was this a terrorist attack? Fleeting memories of the Oklahoma City bombing ruffled through her mind, and she fumbled desperately for the key at the bottom of her briefcase. If trouble had erupted a few blocks away, she wanted to be home with Stacy.

From far away the wail of a siren stretched across to her, and Theo switched on her radio as she drove out of the parking lot. If this was serious, it'd be on the news. She fumbled with the dials for a moment, picking up snatches of conversation and music. Whatever the cause of the explosion, it was bound to wreak havoc with traffic. She'd drive south and steer clear of the gridlock.

There were no urgent news bulletins on the radio, and Theo assumed the explosion had been only an industrial accident of some sort. As whispers of traffic drifted by, she forced herself to concentrate on her book. The information about BioTech and fetal-cell research was gruesome, and Theodore Russell had apparently researched that angle even though it wasn't mentioned in his proposal. Had a bitter employee of BioTech given Russell material that would prove an abortion–breast cancer link? Had Russell omitted the data from his formal proposal in order to protect someone? If he had interviewed Ken Holman and Adam Perry, Theo thought it likely that he had questioned other people, too. But whom?

On an impulse, Theo pulled into a small neighborhood market with a pay phone out front. The phone book was missing, of course, but the grocer inside pulled his phone directory from beneath the counter when she asked to borrow it. She scanned the white pages, then stabbed the book with her fingernail and fumbled for her notebook and pen. BioTech Industries was located in Hillcrest Heights, a Maryland suburb just southeast of Washington. She returned the book to the grocer, bought a soft drink and a pack of gum to thank him for his help, then returned to her car and pulled back out onto the street and drove toward the beltway.

* * *

By three o'clock, Theo had parked the Ford across the street from the modern brick building housing the offices of BioTech Industries. There were no windows in the structure, only a pair of glass doors, and no apparent explanation or description of the business operating inside.

Theo got out of the car, ran a hand through her hair in an absentminded swipe, and took a deep breath. *Look professional, Theo. You can do this.* A jackhammer crew was shredding the sidewalk behind her, and the noise served to hide the ferocious pounding of her heart. Checking traffic, she crossed the street and switched her briefcase from her right hand to her left. She didn't know what she was doing or what she'd find in this place, but at least she was moving forward.

The front door was unlocked, the lobby decorated with ornate cherry furniture and plush carpets. A pair of fine Chinese porcelain vases stood on carved wooden stands, lending an air of distinction without calling attention to their true costliness. A tufted leather sofa offered a place for visitors to sit and wait. For what?

"May I help you?" At the rear of the lobby, a pretty young woman sat behind a large, elegant desk.

"Yes," Theo answered, casually looking around as she walked toward the girl. An electronic key-code pad hung near a door behind the girl's desk. Except for the front doors, there were no other entrances or exits from the lobby.

Theo gave the girl a polite, businesslike smile. "I'm working on a book concerned with fetal tissue research and wondered if you'd have someone available to talk to me. Of course, I'd be happy to give proper credit in my book—"

"I'm sorry, but we really don't have anyone available for that sort of thing." The girl folded her hands across the desk.

"What do you have available?"

"I beg your pardon?"

"What services does your company offer? Do you have a brochure or something I could take with me?"

"We're a private company, ma'am. We don't advertise."

"But surely you have something—"

"We're not a tourist attraction." The girl's smile was more like a grimace with teeth in it. "I'm sorry, I can't help you."

The receptionist unfolded her arms and lowered one hand out of sight behind the desk. *An alarm button?* Theo wondered.

"Miss, if you could just ask someone for me. Surely you have a public relations department or a spokesperson for communications—"

"I'm sorry, we don't."

The door behind the receptionist opened, and a granite-faced man in a white lab coat stepped through the doorway. Looking steadily at Theo, he placed a white, stamped envelope on the girl's desk, then paused, crossing his muscled arms.

"I guess I'll be going, then," Theo said, turning toward the door. She took three steps, then suddenly turned again. "May I leave a name and number in case you think of something?"

As she had hoped, the man had turned to leave when she did. Pausing at the door, he threw the girl a questioning glance. She waved him away with a backward flick of her hand while she looked with exasperation at Theo. "If you wish."

Theo pulled her notepad from her briefcase and jotted down a nonsense name and address, knowing the girl would toss the paper in the trash as soon as she'd left. Confident that she was leaving, the man punched a code into the keypad. Theo listened intently, jotted down the tones at the top of her page, then ripped off the fake address and handed it to the receptionist.

"Thanks," she told the girl, then crossed the lobby and left the building.

Thank God for perfect pitch and piano lessons, Theo thought, humming the five-note key-code sequence to herself. The code to unlock the door at BioTech was an F-sharp, a quarter tone flatter F-sharp, a quarter tone flattened E, a true D, and a true E. The tones rang clear in her memory, but what numbers did they match?

She found a phone booth outside a restaurant across the street and lifted the receiver to her ear. Ignoring the dial tone, she punched in the numbers one through zero and listened to the tones. Three, six, and nine were all in the range of an F-sharp, but each number was pitched a bit higher than the one preceding it. Two, five, eight, and zero were pitched between an E and E-flat, but the tones increased in brightness as the numbers progressed. One, four, and seven were successively brighter Ds.

She pulled out her notepad and looked at the pitches she'd heard at BioTech. A bright F, a slightly less bright F, a slightly flattened E, a D, an E. *Nine, six, eight, one, zero.*

She scribbled the numbers beneath the corresponding pitches, confirmed them by listening carefully as she punched them into the telephone, then called Ann to say she wouldn't be home for dinner.

* * *

In a narrow alley behind the BioTech facility, a white delivery van emblazoned with BTI EMERGENCY SERVICES stood idle.

Several cars were parked in a small lot behind the alley, but Theo was most interested in the white door that led into the BioTech building. A small metal box sheltered an electronic keypad. Would they use the same code for all the doors in the building? Maybe.

Standing in the street, Theo considered her options. She had no way of knowing how many people worked inside BioTech. The cars in the back lot could have belonged to any number of people who worked in the block. *But if you wait until after five, when most businesses are closed. . . .*

A chill pearl-colored mist hung in the air, threatening either rain or snow, and Theo shivered, suddenly cold. An autumn wind had arisen with the promise of dusk, and she remembered the jacket she kept in her car. Why not snuggle into the jacket and wait? She could even grab a sandwich and a cup of soup at the restaurant across the street. There'd be plenty of time to relax, to think things through . . . and pray that God would guide her steps.

The restaurant was a homey mom-and-pop place with gingham curtains and a friendly waitress who greeted Theo with "Just find a seat anywhere, honey, and I'll be with you in a sec." Theo took a booth near the window so she could keep an eye on the situation across the street. At four o'clock, just after her second cup of coffee, the BTI van pulled away from behind the building. At four-thirty, a uniformed security guard locked the double glass-entrance doors from inside the building. At four-thirty-five, the pretty receptionist pulled out of the back parking lot and sped away in a bright green sports car.

The waitress approached with the coffeepot, but Theo put her hand over her cup. "Thanks, but I'm as jumpy as a frog in a frying pan now," she said, smiling up at the woman. "I just need to kill some time, if you don't mind."

"Take all the time you need, honey," the waitress said, taking the plate with the remains of Theo's tuna sandwich. She was an unstylish, soft little woman, with loose wisps of hair that made dark commas on her neck. "We all have days when we need more time for thinkin' and less for doin'."

By five-fifteen the street had begun to wear the deserted look of downtown after dark, so Theo paid her check, waved good-bye to the waitress, and left the restaurant. The jackhammer crew had gone home; streetlights were beginning to push at the gloom of dusk. She walked down the road that led to the alley, then peered through the gathering gloom. Most of the cars were gone. Only two remained in their places, but they were parked far away from BioTech.

She crossed to the door with the confidence of someone who had every right to be there, then pulled her notepad from her briefcase. Her fingers trembling, she tapped the keys: nine-six-eight-one-zero. Holding her breath, she turned the doorknob.

A latch clicked; the door opened. A conflicting rush of anticipation and dread whirled within her, but Theo pulled the door open and darted inside the building.

* * *

A long, white hallway punctuated by sterile-looking glass doors opened up before her. A security camera blinked above the door, and Theo automatically pulled her jacket over her head, then flattened herself against the wall directly beneath the camera. She winced at the thought of her image on videotape. But even if that blinking eye had caught her, no one at BioTech would know who she was. She'd been smart enough not to give her real name to the receptionist. If she got in and out without leaving a trace of her presence, maybe they wouldn't even review the videotapes. They'd never know she'd been there.

Keeping the jacket over her head and her back to the security camera, Theo slipped through the dimly lit hall that smelled vaguely of antiseptic solution. Bold black lettering on the glass door to her right read "Cryogenic Storage," and beside it hung a keypad similar to the one outside. Theo punched in the code she had used at the back entrance, but the door would not unlock. Through the glass she could see several steel-walled storage units and black-topped lab tables.

Conscious that the camera recorded every move, she continued down the hall.

The next glass door read "Ablation and Abscission." She didn't try the key code this time, suddenly aware that she was leaving fingerprints throughout the building. Peering through the glass, she saw a large operating room of sorts beyond the door. Domed lights dangled from the ceiling; several trays had been covered with clean cloths. Near the door, clothing that looked like surgeons' gowns and lab coats lay neatly folded on a table.

She was about to move farther down the hall when she heard pebbly tire noises from the alley. The building around her was silent but for the hum of the overhead fluorescent lights, but the hallway was next to the parking lot, and there was no denying a sudden crunch of gravel outside. Where could she hide? Were all the rooms locked?

Tightening her grip on her jacket, she ran doubled over down the hall, ignoring the keypad locks. A wooden door off the corridor labeled "Counseling" had no keypad; she opened it and slipped inside. Fumbling in the darkness, she found a light switch and flipped it on in the same instant she heard the sound of voices.

She was in a small room furnished with a couch, two chairs, and a chrome, glass-topped coffee table scattered with colorful brochures and magazines. Theo bit her lip and moved toward the wall, hoping to hide behind the couch. Then she spied a small door not more than three feet high—probably a small closet or utility access.

The voices grew louder, and Theo lurched toward the small door, not caring where it went. A dark open space lay behind the door, and she dove in headfirst, curling her knees to her chest and lowering her chin between her knees. She scraped her shin on the door frame but stifled the cry of pain that threatened to spring from her lips. Grasping the smooth inside of the door, she pulled it to her just as someone came into the room.

"This is our counseling room," a masculine voice said. "I hope you'll forgive me for bringing you in the back way, but security has the front locked up tight."

Theo caught her breath. The closet door had no inside handle, and she couldn't pull it completely closed. *Please, God, if you've forgiven me for getting myself into this mess, don't let them see that the door is cracked.*

"We don't mind, Dr. Dunlap," a woman answered. Her voice had the tremulous quality of an older person's. "We're just grateful you're able to meet with us at all."

Theo tightened herself into a ball, willing her body to occupy the smallest possible space. Sweat had begun to bead on her forehead, and her neck protested its cramped position with a shooting pain that ran from her neck down her spine. Sudden thoughts of spiders, roaches, and rats quickened her breathing, and she shoved those thoughts from her mind. She'd backed herself into this corner in order to investigate BioTech Industries, and she'd gone too far to lose all control in an attack of claustrophobia.

Even so, though she hated to admit it, she couldn't deny the overwhelming feeling that Ken and Ann were right: She was in way over her head.

Chapter 24

DR. Griffith Dunlap helped Mrs. Peterson seat her frail husband on the couch; then he waited politely until she took a seat next to him. Mr. Peterson's arms and legs moved constantly in spasm, a symptom of advanced Parkinson's. Sinking into an empty chair, Dunlap noted the way Mrs. Peterson's hand curled protectively around her husband's knee. Good. This was a solid marriage, a devoted couple. No cost would be too great for one to protect the other.

"Of course, Mr. and Mrs. Peterson, you know our program is technically experimental," he said, casually linking his hands. "But we've experienced remarkable results. Last year I had a patient who was so affected with Parkinson's that he could barely walk. Today he has returned to his job as a carpenter and is taking less medication. He's nearly completely weaned from L-dopa."

"That's what we need," Mrs. Peterson answered, her voice warm and fervent. "Harold has deteriorated so . . . so *quickly*, Doctor. I don't want to lose him."

Dunlap studied the man on the couch. Harold Peterson was barely sixty, but Parkinson's disease had sapped his strength and energy. The man's uncontrolled movements kept his limbs in constant motion; it was a miracle that he had been able to walk to the counseling room.

"Other treatments have failed?" he asked softly.

"We've tried everything," Mrs. Peterson answered. "But the drugs have side effects—moodiness, for instance. Sometimes I think Harold's about to lose his mind. We'll try anything new, Doctor. We don't care how experimental it is."

"It will work for your husband, Mrs. Peterson. The fetal cells will blossom in your husband's brain tissue and substitute for the missing dopamine cells. Within months, I'm sure Harold will be back to the condition he was in five years ago."

The woman looked at Dunlap as if he'd just told her he could walk on water.

"Of course, the procedure is still classified as experimental, so your insurance won't cover the expense."

"We know," the woman answered, idly fingering a diamond ring that hung heavy on her slender hand. "We're prepared to meet whatever expenses might be involved."

Dunlap hesitated a moment and grappled with greed. Just how wealthy were the Petersons?

"The expenses will probably run in the neighborhood of five hundred thousand dollars," he said, pulling a brochure from the coffee table. "This booklet will explain how the costs are incurred. There are two operations involved, one to extract the cells for transplantation, another to implant them in your husband's tissue. There are storage and retrieval fees and several laboratory fees as well. The fetal cells must be tested for bacterial infections, viruses—"

"AIDS?" the woman said, lifting wide eyes from the brochure. "I wouldn't want Harold to get AIDS."

"There's no chance of that," Dunlap soothed her. "All our products are carefully screened."

The woman studied the brochure for a moment, then clasped her hands over her purse. "How exactly are the cells put into . . . Harold's brain?"

Dunlap smiled and waved his hand. "It's a routine procedure. We will drill a hole the size of a small thimble into your husband's skull.

The fetal cells will be shot into the brain tissue after we use an MRI scan to determine the exact area of the brain that's been crippled by the disease. Your husband will be awake and alert throughout the procedure."

"Awake?" she gasped.

Dunlap nodded confidently and shifted his weight in the chair. "Absolutely. It's a very safe operation, without even the normal risks one would associate with anesthesia."

"Well, if it's perfectly safe . . ."

"It is, Mrs. Peterson. We have a shining success record. You needn't worry. Of course, your own doctor wouldn't have recommended us to you if he had any reservations at all."

The woman nodded in agreement, but her lips were still pursed suspiciously.

"If you don't feel right about this," Dunlap said, sensing that she needed more to convince her, "we don't have to proceed. You do realize, though, that your husband's condition will only continue to deteriorate." He paused for a moment to let that fact sink in. "Should you agree, we can do the surgery next week, and you'll begin to see improvement quickly." He shifted his weight to his arms as if to rise from the chair. "We all have money, Mrs. Peterson, but money can't buy time. Each day you wait is a day that can never be regained."

Mrs. Peterson took her husband's hand and looked straight at Dunlap. Her eyes were bright and fierce with pain. "All right. We'll do whatever we have to, Doctor. You just tell us what to do and how much we should pay."

Dunlap stifled a smile and forced a look of compassion onto his face. "Next week, then. Call my office tomorrow and ask to speak to Miss Landry, my assistant. She'll take care of everything we need to arrange a date for your husband."

"You'll want the money then?"

Dunlap shrugged as if money were the least of his concerns.

"Miss Landry handles all of that. I just want your husband to get better."

Dunlap stood and opened the door for Mrs. Peterson, who helped her husband up from the couch and propelled him through the doorway. The doctor was in the midst of polite leave-taking when Scotty Salago entered the hall.

Scotty, Dunlap noted, had the good sense to wait until the Petersons were outside the building before he spoke. "How's it going, Doc?"

"What are you doing here?" Dunlap snapped, turning to him.

"Calm down, Doc," Scotty said, his voice low. He leaned forward, suddenly serious. "The boss sent me over. You've got a visitor in the building. Security cams picked her up."

Dunlap felt himself staring incredulously. "Someone in *this* building? How in the—"

"In the counseling room," Salago answered, grinning. He jerked his thumb toward the room from which Dunlap had just come. "Cameras caught her flying down the hall when you came in with the old folks. Gotta still be in there."

Dunlap straightened himself. "Well, what does Reyes want to do?"

Scotty combed his greasy black hair with his fingers, then pocketed his hands in his suit coat. The grooves beside his mouth deepened into a full smile that was lazy and smug. "That's the easy part. He wants us to call the cops."

Dunlap chuckled. "The police?"

Scotty nodded slowly. "Yeah. And I can't be here when they come, so you'll have to hang around so she don't get into anything, OK?"

"I'll make the call myself."

"That's good, Doc," Scotty said, sauntering toward the back door. "Just play it cool, Reyes said, and act like you've caught a common trespasser." He shook his head. "The boss was excited when he saw who it was. Said he couldn't have rigged it better if he'd tried."

* * *

Theo heard the click of the door as the doctor and the couple left, then waited five minutes before unfolding her cramped arms and legs and easing them through the tiny closet door. She groaned when she realized she had left her briefcase outside on the floor. But it had been partially hidden by the couch, and no one had remarked on it.

Everything else in the room appeared just as it had, except that one of the brochures lay open on the table. She picked it up and stuffed it into her briefcase. *And that receptionist told me BioTech didn't have any publications,* she thought. *I guess these aren't for general public consumption.*

BioTech's purpose and function were now abundantly clear. The company existed to collect body parts from aborted babies and sell them to people who were desperate for a last chance at health. No wonder Ken Holman had been repulsed. But what a fascinating new angle this would bring to her book!

Burning with excitement and nervous energy, Theo crept to the door and pressed her ear to the wall. Not a sound disturbed the stillness of the hallway. How could she be sure that everyone had left the building?

She reached for the cool metal of the doorknob and turned it slightly. It opened easily. She reached for the light switch on the wall and flipped it so no telltale beam of light would shine out into the dim corridor as she cracked the door and peeked out.

The hallway was empty, but bright light shone from a glass door near the exit. The doctor must be in the lab.

Theo closed the door and stood in the darkness, thinking. She was neither a professional spy nor a sprinter. She could make a run for the door, but what if she tripped and fell? Or she could wait for the doctor to leave and make her escape in relative obscurity, but what if the man planned to work all night? Could she slip by the glass door of the lab unnoticed?

Maybe. She could have set off an atom bomb next to Matt when he watched a football game, and he wouldn't have noticed. If this guy was concentrating on his work—if he was even playing a computer game, for that matter—she could probably slip by.

Taking a deep breath, she eased the counseling room door open again. Like a swimmer about to plunge into freezing water, she steeled her nerves and looked out on the course ahead. She'd have to run fifteen, maybe twenty steps to the laboratory door, then make a quick duck behind the wall. From there it was only five, maybe six, more steps to the exit. It was past seven o'clock and dark outside, so she could probably get to her car without being seen. If she were smart and quick, she could be out and home before anyone at BioTech Industries even knew she'd been around.

One, two, three! Throwing the door wide, she flew out into the hall, remembering too late that she should keep her jacket over her face. She sprinted for the safety of the wall on the other side of the brightly lit lab door. A sudden whirring sound made her look up. The surveillance camera broke from its usual slow rotation and centered on the hallway. The cold black eye of the camera widened and seemed to focus on her.

At the same instant, the silence of the night was shattered by wailing police sirens. As Theo froze in the hallway, half-blind with unreasoning terror, the laboratory door opened. A tall, dignified man in a lab coat regarded her with somber eyes and pointed toward the exit door leading to the alley.

"Out there, my dear," he said, an ironic sneer hovering about his heavy mouth. His dark eyes impaled her where she stood. "You'll find the reception party outside."

As Theo froze, her mind and body numbed by fear, the doctor moved toward the door and opened it. Three uniformed police officers stood outside in a blaze of flashing white and red lights, their guns drawn.

Chapter 25

GOD, *help me. God, help me....*
The phrase played over and over in Theo's mind as she was handcuffed, placed in the back of a police car, and taken to the Hillcrest Heights police station. As she stood in front of the officer in charge and demanded to see a lawyer, a sword-thin policeman approached the desk.

"Metro PD wants this one right away. Take her to District headquarters and deliver her to a guy called Datsko."

The man who had been questioning Theo pushed back his chair and hitched up his belt. "How'd you get such pull?" he asked, his blue eyes narrowing in speculation.

"I don't know," Theo managed to whisper. The arresting cop escorted her back to the police car, and within thirty minutes she stood in the central headquarters of the Metropolitan Police Department. The scene reminded Theo of something out of Dante's *Inferno.* Never in her entire life had she seen such an assortment of bizarre people or heard such language.

Ann would just die if she could see me now. And Ken—he'd be glad he got rid of me at lunch.

Howard Datsko gave her a grim smile as an officer led Theo to his desk. He carried one arm in a sling but otherwise seemed in good health. "Nice to see you, too," he said abruptly, gesturing toward a chair where the Maryland policeman parked her. "And remind me not to ride in the same elevator with you if we have to go downstairs."

"I'm glad you're all right," Theo volunteered. "I thought you were dead."

"Nice of you to send a sympathy card, then. And nicer still to run away from the scene."

"I didn't run; that guy was trying to kidnap me. I barely managed to get away from him myself."

She shifted her shoulders and grimaced in the handcuffs, and the Maryland officer bent down to take them off. "Thanks, buddy," Datsko said, grinning up at him. "I owe you one."

"Forget it," the officer replied, resting his hands on his belt. He gave Theo a frankly admiring smile. "I wish all our perps were as polite."

Theo felt her cheeks burn and looked up to see Datsko staring at her. "What?" she snapped, suddenly annoyed. She hadn't done anything worth all this fuss.

"Nothing," he answered, clearing a space on his desk with a sweep of his arm. "I just can't figure out how someone like you keeps turning up on the wrong side of the law. You look like a Sunday school teacher."

"I am," Theo whispered, thinking suddenly of Stacy. Good grief, what if *this* story hit the paper? She'd just have to be nice to Datsko and beg him to do whatever cops did to keep stories away from the press. After all, in the eternal scheme of things, her wrong was the size of a mustard seed compared to the mountainous evil perpetuated by BioTech Industries.

"So," she asked, looking up at Datsko, "how did you survive that gunshot? You got nine lives or something?"

"Bulletproof vest," he said, picking up a sheet of paper in front of him with his good hand. "But at that range, the impact still broke my collarbone. So I'll be pulling desk duty for a while, but that's OK. Seems like a desk is the place to be if I want to apprehend the dangerous and felonious Theodora Russell."

"I'm neither dangerous nor felonious," Theo said, lifting her chin. "I was at BioTech doing research for my book. I know going into the building was a stupid thing to do, but I didn't take anything, and I didn't hurt anything. So if you'll let me call a lawyer—"

"Right now I couldn't care less about what you were doing at BioTech," Datsko answered. "I want to know why you bombed Dunlap's clinic."

Paralyzed by astonishment, Theo could only stare at him.

Datsko grinned. "Surprised that the long arm of the law caught you so quickly? It wasn't hard, little lady. But I must admit that at least one thing puzzles me. How does an ordinary civilian woman pick up plastic explosives? You know of a terrorist boutique someplace near here?"

"I-I don't know what you're talking about," Theo stammered, her mind racing.

"Your purse was found near the timer of a bomb that exploded yesterday at Dr. Griffith Dunlap's Family Services Clinic."

Griffith Dunlap? The elderly woman at BioTech had called the man in the lab coat Dr. Dunlap. Theo shook her head. "The guy who shot you in the elevator stole my purse."

"I didn't see any theft."

"How could you? You were out cold on the floor. It should be in the police report."

Shifting uncomfortably in his chair, Datsko rested his sling on the soft paunch of his belly. "We know that you're an antiabortion activist."

"I'm pro-life. I'm not anti anything unless it's wrong."

"According to Pam Lansky of the *Post*, you think just about everything is wrong. She says you're a bloomin' fanatic."

"Pamela Lansky's the fanatic. She's probably the type who won't wear wool because shearing embarrasses the sheep, and yet she favors murdering the unborn."

Datsko raised a bushy brow. "Those kinds of comments will get you in trouble, lady. Look at the facts: Theodore Russell's proposal—which you admitted taking—was found in your purse, burned but readable."

Theo took a quick, sharp breath. "Impossible! I mailed that proposal back to Evelyn Fischer a week ago!"

Ignoring her, Datsko lifted his index finger. "You were caught trespassing at BioTech Industries, a place that distributes abortion leftovers. We know from the evidence that the bomb was planted on Sunday night. There is some question about how you got by the alarm, but the security system at BioTech didn't seem to give you any trouble."

"Wait a minute here," Theo said, pressing her hand to her forehead. "None of this makes any sense at all. If you found that proposal in my purse, it had to be a copy because I sent the original back. You can call Evelyn Fischer and ask her! And I don't know anything about security systems; I only got into BioTech because they had one of those keypad things. I don't know anything about bombs or explosions, and I'm certainly not a terrorist—"

She stopped when a distinguished-looking man in his late forties shouldered his way through the confusion in the room and stopped beside Datsko's desk. He stared at Theo for a long minute, his eyes narrow and speculative, then shifted his gaze to the police officer. His expression was so twisted that Theo did not recognize him until he spoke.

"I'm Dr. Griffith Dunlap," he said, the memory of his voice edging Theo's teeth. "I understand that this trespasser also bombed my clinic."

"Allegedly bombed your clinic," Datsko corrected. "And I doubt she could have done it alone. We'll be checking out possible accomplices and links with antiabortion groups—"

"Bloodthirsty terrorists." The doctor's pale blue eyes fastened on Theo again, and he stiffened. "Young lady, it's beyond my ability to understand why you would choose to hinder my work. My clinic helps women who could not otherwise afford safe, inexpensive health services, and BioTech Industries is responsible for helping thousands of people lead normal, healthy lives."

Theo looked away, covering her mouth with her hand as she collected her thoughts. She had just passed through a day and night unlike anything in her prior existence, and her senses reeled at the dreamlike lunacy of it all.

But if this nightmare was brutal and blunt, she could be, too. "Well, Doctor," she said, looking up to return his harsh gaze, "it's beyond my ability to understand lawful genocide." She glanced over at Datsko. "I'd love to carry on a philosophical discussion with the doctor, but I'm really tired. I just want to go home."

Datsko looked over at Dunlap. "You're pressing the trespassing charge?"

"Indubitably." The doctor eyed Theo with cold triumph.

"Then, Mrs. Russell," Datsko went on, "you are officially under arrest. I suppose you know you have the right to remain silent. Anything you say can be used against you in a court of law—"

"I don't think I should say anything else until I have a lawyer present," Theo answered, trying to maintain her fragile control.

"So call one," Datsko said, standing. "The night is young, and I've got other work to do. Unless you can find someone to bail you out tonight, I've gotta lock you up until morning. You got someone to call?"

Despite her show of bravado, the words "lock you up" lifted the hair at the back of Theo's neck. She nodded dumbly, then dialed Ann's number on the phone Datsko thrust toward her.

Barreling his chest in indignation, Dunlap nodded severely at Datsko, promised to call him later, and left.

Suddenly limp with weariness, Theo told Ann what had happened and asked her to call Adam Perry . . . and Ken Holman.

TUESDAY
October 29

Chapter 26

IT was after midnight before she was ushered into the jail. Theo wanted nothing more than to lie down, close her eyes, and plunge into sleep, but there were no cots in the large holding cell. Two scratched and initialed benches stood opposite each other like lonely testaments to the sorrowful lives who had passed over them; the painted floor shone dully in the bright overhead light. Sitting on the cold cement, Theo stared for what seemed like hours at the drain in the center of the floor. Better to look at the gaping hole and think than study the pitiful representatives of womankind in the cell with her: several prostitutes, a woman in a blood-splattered blouse who kept moaning that she had just stabbed her man, and a glassy-eyed teenager high on something.

And then there's me, Theo thought, pulling her knees to her chest. *The mad bomber.* Tears stung her eyes as she stared at the floor. *OK, God, you win. I should have listened to Ken. I should have paid attention to Ann. I'm not an investigative reporter; I must not know how to do anything. Good writers don't end up in jail. The other Theo Russell was a definite eccentric, but I don't think he ever spent a night in the holding tank.*

In all her thirty-two years, Theo had never come this close to the underbelly of life, and the sound and smell and presence of these women both frightened and fascinated her. How could anyone think she was like them? She was *clean,* for heaven's sake. She obeyed the law, went to church, actually read the newspapers, and voted. A law-abiding, upstanding citizen, warmhearted, sensible, and until yesterday, shockable. . . .

Why, God? She lowered her head to her knees and closed her eyes. *You put me in this mess, so now you've got to get me out. All I wanted was to sell a book; then I just wanted to help Janette. But I can't even take care of Stacy if I'm in jail. . . .*

After passing a night woven of eternity, a female police officer appeared outside the cell and called Theo's name. Theo staggered to her feet, walked swiftly and gratefully through the stares of the other women and a cloud of profanity, and hung her head as she was led away.

The officer led her to another desk, where her briefcase was returned to her. Ken Holman and another man waited on the other side of a railing.

"Thank you for coming," she murmured as she joined them, her voice threatening to break. She extended her hand to the lawyer. "I suppose you're Adam Perry. How'd you get me out? Do I owe you my firstborn child?"

"Bail for the trespassing charge was low," the lawyer said, shaking her hand. "And they haven't formally charged you with bombing the clinic. Your purse was found at the scene, but unless they can prove you had help, no one seriously believes that you know how to set a bomb with plastic explosives." The man gave her a searching look. "Or at least Ann Dawson assures me that you don't. Do you?"

"No." Theo shook her head. "I don't know a thing about explosives. I told Datsko my purse was stolen by the man who shot him, but I don't think he believes me."

"I wouldn't be so sure," Perry said, opening the door to the street. "Howard Datsko's a good cop with at least twenty years under his belt, and he knows a setup when he sees one. I'd say the fact that you haven't been charged is encouraging. And the report about Datsko's shooting confirms your story about the purse. If they seriously believed you bombed that abortion clinic, you wouldn't be here. You'd be looking at a million plus for bail."

They stepped outside, and Theo breathed in the delicious, clean air of autumn. After the sordid smells of the jail, the crisp atmosphere was invigorating. The rising sun had swallowed up the chilly wind of the previous day; tires hissed steadily on the asphalt, a blessedly normal sound.

"Where do you want to go?" Ken asked.

"I want to go home," Theo said, realizing suddenly that she hadn't slept in her own bed in three nights. Her eyes were burning, and her bones ached.

Ken seemed to realize how fragile she felt. He nodded at Perry. "We'll be in touch later. Thanks, Adam, for coming down so soon."

"No problem," the lawyer said. He gave Theo one last look and a quick smile, then headed off into the rising stream of pedestrian traffic.

"I'll get us a cab," Ken said, taking her elbow.

"My car," Theo whispered, suddenly remembering where she'd left it. "I think it's still at BioTech. In Maryland."

Ken arched his brows and shot her a half-smile. "OK. We'll take a cab to Maryland, and then I'll take you home."

＊ ＊ ＊

It was midmorning by the time they reached her car. Grateful for his willingness to drive her home, Theo slid into the passenger's seat and tried to keep her distance from Ken. She felt filthy and knew she probably carried the stale smells of vomit, urine, and sweat in her clothes.

Ken calmly slid behind the wheel and put out his hand for the key. She gave it to him and mumbled directions, then leaned her head on the door window and closed her eyes. "I can't believe any of this is happening," she breathed. "I'll be so glad when it's over."

"I know you will." Ken answered, starting the car. "But I'm afraid it's far from finished. Pam Lansky heard about the explosion at Dunlap's clinic from a police scanner. She was there when they found your purse. She also heard about the police picking you up last night at BioTech."

Theo lifted her head and made a face. "So the story will be in tomorrow's paper?"

Ken took his eyes from the road long enough to give her a grim smile. "It's in this morning's. She's taken more than a passing interest in you, and she writes with a particular passion. You should take a piece of advice from Tommy Lasorda: Never argue with people who buy ink by the gallon."

Theo groaned and let her head fall back against the window. "What did the article say?" she whispered, not sure she wanted to know.

"Just the facts—Lansky was careful not to actually state that you were guilty. But she covered the explosion at the clinic, your arrest at BioTech, plus she threw in your comments about the pro-life cause." He shook his head. "It doesn't look good. And I don't know how you'll feel about this, but Lansky reported your address and age. You've got no more secrets, honey."

Theo felt the hot pressure of tears behind her eyelids. "Well, Doctor, if I didn't run you off yesterday, I suppose I will today."

"I don't think so." His hand slid over the seat and squeezed hers. "In a way, I feel responsible for part of this. If I hadn't told you about BioTech and given my notes to Theo Russell, none of this would have happened."

"But yesterday you tried to talk me out of pursuing the story. And you certainly didn't tell me to break into BioTech."

"No." He shot her a curious glance. "I won't even ask how you managed that. If you're a part-time spy or something, I don't want to know."

She gave him a rueful smile. "Perfect pitch, that's all. Easy as pie, if you're born with it."

He shook his head in bewilderment.

"I don't know what I'd do without you," she said, clasping his hand as a sudden rush of emotion swept over her. "The police said the bomb at Dunlap's clinic was set on Sunday night. That was the day after I sprained my ankle, remember? You'll have to tell them I was in no condition to run around setting bombs. I was at Ann's house, asleep on the couch."

"I'll tell them." He squeezed her hand. "But I don't know how good a witness I'll make. Prosecutors take a dim view of witnesses who are falling in love with the defendant."

A warm flush colored her cheeks when his eyes met hers, and despite her exhaustion, a sense of tingling delight began to flow through her. "Maybe you're right," she whispered, closing her eyes against the unguarded emotion. "Right now I don't think anything I say would be very credible. Maybe we're both too mixed up to know what's going on . . . or what we're feeling."

"Maybe," he answered, but his grip on her hand was strong.

✳ ✳ ✳

Ken slowed the car as he turned onto Theo's street. "Looks like something's going on up ahead," he said, leaning forward against the steering wheel. "Is your street always this crowded?"

Theo lifted her head. They'd been riding in silence, and she had almost fallen asleep, but the sight of a mob in front of her house brought her instantly awake. At least half a dozen women swarmed over her lawn and churned in her driveway, brandishing posters covered with pictures of bloody coat hangers. Other posters featured Theo's name in conjunction with unprintable words.

Ken parked the car on the street two doors down from Theo's house. "Stay here," he told her. "Keep low while I see if I can clear a path to your door."

After slipping out of the car, Ken walked toward the angry women with his hands raised. "Oh, yeah, I could get a fair trial in

223

this climate," she whispered to herself, sinking lower in her seat. "With my luck, most of those women would be on my jury."

Ken talked for a few minutes, the women shouted back, but finally they vacated the lawn and driveway and stood on the sidewalk, their faces contorted with rage and hate. The posters turned and faced the car, like radar screens homing onto a signal.

Ken returned to the car and opened her door. "You can come out. I'll walk you in."

"What did you say to them?"

"Simply that I'd call the police if they didn't get off your property. Come on, Theo. The longer you wait the harder it will be."

Theo slipped out of the car and ran toward her door, ducking under the protection of Ken's arm. The roar of the crowd escalated into a frenzy as she slipped past, and Theo resisted the mad impulse to stand and roar right back at them. Her impulsiveness had thrust her into too much trouble already.

She and Ken ran past the garage and hurried up the sidewalk, but the sight of the front door stopped them in their tracks. Someone had hung a twisted coat hanger over the doorknob. On the door were painted the words NEVER AGAIN with something that looked like blood.

Theo turned and buried her face against Ken's shoulder; then a quiet click compounded the moment of horror. Standing only a few feet away, a photographer had shot a picture of her in Ken Holman's arms.

Chapter 27

HOME.

Theo closed the door and leaned against it, breathing in the comfortable scents and sights of her house. Despite the fingerprint ink stains on her fingertips, the steady *ticktock* of the schoolhouse clock in the hall, the electric hum of the refrigerator, and Stacy's worn teddy bear on the bench by the door reminded her that she was Theo Russell, mother and homemaker. She was not a bomb-toting renegade.

Had it been only twenty-four hours since she left the house for lunch with Ken? A lifetime had passed since then.

Relishing the solitude, Theo lingered a moment at the door. After chasing the photographer away from her front porch, Ken had assured Theo that he could catch a cab at the end of the street. He told her good-bye and slipped through the mob. *He was probably glad to be away from here,* Theo thought, listening to the chanting of the protesters. She closed her eyes, mentally wishing them away. After a moment, she shook her head, then moved into the kitchen and dialed Ann's number.

"Hi, I'm home," she said after Ann picked up the phone. "How's Stacy?"

"She's fine. How are *you?*"

"OK," Theo answered, leaning against the wall. "I'll tell you about it later. Right now I want to take a shower and clean up and

225

take a nap. Then I'll slip over and pick up my little sweetie if the mob is gone." She bit her lip. "You can't believe how I've missed her. I feel as if I've been gone a year."

"Go out through your back door when you come. That mob outside is vicious—I wouldn't let Bethany walk through them to go to school."

Theo groaned. "I'm sorry. I'll bet the neighbors hate me. When did the rabble show up?"

"About eight. They pulled up in a van and have been growling ever since. The word must be out on the fruit-and-nut grapevine."

"And they think *I'm* a fanatic," Theo murmured, moving to peek out her front window. "It's like the National Organization for Women's goon squad is on my front lawn."

Ann laughed. "I don't know about that, but the brochures they're tossing at passing cars were published by the National Committee for Choice. I ran out to get one that blew onto our lawn. Pure propaganda."

"That's just great." Theo paused and looked again at the protesters' angry, distorted faces. "Keep Stacy away from the windows, OK? I'll come and get her later when things calm down a little bit. I don't want her upset by all this."

"I don't blame you," Ann said. "But don't worry about her. She's playing with my pots and pans and having a ball."

Theo caught sight of her reflection in a windowpane. Her eyes were ringed with black circles; she felt as hollow as her eyes looked.

"So what are you going to do?" Ann's voice sounded worried. "You're not thinking about trying to interview any of those people, are you?"

"No," Theo answered, laughing tonelessly. "I'm not *that* demented. I'm going to take a shower and make some notes. I'll be over when the horde calms down a bit."

As she hung up the phone and moved toward her bedroom, Theo noticed how the intrusive noise of the protesters wrapped around the little house like water around a rock. The sound of their chanting irritated her sleep-starved nerves. She needed rest and a warm hug from Stacy. She needed to do laundry and maybe cook dinner. A healthy dose of normalcy would set her life back on course.

She paused in the hall, a frown creasing her forehead. Her bedroom door was closed. Theo never closed her door unless . . . she smiled, remembering that she'd left a window cracked after yesterday's hot shower. A breeze had probably slammed the door. She gripped the doorknob, felt the cold metal under her hand, and realized her heart was pounding.

What are you afraid of? You're home.

She turned the knob and opened the door. Nothing moved but a curtain from the open window near her small bathroom. *Good grief, Theo, you're as jumpy as a kangaroo on a trampoline.* She smiled at her unreasonable fear and walked confidently into the room, then stopped as a wave of shock slapped over her. On her bed, in the middle of her grandmother's quilt, lay a large glass jar, which imprisoned a tiny baby, its skin a deathly gray, its arms and legs curled upward in a fetal posture.

She balled her hands into fists and released the scream that had been clawing in her throat for hours.

✳ ✳ ✳

Dear God, why this? Why would you allow someone to come into my house and leave this horrible thing?

In fear, frustration, horror, and pain, Theo cried out to God. Totally alone, with no one to overhear, she vented the feelings that had spun out of control. Even the pain of losing Matt resurfaced as she wept, for if he had not died she would not be alone, she would not have to face the financial pressures that were compelling her to write this impossible book. Money and Janette were driving Theo—need and responsibility. If Janette were not sick, if she hadn't become pregnant at sixteen, if Theo's parents hadn't been such blasted *hypocrites*. . . .

"God, you're not fair!"

Deep sobs racked her insides, and she wept aloud, curling into a ball on the floor of her bedroom. For over an hour she cried, expending her frustration and grief until the tears would no longer come. When her emotions and anger were spent, she lay still on the floor, her hands clenched into the carpeting.

In the silence of her soul, a quiet voice began to speak: *Don't be afraid, for I am with you. Do not be dismayed, for I am your God. I will strengthen you. I will help you. I will uphold you with my victorious right hand. See, all your angry enemies lie there, confused and ashamed. You will be a new threshing instrument with many sharp teeth. You will tear all your enemies apart, making chaff of mountains. You will toss them in the air, and the wind will blow them all away; a whirlwind will scatter them. And the joy of the Lord will fill you to overflowing.*

With a shiver of vivid recollection, she knew she had heard those words before; her pastor's Sunday sermon had centered on that passage from Isaiah. But what was God saying to her now? She didn't *want* to be a threshing instrument with sharp teeth, and she certainly didn't want to tear anybody apart. She just wanted to take care of her daughter and help her sister as best she could.

Gathering her strength, she wiped her cheeks, sat up, and stared again at the pathetic form in the jar. Downy hair covered the skin; delicate pearl-colored nails dotted the ends of the fingers. Somebody's child. A soul dispatched to heaven before it had even drawn a breath.

Just like Janette's baby.

Just like millions of others.

Theo stood up, respectfully covered the jar with a scarf from her closet, then carried it into the living room.

"I may not understand all the reasons, but I'll trust you, Father," she whispered, closing her ears to the sound of the protesters outside her house. "I will not fear if you are with me. And I'll be a threshing instrument, or whatever you want me to be."

Girding herself with resolve, she moved through the house with the precision of a drill sergeant, testing locks on windows and doors and locking any that were open. When every possible entrance was as secure as she could make it, she shut herself into the bathroom.

After showering, she slipped into an oversized shirt that had belonged to Matt, then set her alarm, crawled into bed, and slept deeply and dreamlessly for three hours. At two o'clock, her alarm clock buzzed. Awareness hit her like a punch in the stomach, and she got up, padded to the kitchen, and pulled a cup of yogurt and a diet cola from the refrigerator. Peering through the lace curtain in the living room, she saw that the protesters were still outside, their posters fighting the October breezes, their faces stiff with anger and red from the wind. But they marched quietly now, in groups of two and three, up and back on Theo's sidewalk.

She gulped the cola, ate the yogurt, then walked purposefully to her office. Her computer stood before her empty chair, waiting. She took a seat, flipped the power switch, and drummed her fingers on the desk as the computer booted up.

Her troubles had begun with her desire to write.

If she was any good, her desire to write could end them.

She paused only a moment to think before typing "My Side of the Story." The *Post* ran a weekly guest editorial column. Considering all the innuendo they'd recently published about her, they ought to print her view of the situation. She began to write, and her thoughts and feelings flowed with uncommon ease through her fingertips and across the computer screen. She wrote of her concern for women like Janette, her conviction that life is precious, and her love for Stacy, an "imperfect" child:

> Until two weeks ago, I would have told an interviewer that while abortion was not *my* choice, it was an option I could not

deny other women. Even though I am a Christian, my feelings were ambivalent, falling somewhere between conviction and casual acceptance. But the events of the past few days have taught me that our moral choices do affect others. Right moral choices strengthen us; when morals are discarded, the very fabric of our society—even our individual character—is irreparably weakened.

Pregnant women ought to be told that they carry life within them. They ought to be told that aborting any pregnancy increases their chance of having breast cancer as much as 50 percent or more. They ought to be told that the abortion of convenience is against nature.

I did not intend to be the trumpeter of this message; I wanted merely to write a book on an interesting development in medicine. But the forces that work against society's common good have convincingly aligned themselves against me. As I write this, pro-abortion protesters stand outside my home, their faces set in rage, their fists lifted to threaten me. Why aren't they talking about "tolerance" now?

Though I have not lifted a hand against anyone in the prochoice movement, someone entered my home and left behind a jar containing an unborn baby. Perhaps to whoever left it, that fetus was a mere specimen, a conglomeration of tissue, but it is a human child. That baby deserves respect; that child deserved the same life, liberty, and pursuit of happiness guaranteed to every American under the U.S. Constitution.

In 1988 an ethics panel of the National Institutes of Health suggested that human fetal tissue be given the same respect accorded to other cadaveric human tissues. Have we twisted logic to the point where we recognize the humanity of cadavers but not fetuses? In death, the NIH suggests, we should give unborn babies the respect they deserve. In life, we give them nothing.

Theo stared at the computer screen for a moment more, then switched on her printer. Let the *Post* print it, if they dared.

> *"Five, six, seven, eight,*
> *Theo Russell's full of hate!*
> *Seven, eight, nine, ten,*
> *Send her back to jail again!"*

Theo stood and observed the protesters, who renewed their earlier chants. She sighed and moved away from the window. There was no way she could mail the editorial today; she'd have to fax it. She wasn't about to venture down to her mailbox as long as the milling mob continued its chanting surveillance outside her house. One of the neighbors had called the police, but when the officers arrived, the women only caused a scene and moved into the street. Theo hadn't gone out. She'd had more than enough dealings with the police in the last twenty-four hours.

She went back to her computer and pulled up the file with her letter, preparing to send it to the *Post*'s editorial fax line. A small family photo taped to the side of her monitor caught her eye, and the pain of missing Matt struck her like a cold slap. Why had God taken him when she needed him so much? On days like today she needed his protection, the security of his arms, the calm assurance he had always seemed to project. She wouldn't be half as worried or feel so lonely if he were here.

She bit her lip and resisted the temptation to lower her head to the desk in despair. She had work to do. Ann's nebulous suspicion that someone wanted to silence her was more than a crazy notion now. Somebody had tried to frame her for bombing the abortion clinic. But who would do such a thing? And why?

She typed in the *Post*'s phone number and listened to the high-pitched squeal of the computer fax. As the machine warbled and began its transmission, she picked up her notes about Russell's

231

proposal. As she'd hoped, she had copied down the agent's name and phone number.

Though she didn't know where this trail would lead, it had begun with Theodore Russell. Maybe Madison Whitlow would have some answers.

* * *

Madison Whitlow ignored the ringing of the telephone and stared out his office window. Crowds of pedestrians clogged the sidewalks below him; cars and taxis jammed the streets. Dwarfed by the taller, broader building to the east, his office never received any sun, and Madison's mood was as sad and gray as the building he worked in. He'd just come from Theo Russell's memorial service. Now the task of emptying the novelist's house loomed before him.

Blast Russell, Madison thought, flexing his hands. *Why did he have to name me executor of his will? Didn't the guy have any other friends?*

The phone persisted, and finally Brittany, his secretary, came rushing in to answer the call. As she sat at her desk and greeted the caller, Madison turned to look at her and allowed himself a wry smile. As one of his more recent romantic conquests, he'd been surprised to find that she was actually a fairly competent secretary. "You say your name is Theo Russell?" she said, strengthening her voice. Madison shifted his eyes from her legs to her face and felt a little spasm of panic shoot across his belly. Brittany lifted an eyebrow and pointed to the phone, then circled her index finger in the area of her right temple. "Just a moment, ma'am. I'll see if Mr. Whitlow is in."

Brittany pressed the hold button and crossed her legs. He'd hired her for those legs, but the sight of them gave him no comfort now. His hands gripped the edge of his desk; a hard knot of fear grew in his stomach. Two nights before, a dark figure in a ski mask had appeared in his bedroom. While holding a knife to Madison's throat, the intruder had threatened to gut him from stem to stern if he was ever linked in any way to Theodora Russell.

Brittany pouted prettily. "It's no one important, just some woman trying to be cute by saying she's Theo Russell. Do you want me to tell her to take a flying leap?"

"No." Madison shook his head. The phone in her hand seemed suddenly alive, reptilian, repulsive. "No. I won't talk to her. Tell her anything; say I'm out of the country."

"I ain't gonna lie for you, Madison," Brittany said, but she smiled as she said it.

She clicked the phone again. "I'm sorry, but Mr. Whitlow's away from the office for a few days." She winked at Madison. "Can I take a message?" She scribbled on a scrap of paper, hung up, and thrust the paper at Madison.

He stared at it, unable to move.

"She says it's urgent, and you should call her when you get in," Brittany said, thrusting it toward him again. Her smile dipped. "Last month's girl?"

"No," Madison answered, forcing himself to take the message. He fumbled in his pocket for his lighter, then lit the corner of the page. As Brittany watched in blue-eyed amazement, the message crumbled into flame.

He let the ashes fall into an empty trash can. "If anyone ever asks you, you never heard of that woman, do you hear? I never called her. She never called here. We don't know anything. Got it?"

Brittany nodded. "Gee, Madison, what on earth—"

He grabbed his overcoat. "It's stuffy in here. I'm going out for a walk." He slammed the door on his way out.

Chapter 28

KEN Holman found himself listening to his patients' troubles and symptoms with a detached air. Still reeling from the incredible events of the past few days, his concentration was drawn away from his work by the unnerving realization that he and Theo Russell had become more than friends. After that disastrous lunch yesterday he had been sure he'd seen the last of her, but she'd called and he'd come to her aid like the proverbial knight in shining armor. It felt good to be useful, to be needed.

Still, he was no young schoolboy. He realized the circumstances were extreme and Theo might not be acting like herself. What would she feel about him, if anything, when the present crisis was over? And what would he feel about her?

Now, he admitted, he definitely felt responsible for her. His research had formed the basis of Theodore Russell's proposal, so ultimately Theo had found herself in trouble because of Ken's work. But beyond responsibility, he wanted to help Theo because he liked her. Except for his wife, he'd never met a woman with such fierce determination. Even though he had to admit she was stubbornly independent and entirely unpredictable, she was also intelligent, astute, and compassionate—all the things he admired.

But was he ready to love again? Theo Russell had a five-year-old child he had never met, and children complicated things. A five-year-old was old enough to feel threatened by a new person in Mommy's life; five-year-olds weren't always old enough to understand that Mommy needs friends, too.

Face it, Ken told himself as his latest patient described her battle with overeating, *a five-year-old who's set against you can make life pretty miserable.*

He recommended that his patient learn to eat only when she was hungry and stop when she was full; then he slipped out of the examination room. Darting into his office, he placed a quick phone call to Adam Perry. Fortunately, Adam was in.

"Hi, Adam. I hate to interrupt, but I'm in between patients. I've got a quick question."

"Shoot."

"What do you really think about Theo's case? Will she be charged in the bombing? There's no way she could have blown up a clinic."

Perry paused. "I don't know how it will come down, Ken. If they do charge her, things don't really look good. The police know about her involvement with that novelist's work, so right off the bat she looks unethical. And then there's that interview where she admitted being pro-life. And the strange situation where that cop was shot— once again, Theo Russell was in the wrong place at the wrong time. And she's admitted to trespassing at BioTech Industries. I'd love to paint her as the typical American housewife, but the evidence suggests she's not exactly Susie Homemaker."

"But I can testify that she had a sprained ankle. There's no way she could have been out setting bombs."

"Were you with her that night? All night?"

Ken heard the veiled question in the lawyer's words. "Certainly not. There's nothing going on between us."

"Yet."

Ken paused. "Right. Not yet."

"Well," Adam said, with dark promise in his voice, "the situation won't look at all innocent if the press or the police find out you two are involved. You may find yourself under investigation. It's well known that you've taken an antiabortion stance in your practice—"

"Theo and I are friends."

"Well, Ken, keep it that way, and we may have a chance."

* * *

Across town, Victoria Elliott looked out of her office and saw Pam Lansky coming her way, a sheet of paper in her hand. "Just look at this!" Pamela crowed, holding the paper aloft. "Give a zealot a rope, and she'll hang herself with it every time. Read this, Victoria, and then tell me that Theodora Russell isn't a raving right-winger."

With a triumphant flourish, Pam dropped the page on Victoria's desk. It was a letter to the editor, brief and neatly typed, from Theodora Russell. Victoria read it quickly, then again slowly, and realized that Theo Russell was actually a very competent writer. After her second reading, she lowered her chin and peered at Pam over the top of her glasses. "So? This is a well-written opinion piece. We've published letters that were far more outrageous."

"What?" Pam leaned forward, spreading her hands on Victoria's desk. "You can't seriously mean that you would consider it! The *Post* was never intended to be a mouthpiece for Neanderthals in the right wing—"

"I doubt that Ms. Russell considers herself a Neanderthal," Victoria replied, leaning back in her chair. "And if I were an editorial-page editor, sure, I'd consider running it. There's nothing here that's libelous or factually incorrect. This is a very usable piece."

Pam snatched the letter from Victoria's desk. "I'll use this, I swear I will, the next time that nut does something." She held the page with two fingers as if it were a filthy rag. "I couldn't ask for anything better than this. She'll convict herself with her own words."

"I'd like a copy of that," Victoria said, motioning to the letter. "For my files."

"OK." Pam frowned at the page, then grinned back at Victoria. "Isn't life grand? I was just thinking I'd hit a dead end because that woman certainly won't talk to me anymore, and then, *wham!* Editorial sends this copy over to me."

"Serendipity," Victoria said, resting her chin on her hand.

As Pam stalked toward her own desk, Victoria lifted a hefty phone book from a drawer. The return address on the letter had been Washington, D.C., and after a moment, Victoria found the phone number for T. Russell on Pineview Lane.

She punched in the number and was relieved when a woman answered.

"Hello?" The voice was hesitant, cautious.

"Mrs. Russell," Victoria began, trying to inject a note of honest warmth into her voice, "I'm Victoria Elliott, city editor at the *Post*. I have just read your editorial. Very impressive."

"Thank you. Are you going to print it?"

"I don't know; that's not my decision." There was a sigh at the other end of the phone, but Victoria pressed on. She swiveled her chair away from the open room where Pam Lansky was diving like a dervish into a pile of paperwork. "I was very interested in what you had to say, Mrs. Russell, because years ago I had an abortion. Last year I had a mastectomy."

Silence at the other end of the phone. Then, "I'm sorry."

Victoria gripped the phone more tightly. "For personal reasons, I'd really like to talk to you. Can you meet me tonight for dinner? It'll be my treat."

"I don't know," Theo answered. Her voice faded, as if she was pulling away from the phone, then strengthened. "Thanks to your newspaper, the street in front of my house is filled with protesters. And I really need to spend some time with my daughter."

"You have a daughter? You're blessed. I tried for years to have a child but couldn't. The abortion left me sterile." She paused, allowing her words to sink in. "Please, we'll meet quietly. If you can slip out, meet me at Pepe's Café in Georgetown at eight o'clock. Surely you can get away by then."

"I hope so." Theo paused. "All right, Ms. Elliott, I'll meet you. How will I know what you look like?"

Victoria laughed. "Oh, I'll be easy to spot. I'm black, twenty pounds overweight, and every day of forty-five. I'll look forward to meeting you, Mrs. Russell."

She swiveled to replace the phone in its cradle and saw Pam Lansky in the doorway, staring like a lunatic over the asylum wall.

Victoria ignored the warning systems clanging in her brain. "Can I help you, Pam?" she asked, holding the younger woman in a firm gaze.

"Theo Russell? *You're* meeting with Theo Russell? That's my story, Victoria!"

"I'm not going to touch your story," Victoria answered. "If you must know, I'm meeting her for personal reasons on my own time. I'm interested in what she has to say."

If anything, Pamela looked even more aghast. "You *agree* with her?"

Something in Victoria snapped. In a flash of defensive spirit she stood to face the younger reporter. "Listen, Pam, when you've been through what I've been through, then you'll have earned the right to judge me. But you don't know what it's like to have a surgeon cut your chest away, and you don't know how it feels to have more yesterdays than tomorrows." She looked past Pam and stared at the bustle of the news office. Her voice softened. "Are you familiar with the idea that if a man causes a single soul to perish, it is as if he has destroyed a whole world? You'll find it in the Torah."

"I'm not Jewish." Pam's voice was dry. "Why should I care what the Torah says?"

Victoria swiveled her dark eyes toward the reporter. "Because it contains wisdom. He who kills one soul kills all the children and children's children that might have come from that person. A baby girl's ovaries contain all the eggs she will ever have—a link in the chain of life from which would come her children and grandchildren. Considered in that light, doesn't abortion strike you as a terribly profound thing? I've heard you say that you won't sleep on a feather pillow because the feathers are plucked from living geese, and yet you defend the abortion rights movement—"

"That's all I want to hear." Pam fastened Victoria with a hard glare. "I don't have time for sentimental musing, and I'm really afraid that you're losing your objectivity, Victoria."

"I am?"

"Yes." Pam spat out the word in contempt. "I shouldn't have to remind a city editor, but we're not here to make news—we report it. Both sides of an issue. I allowed Theo Russell her say. My conscience is perfectly clear."

With an abrupt lift of her chin, Pam turned and left. Sighing, Victoria turned and leaned on the edge of her desk, her back to the bustling office.

* * *

Pam Lansky slid into her chair and grabbed the telephone as momentum carried her toward her keyboard. When the arm of her chair had come to rest against the edge of the desk, she deftly punched in the four-digit extension for Ronald Jameson, editor in chief at the *Post*.

Jameson was the perfect boss. Though he had the temperament of an underfed grizzly, he stayed out of his editors' and reporters' way unless there was a conflict. Then he entered the fight snarling and slashing until one party was vindicated and the other silenced.

Jameson answered the phone with his usual gruffness.

"Hi, Ron, Pam Lansky here. I hate to involve you in this, but I think the stress of the last year has really affected Victoria. She's losing her judgment. I don't know, maybe she needs a vacation or something, but she's meeting tonight with that antiabortion zealot

Theo Russell—for *personal reasons,* she says. You know that won't look good for the paper if it gets out. Heaven help us if the *Times* gets wind of it. I think her perceptions are being colored by this entire abortion–breast cancer debate."

Chapter 29

THE shadows of the houses across the street stretched to fill the road as the sun set, and by six o'clock Pineview Lane wore its usual deserted look. Relieved that the protesters had finally gone home, Theo slipped quietly through the gathering darkness to Ann's house where she was met by a feverish little girl who gave her a weak hug.

"She's missed you," Ann said, watching the reunion with concern. "And she's been running a fever since noon. With everything that's going on I didn't want to worry you, but despite steady doses of aspirin, ten minutes ago her temperature was a hundred and one."

"You're kidding." Kneeling, Theo pressed her palm to Stacy's hot forehead, then felt the child's burning stomach. Guilt raked her heart. "My poor baby. I should have been here."

"What could you have done? I would have brought her home, but with that crowd. . . ."

"I'm glad you didn't upset her. I didn't think those women would ever leave." Theo spied Stacy's security blanket, scooped it off the floor, and carried her daughter to the sofa. Sinking onto the couch, she pressed her cheek to her child's burning forehead.

"Do you think they'll be back?" Ann asked, moving toward the window. "Bethany's been a nervous blur all day. The folks on Pineview Lane may never be the same after this, you know."

"I'll personally apologize to everyone on the block," Theo said, watching Stacy's heavy eyelids close in sleep. "Goodness, Ann, she's hot. I ought to call the pediatrician. It could be just one of those twenty-four-hour viruses, but what if it's not?"

"Call him," Ann said, perching on the edge of her favorite chair. "But unless he's a saint, he'll tell you to give her aspirin and fluids and call him again in the morning if she's not better."

Theo hugged Stacy close. "I was supposed to meet someone for dinner. Can you believe it, Ann? I wrote an editorial and faxed it to the *Post*. An editor saw it and called me right away. Years ago she had an abortion, and last year she had breast cancer. She had to have a mastectomy."

Ann sat back with a whistle of surprise. "You're kidding. If you're still serious about doing the book, you ought to talk to her."

"I am still serious." Theo ran her fingers over Stacy's silky hair. "This morning I was ready to give it all up, but then I prayed and somehow . . . though I can't really explain it, I just know God wants me to go through with it." She laughed softly. "My own fiery furnace, I guess, and it's more than a little scary. But I won't let anything hurt Stacy, and I don't want to leave her tonight if she needs me."

"She'll be fine with me," Ann promised, sitting up. "If her fever spikes or if she gets worse, I'll take her to the emergency room and call you."

"Are you sure?" Theo looked up from her daughter's sleeping face. "Lately I feel as if I'm always leaving her."

"Don't OD on maternal guilt now," Ann said, her voice gentle. "You're a good mother, Theo. You're home more often than most mothers are. Go on. But be careful of this editor. That paper has done nothing but blast you, and you're in serious trouble now. You need to steer clear of anything else that's going to stir up the waters."

"I'll be careful," Theo whispered. She ran her fingers over Stacy's forehead, wavering between opposing desires. "I won't be gone long. But this woman will be another voice to validate the link between breast cancer and abortion."

A smile found its way through the mask of uncertainty Ann had worn for days. "If you think this is right, then follow the commercial's advice, honey, and just do it. But if you're going to invest your time in this book, do it for the right reasons. If you're doing it for money, it's not worth it. And if you're doing it to make a name for yourself—well, you've had your fifteen minutes of fame. Can you tell me it's been fun?"

Theo shook her head. "It hasn't been fun, but it's important. And I think that if I tell the truth and reveal the facts, I'll be cleared of all this crazy stuff they say I've done. Truth is powerful, Ann. They can't fight against truth, but I've got to get the word out. I can't give up and hide this story—"

"Under a bushel," Ann finished. "I know."

Theo sighed and leaned her head back against the comforting softness of the sofa pillows. Suddenly she felt very tired. "Do you think I could take a nap right here with Stacy? Can you wake me up at seven? As long as I'm at Pepe's by eight, I'll be OK."

Ann got up from the chair and dimmed the lamp in the living room. "Snooze on, fearless crusader," she whispered, moving toward the kitchen. "I'll wake you up. Just get some rest."

* * *

Theo felt a hand on her shoulder and opened her eyes. The clock on the piano read seven o'clock. Unbelievably, chanting came again from the direction of the street.

"They're back," Ann said, moving to the window where Bethany peered out through the lace curtains. "With candles and thermoses. It's like a vigil."

Theo shook the heavy veil of sleep from her eyes and sat up to peer out the window with Ann and Bethany. A line of eight women stood on the sidewalk facing her house, lighted candles in their hands. Despite their demure appearance, they were chanting, "One, two, three, four! Women will be slaves no more!"

Bethany looked up and gave Theo a lopsided grin. "At least they're not singing 'Kum By Yah'."

"Or 'I Am Woman, Hear Me Roar'," Ann said, laughing.

Stacy suddenly sat up and pointed a chubby finger toward the glowing lights out the window. "What, Mama?" she asked, blinking.

Theo hugged her daughter. "Pretty lights," she said. "Like Christmas."

Bethany snorted at Theo's reply, and Ann moved away from the window. "They don't know you're here," she said, fumbling in her purse. "You can take my car. I'll give you a scarf to cover your hair, and maybe nobody will notice you as you leave. Just don't let them throw things at my car, OK? It's the only one I've got, and Bethany's itching to drive it next year."

"I'll take care of it," Theo answered, giving Stacy a quick kiss. "Make sure Stacy's in bed soon, OK? She doesn't feel as hot as she did before, but keep an eye on her. And I just realized, I know a saintly doctor. I think I'll call Ken Holman and see if he'd mind dropping over to take a look at her."

Ann twinkled. "Your doctor friend will make a house call for you? Just how chummy are you two?"

"I haven't had time to think about it," Theo said, standing up. "Just let him in if he comes by, OK? He's tall, with sandy hair and very nice eyes, so don't zap him with pepper spray if he rings your doorbell." She paused to press her hand to Stacy's forehead, but the little girl seemed better and was laughing at Bethany's funny faces. "It's probably nothing, but I'll call him now."

"OK." Ann stood for a moment in the doorway of the kitchen, an anxious frown on her face, and Theo gave her a confident smile.

"There's nothing to worry about," she said. "I'm just going to meet a woman for dinner. What could possibly go wrong?"

＊ ＊ ＊

Safely inside a booth at Pepe's Café, Theo ordered a cup of coffee and a buttered croissant, then sat and stared out the window at passing cars. By her watch eight o'clock had come and gone five minutes earlier, but there was no forty-five-year-old black woman in the restaurant who seemed interested in company. In fact, there weren't many people in the café at all. Two men in overcoats had come in behind her and taken a booth two rows away, an elderly couple sat across the restaurant and ate slowly without speaking, and a coarse, insolent-looking man with heavily tattooed arms sat at the counter working on a meal of steak, potatoes, and biscuits.

Theo watched the window and thought of her last conversation with Ken Holman. He had been so kind! She'd had to call his answering service, but he returned her call within two minutes and was very concerned when she described Stacy's fever. He had been the one to suggest that he drive out to look at Stacy and joked that while pediatrics wasn't his specialty, if he was going to play knight in shining armor, he might as well come to the aid of the distressed damsel's daughter, too.

Like Ann, he was quick to caution her when Theo told him she was on her way to meet the *Post* city editor at Pepe's Café. "Don't you think you should just lay low for a while?" he asked, concern in his voice. "Honestly, Theo, there's such a thing as becoming too involved."

But she insisted that this meeting was important, and he didn't argue. Had he given up because he didn't want to push her or because he didn't care enough to force the issue? It was an interesting question, and Theo pondered it as she stirred sugar into her coffee and watched the parking lot.

Rain had begun to fall outside, and a car pulled off the highway and into the lot. Theo held her breath as the car's headlights shone toward her through the rain, then cut off. A black woman in a beige trench coat got out of the car and struggled to hold a newspaper over her head as she slammed the car door shut with her hip. Ducking under the tented newspaper, she took a few mincing steps in too-high heels, then paused before a rapidly deepening puddle.

Theo glanced toward the kitchen, hoping to get the waitress's attention. This had to be Victoria Elliott, and after walking through this chilly rain, she'd certainly want hot coffee or tea.

Somewhere out of Theo's vision, a car engine roared to life. Theo saw its headlights cut through the rain, lighting the woman's path. She glanced up at the car as if grateful for the light, and Theo saw that the woman fit Victoria's description.

The twin beams disappeared, but Theo scarcely noticed. She was watching the woman splash through the parking lot. Then a dark shadow moved into the lane where Victoria Elliott negotiated the puddles in her path. Victoria saw the approaching vehicle and paused for a moment; the dark sedan slowed. A white hand from inside made a motion, giving her permission to cross.

As Victoria took three rapid steps forward, the car engine growled and the vehicle lurched forward, careening toward her. Theo caught a glimpse of the woman's startled face, then heard the sickening thud of a body tossed upon the hood of a car. As Theo blinked in horrified amazement, the air filled with the screech of steel-belted radials and the scream of an engine as the car rounded a curve and flung the woman onto the wet asphalt.

Theo burst out in full-throated shrieking before she fully realized what had happened. She was certain every eye in the restaurant had turned toward her, but all she could do was point out the window at the still form lying in the rain.

✳ ✳ ✳

Pandemonium broke out in the restaurant. A waitress sprang to call 911, the two men in overcoats ran outside, the old couple huddled in the booth as if fear held them fast to their seats. The tattooed wonder stood at the window, cursing frequently, with a vague note of awe and regret in his voice. "I wish I'd seen it," he kept saying over and over. "Man, if only I had seen it!"

Both waitresses and the cook huddled together in a small group at the door, driven forward by curiosity but bound by the rain and their duties. No one ate.

Theo's hand shook when she tried to lift her coffee cup to her lips. Someone had just murdered Victoria Elliott. This was not a warning, like the fetus left on her bed. This was homicide, as serious as the bombing of the medical clinic. But why would someone want to kill a newspaper editor? And who had known about their meeting? Only Victoria and Ann. And Ken.

Ken Holman. A whisper of terror ran through her as she considered his name. Why would Ken want to kill Victoria Elliott? It didn't make sense. But only he and Ann had known about this meeting, and he had tried to persuade Theo not to come. In fact, he'd been trying to talk her out of working on the book for days. But why? He'd been the one to give the information to Theodore Russell. . . .

He had access to fetuses in formaldehyde, memory reminded her. *Didn't he tell you he'd seen them in medical school? He knew you would be staying at Ann's house the night the bomb was set at Dunlap's clinic. Are they competitive rivals?*

"No," she groaned, closing her eyes. Suddenly her mind blew open, and a cold shiver passed over her as she double-checked her memory and fit the pieces together. When Ken Holman gave the information about breast cancer and abortion to Theodore Russell, there was no lawsuit. But since that time, Adam Perry had filed a multimillion-dollar lawsuit on behalf of Holman and his late wife.

Millions of dollars. People have killed for far less.

Ken Holman didn't want Theo to publish her book because the resulting publicity would hurt the lawsuit! If Theo's book was released before the wheels of justice had finished with Ken's case, his lawsuit would be just one of hundreds filed, like the scores of women who settled with the makers of faulty IUDs and the manufacturers of breast implants. The award would be thousands instead of millions, and Ken would be just another victim who'd lost his wife, not the great researcher who had instigated the suit on behalf of women everywhere.

A thunderbolt of understanding jagged through her. What a fool she had been! She had actually begun to believe that he was concerned for her, that he had seen something in her that he respected, that he really believed in her work . . . that he *cared* for her. And she had just sent him to check on Stacy! Perhaps he's heading to Ann's house now.

Anxiety spurted through her as her thoughts raced. He would tell Ann that Stacy was ill, that she needed to be in a hospital. He would volunteer to take her himself, and Ann would agree, knowing that Theo trusted him.

Theo slipped into her coat and turned to slide out of the booth, then remembered the check. She yanked a five-dollar bill from her purse. The waitresses and cook were still at the door, so Theo slid the bill under the edge of her plate and slipped to the end of the bench. One of the two men in overcoats, Theo noticed, had reentered the restaurant and sat on a long bench inside the door. He quickly averted his eyes when she caught him watching her.

Suppose Ken Holman was not acting alone? Of course he wasn't! Adam Perry was in on the plot, too; there was little doubt that he wanted to win the case. He was a lawyer, and lawyers knew all kinds of criminals. They knew who could be paid to break into a woman's home, shoot a cop in an elevator, and follow a woman to her dinner appointment just to make certain that the appointment was never kept.

Prickles of cold dread crawled along her back, and Theo took a deep breath to calm herself. Picking up her purse, she stood and casually walked toward the restroom. Once there, she waited until she heard the wail of sirens in the parking lot, then scooted out of the ladies' room and through the back door of the restaurant. Though the emergency alarm on the door blared loudly, no one ran after her as she sprinted through the rain toward her car.

Chapter 30

PEERING through the peephole in her door, Ann saw a tall and rakishly good-looking man in a khaki-colored raincoat. He carried a black bag in his hand and regarded the door with a look of calm acceptance. He knew she was evaluating him.

With a flush of embarrassment, Ann opened the door and smiled at her visitor. "You must be Dr. Holman. Theo told me to expect you."

"And you must be Ann," he said, extending his hand. "It's nice to meet you in person."

Ann shook his hand, then jerked her thumb toward the protesters on the street. "They're still here, as you can see. I was hoping the rain would wash them away."

Ken glanced over his shoulder at the protesters; then his smile flattened out. "I'm afraid those folks are like death and taxes: inevitable."

Ann moved out of the doorway to let him in, took his wet coat, and found herself wishing that she could find as handsome a prince. Things had been difficult for Theo in the past few days, but her discovery of this man had certainly tipped the scales in her favor. Maybe Ken Holman would be the silver lining in the clouds.

"Where is the little girl?" he asked politely, interrupting her thoughts.

Wordlessly, Ann pointed to the living room where Stacy slept on the couch. "She fell asleep after Theo left for her dinner appointment," Ann explained, raking hair off her forehead. "I know she ought to be in bed, but I hated to move her."

Ken Holman was staring at Stacy as if he'd never seen a child before. "This is Theo's daughter?" he said, looking at Ann with frank wonder in his eyes. "She didn't tell me . . . she never mentioned that Stacy was—special."

Ann sat on the edge of a chair. "She wouldn't. She's accepted the Down's syndrome as just another part of life and considers herself lucky to have Stacy." She motioned toward the hall. "I'll go turn down the extra bed in Bethany's room if you'll carry her in there for me. That way after you wake her up, she'll be all tucked in."

Ken Holman nodded and lifted Stacy into his arms as Ann stood and led the way down the hall. When the doctor began to softly sing a lullaby, Ann found herself hoping he had a brother.

* * *

In a booth at Pepe's Café, Howard Datsko awkwardly flipped open the cover of his notepad with his left hand. The blasted sling he still wore was definitely making life more complicated. Across from him sat two undercover officers, Greerson and Stockton. Datsko regarded them with a level gaze.

"OK, so our gal sat there and watched the window, then screamed when the Elliott woman got hit, right?" he said, glancing from one man to the other. "Then what'd she do?"

"She went into the ladies' room," Greerson replied, raising a coffee cup to his heavily mustached lips. "She was pretty upset. Everybody was."

"And then?"

"She must have gone out the emergency exit," Greerson explained, his face brightening to the color of a tomato.

"Isn't there an alarm on that door?"

The two officers looked at each other. "I don't know," Stockton

254

answered, folding his arms. "I was outside with the victim. He stayed inside with the woman."

Greerson flushed. "I couldn't hear anything in all that ruckus. People yelling, the sirens—it was mass confusion here."

"Did she realize you two were cops?" Datsko asked, glaring at the pair. "What made her run?"

"Scared, probably," Stockton said. "I saw her face right after the Elliott woman was hit. She was scared spitless."

Datsko picked up his pencil. "OK. What was she driving?"

"A green Altima, late model," Greerson answered. "The neighbor's car, registered to Ann Dawson. She left the neighbor's house at seven-fifteen."

Datsko flipped the cover of the notepad and slid it into his pocket. "OK, maybe she made you, maybe she didn't, but she's gone. Any idea where she might go? Any idea why she wanted to meet Victoria Elliott here? Did she say anything to anyone? Maybe one of the waitresses?"

"She was quiet and alone," Greerson muttered. "And we don't know anything about the case because we weren't told anything. We're supposed to shadow; you're supposed to detect. Besides, a woman was killed here tonight. Aren't you going to ask any questions about *that*?"

Smart aleck. Datsko slapped his good hand onto the table in annoyance. A murder had just been committed, one that was probably tied into the clinic bombing and Theodora Russell, and the two cops he'd assigned to follow her probably couldn't find their heads without a mirror.

"There are ten cops and two homicide detectives out in the parking lot," he snapped. "And I ain't Homicide. Look, this woman's not Houdini. Get on the road and find her. Put the word out on the radio; have someone try BioTech again. If nothing turns up, go back to her house and wait like you did before. She can't be too hard to find. She's a Sunday school teacher, not America's most wanted!"

Greerson and Stockton looked at each other like imbeciles, and Datsko stood up and left them alone. The sling around his neck irritated him, so he jerked it off over his head, ignoring the sharp stab of pain that ripped across his bruised chest. *If you want to get a job done right,* he told himself as he moved toward his car, *sometimes you gotta do it yourself.*

* * *

Scotty Salago nosed his black Mercedes onto Pineview Lane and parked half a block from Theodora Russell's house. All was quiet. A cool wind blew remnants of rain from the trees overhanging the neat sidewalks, and the street shone clear and clean. Scattered sheets of wet paper clung like gray laundry to the Russell woman's lawn, probably remnants from the protesters the boss had sent over. Apparently the rain had chased everything but their garbage away.

He knew she'd be home soon. She may have been hysterical when she realized what had happened to that lady from the paper, but Theo Russell had a kid, and that kid was still next door. One of the women in the group of protesters had kept a careful eye on the street all day, and Reyes had called Scotty late that afternoon with explicit instructions. He was to pick up the woman and bring her to her senses. Her meddling, Reyes said, had gone on long enough.

Scotty waited ten minutes, humming under his breath; then a car's headlights broke the darkness at the end of the street. Cursing softly under his breath, he ducked. The car slowed, then suddenly accelerated after passing the Mercedes. Scotty lifted his head. With a squeal of rubber, the green car pulled into the next-door neighbor's driveway, and a thin woman with short hair rushed out and sprinted to the front door. The woman fit Theo Russell's description, and for a moment he was stymied. She had escaped him by driving another car and going next door, but there was more than one way to snare a rabbit.

Scotty slipped out of his car and walked casually down the street.

Still humming, he turned into the driveway of Theo Russell's house, walked up her front sidewalk, and hid himself among the greenery growing in the shadows along her front porch.

She ain't so smart, he thought, lighting a cigarette in the dark. *Didn't even leave a porch light burning.*

* * *

Ann nearly dropped the cup of coffee she was offering Ken Holman when Theo burst through the front door, her face and hair wet with rain. "My gracious, Theo, what's wrong?"

Theo didn't answer but slammed the door behind her and moved into the living room, her eyes fixed in a deathly bright stare upon the doctor. Confused, Ann cast a quick glance at Ken Holman, but he was watching Theo with as much amazement as Ann.

"Go to your room, Bethany," Theo commanded in a no-nonsense voice. Bethany looked to Ann for assurance, but Theo lifted her arm in an imperial gesture. "Go now!"

"Go," Ann whispered, frightened by the gleam in Theo's gaze.

Bethany rose from the couch without comment and ran for her room.

"Theo, what happened at your dinner?" Ann asked as casually as she could. Something had gone very wrong, for a desperate, angry light glittered in her friend's eyes. Struggling to mask her fear, Ann painted on a warm smile. "Did you learn anything—useful?"

"I certainly did," Theo answered. Her face had emptied of expression; her hands clenched into tight fists at her sides. Ann couldn't imagine what had happened, but a palpable icy anger surrounded the woman standing there. The room was chilled with it.

"What happened, Theo?" Ken asked, his face clouded with uneasiness.

She didn't answer but slowly crossed the room, keeping her eyes fixed on Ken. When she reached the desk, she pulled the key from its drawer.

"Theo," Ann warned, an increasing uneasiness rising from the bottom of her heart, "tell us about it. Stop what you're doing and talk to us."

"I'll talk in a minute," Theo said, unlocking the drawer. Ann leapt to her feet, knowing what was in Theo's mind, but she was too late. In one swift, deliberate movement Theo pulled out the gun. With both hands on the revolver and her arms extended, she aimed the weapon squarely at Ken Holman.

"Theo!" Ann screamed, horrified.

"Where's my daughter?" Theo demanded, her eyes as hard as flint. "And why did you kill Victoria Elliott?"

"What?" Surprise siphoned the blood from Ken's face. His broad hands gripped the arms of the chair.

"Don't try to lie to me! An hour ago a black sedan ran down Victoria Elliott at the restaurant, and now that same car is parked outside. So I'll ask you again. What have you done with my daughter?"

Chapter 31

STACY'S here, in bed, honey. Put the gun down."

Theo tilted her head, listening to Ann's voice as if it came from far away. The only reality she cared about at that moment was the cold steel of the gun in her hand and the wide eyes of the man before her.

"He's going to try to take Stacy," she said, afraid to take her eyes from Ken Holman. "He wants me to stop working on the book, and he knows I will if he hurts her. Look in my pocket; you'll find the note he left on the car. Pull it out; you'll see what I mean."

"Theo, this is crazy." Ann lowered the coffee cup in her hand to the coffee table then walked toward Theo, hesitating only when Theo stretched the gun further in Holman's direction. "The doctor didn't do anything but give Stacy some medicine and check her lungs and throat," Ann whispered. "I was here; I saw everything." Her voice broke; Theo realized her friend was certain she had lost her mind. "What are you thinking? Please give me the gun."

"Look at the note!" Theo demanded, not taking her eyes from Ken's face. "In my right pocket."

Ann didn't argue. Pressing her lips together, she slipped her hand into the coat pocket and pulled out the wet slip of paper Theo had found plastered to her windshield.

"Tonight, the woman," Ann read, disbelief echoing in her voice. "Tomorrow, the little girl. Unless you stop."

"He can't take Stacy; she's all I have," Theo said, voicing the thought that had been running through her mind like a broken record on her desperate drive back to the house. She jerked her head toward the window. "Look outside, Ann, and you'll see that I've never thought more clearly. There's a black Mercedes parked on the street—it has a red sticker on the inside window. That same black car ran over Victoria Elliott tonight before she could even come into the restaurant. Nobody knew I was planning to meet her except you and Ken. And while I was inside waiting for Victoria, he put that note on my windshield."

Theo's arms began to tremble, and she made an effort to steady them. He mustn't see that she was bluffing with an unloaded gun. She wanted him to confess, to explain why he had set about to destroy her life. Was it only the money he'd lose if other women joined in his lawsuit? Or had he decided to use her in some kind of attack against Dr. Dunlap? The pieces weren't fitting together perfectly, but there was a pattern. He had to be involved somehow.

"Listen, Ann, and tell me if this doesn't make sense. Ken planted the bomb at Dunlap's clinic, maybe because they just don't get along, maybe they are rivals. And he told me about BioTech, *knowing* I'd go there and do something to get into trouble. He even—" Theo felt her control wavering as angry tears filled her eyes. "He even pretended to be *interested* in me so he'd make a weak witness for me in the eyes of the court. It all fits, Ann. He left the dead baby in my bedroom when he knew I was staying at your house. Someone in cahoots with him shot Datsko in the hotel elevator—"

"OK, Theo, maybe you're right," Ann whispered, a slight patronizing tone in her voice. She dropped the note on a table and put her hand on Theo's arm. "But this isn't the way to handle things. Put the gun away, and let me call the police."

"I want you to call the police," Theo said, keeping the gun on him. "I want Datsko to hear the truth for a change."

Ken held out his hand. "Theo, stop and think. I don't have a car parked outside. I hate driving in the city, so I took a cab here."

Ann's voice was insistent in Theo's ear. "Listen, honey, I know men, and you've got this one all wrong. He was as gentle as could be with Stacy—"

"No! He would do anything to shut me up!" Theo's hand shook with every word; the point of the pistol wavered. "But I won't be quieted, Ken. You wanted to tell the truth at first, but the thought of the money got to you, didn't it?"

"No," Ken muttered, his face ashen. "I still want to tell the truth, Theo, because of women like my wife and your sister."

He put his hands on the seat of the chair as if to stand, and Theo steadied her grip on the gun. "Don't move."

"I'm calling the police," Ann said, darting into the kitchen.

Ken raised his hands in a "don't shoot" pose and sank back again. "Why, Theo?" he asked, a tinge of sadness in his eyes. "Why would I want to hurt you? I've been trying to *help*—"

"It's all been very convenient for you, hasn't it?" Theo snapped. But at the wounded look in his eyes her knees felt weak, and she sank onto the sofa, though the gun never wavered in its focus. "I don't know exactly why you're doing this, but I suspect it has something to do with your lawsuit against Dunlap's clinic. I think you want to be the first, the one with all the publicity and the million-dollar award, the bellwether case—"

Ann stepped back into the living room. "The police are coming. They'll take care of everything," she said. "And we're listening to you, Theo, but you need to let me have the gun."

Theo lifted a brow and cast her a questioning glance. Why did Ann want the gun so desperately? It wasn't loaded, but Ken didn't know that. And it gave Theo an edge, something to keep the beast at bay until the police arrived.

"We need to let the police investigate and find the truth," Ann went on in her reasonable, coaxing tone. "But I'm the one who took the gun safety course, so let me hold it while we wait for help."

Theo smiled, understanding. This was all part of the act to keep Ken thinking that the gun *was* loaded, that Theo was upset enough to use it.

"I'm OK," she said, keeping the dark metal barrel pointed at the doctor. "Cool as a cucumber." She lifted her chin and stared at Ken, but her thoughts began to whirl in a confused cyclonic rush. *This man framed me somehow. He pretended to care for me. He could have hurt Stacy, but he didn't. He could have hurt me, but he bailed me out of jail and—*

She heard rather than saw him rush from the chair; apart from all conscious thought, her fingers instinctively closed around the trigger. An explosive crack ripped through the house, and Ann screamed.

The explosion echoed back from the walls, battering Theo as a hot and bitter odor filled the air. Ken Holman fell to the floor, a slowly widening red spot darkening the light gray of his trouser leg.

The gun *was* loaded. Ann had lied.

Theo's heart went into sudden shock. Around her, the room fell eerily silent. The only sound was Ken's groan of pain as he struggled to sit up and survey the damage to his leg. His breath hissed through his teeth, and he grimaced up at Ann, pressing down on the tear in his pant leg. "I'm afraid she's clipped an artery," he said, his voice remarkably steady and matter-of-fact. "Have you a belt or something?"

Theo dropped the gun; it fell to the carpet with a dull thud. "Ann," she moaned, pressing her hand over her mouth.

But Ann had rushed to the coat closet. She threw Ken the wide fabric belt of her raincoat, then ran for the phone. "I'll call an ambulance," she yelled.

A sudden wave of nausea swept over Theo. She'd done it now. Time for the police to add *homicidal maniac* to her wanted poster.

Here was the gun, still warm from the accidental blast, still laden with her ink-stained fingerprints.

But maybe he deserved it. He was going to hurt Stacy . . . or try to take her. And he did other terrible things; he wasn't finished yet. . . .

As Ken groaned on the floor, Theo picked up the gun, stuffed it into the pocket of her coat, and slipped out the front door.

※ ※ ※

She needed to think. She needed time, and she needed distance. She had to get home, pack a bag, and get away. When it was safe, she would send for Stacy and hire a good lawyer. One who had nothing to do with Adam Perry or Ken Holman.

As she ran, Theo fumbled in her jeans pocket for her front door key.

Should she wait for the police? No! They'd take one look at the good doctor's wound and haul her off to jail again. And she wasn't going to spend another night in that putrid place, especially not for an accident. The police hadn't believed anything else she'd tried to tell them, so why should they believe her now?

The rain had left dark mirrors of puddles on the glistening asphalt of her driveway, and Theo splashed through them, finally bringing the house key up from her pocket. Her hand trembled; the key wouldn't fit into the lock. A slight breeze rustled the vines growing near the porch; then a distinct, heavy footfall sent icy fear twisting around her heart. She froze.

"Ann?" she asked, hopeful. A faint moonlit shadow fell across the door, and Theo whirled around.

A man stood there, a stranger she'd never seen before. Instinctively, she thrust her hand into the pocket with the gun, grateful that the fullness of her coat hid the telltale bulge.

"Theodora Russell?" The man bobbed his head in an odd imitation of a courtly bow. "Salago's my name, Scotty Salago. I'm supposed to take you to a meeting tonight. My employers would like to have a word with you."

"Your employers?" Fear, like the quick, hot touch of the devil, shot through her; then her pulse quickened as an insane feeling of wild aggression surged through her heart. Why should she be frightened of this man? She had a *loaded* gun. This man and whomever he worked for had destroyed her life; it was time for the insanity to stop.

I can do this, I can stop it all now. . . .

Fingering the reassuring lump of metal in her pocket, she regarded her visitor with cool interest. "Mr. Salago, I'd be more than happy to meet your employers. Am I to assume they're the primary reason I've been spending so much time with the police?"

He bobbed his head again. White teeth gleamed in the semidarkness as his mouth curved in a mirthless smile. "I suppose you could say that."

"I knew Ken wasn't doing this alone. So there are several others?"

Salago extended his arm to the street. "You'll see soon enough, lady. My car's waiting at the curb."

She peered past him. The street was dark and empty but for the black Mercedes, the one she'd seen in the parking lot of the café.

Her heart thumped against her rib cage. "That's *your* car?"

He smiled and nodded. "Sure. And I'm glad you're being so agreeable about this. I'd hate to hurt a pretty lady like you. It was too bad I had to dent my bumper on that woman back at Pepe's, wasn't it?"

Despite her show of bravado, Theo's heart went into sudden shock. *Dear God, this man is the murderer! But what about Ken?*

"So come on," he said, taking her arm. "And come quietly, or I've got orders to send some of my other people to take that sweet little girl of yours. And you wouldn't want that. My guys are a bit uncouth, and—well, they can be very nasty."

Theo's capacity for fear had reached its limit. Her emotions veered crazily from bravery to terror to fury. "Listen here," she said, yanking her arm from his grasp. She pulled the gun from her pocket and lifted it to his face. *Please, God, don't let me pull the trigger again. . . .*

Salago's hands went up automatically; his mouth gaped in surprise. "I'm the one with the gun, do you see?" Theo snapped, her arms trembling. "And *I'm* calling the shots tonight. I want to meet these men; I want to know what they're doing and why they're doing it and why they chose to ruin my life. You're going to take me to them, and no one's going to come near my daughter. *Do you understand?*"

He nodded, and the mad rush of adrenaline made Theo dizzy. She nearly laughed aloud as a sudden inspiration seized her, probably a result of watching too many television cop shows.

Still holding the gun to the man's face with one quivering hand, she clumsily patted his coat with the other. Her probing hand jerked back as if burned when she felt a solid bump under his left arm.

"What's that?" Keeping the gun aimed squarely at his nose, she jerked her chin upward. Salago sheepishly opened his coat and gingerly pulled a revolver from its holster. Theo took it, jammed it into her pocket, then motioned toward the street. "OK, Mr. Salago," she said, gathering her slippery courage. "Now I'm ready to go with you."

Linking her arm through Salago's, Theo kept the gun pointed at his ribs as she led him toward the car. "Don't try anything," she told him, defiance pouring from her eyes. "I've already used this gun once tonight, and I'm just mad enough to do it again."

"That time of the month, eh?" Salago said, giving her a sidelong glance.

"Shut up and get out your keys." As they approached the car at the curb, Theo heard the wail of emergency sirens in the distance.

✳ ✳ ✳

When Datsko heard the police dispatcher report a code ten-fifty-seven—firearms discharged—on Pineview Lane, he floored the accelerator on his '78 Lincoln Continental and smiled as the Beast blew past the other drivers on the wet asphalt. The moon was full, the evening had been eventful, and his instinct told him something big was about to break. Unless he missed his guess, Theo Russell had been badly shaken tonight at Pepe's. Shaken enough, maybe, to make a mistake and do something foolish.

Pineview Lane was quiet when he pulled onto the street. He glanced at the note he'd made from the dispatcher's report—the house reporting the emergency call blazed with light. Next door, Theo Russell's house lay quiet and still under the cloak of darkness. But movement caught his eye. By the dim glow of an overhead streetlight he could see a man and woman walking arm in arm down the driveway. Were they friends of Theo Russell's who'd found her house empty?

Datsko pulled into a neighboring driveway as if he lived there, shut off his lights, and cut the Beast's engine, all the while watching the couple. Then they did a very strange thing. They parted and in unison slid into a black Mercedes parked at the curb, the man in front, the woman in back.

The car started and the lights came on, blinding Datsko for a moment. He stepped out of the Lincoln, whistling, and took three steps toward the house, the picture of a tired father after a long day's work.

The Mercedes edged down the street, then accelerated as the whine of sirens filled the quiet of the night. Datsko did an about-face, ran into the road, and squinted at the retreating sedan's license plate.

Returning to his car, he called the license number in as an eleven-fifty-four, a suspicious vehicle. Before he had finished the call, a fire truck and an ambulance pulled onto Pineview Lane and stopped before the brightly lit house. Uniformed paramedics loaded with bags and a stretcher rushed toward the door.

Datsko smiled and blew into the microphone of his radio for luck.

THE front door of the house stood wide open, and Datsko stepped inside without knocking. The scene was quieter than most domestic disturbances; no one was cursing, screaming, or throwing things.

A quick glance around told him there was no sign of Theo Russell.

A petite brunette was sitting on the carpeted floor, her eyes wide with horror and her hands bloody. The victim, a bearded man in his middle thirties, sat across from her, his back propped against the sofa, his blood pooling atop the beige-colored rug beneath him. Two emergency technicians knelt by his side, and he was calmly talking to them, one bloodstained hand holding a compress to the wound in his thigh.

Datsko zeroed in on the woman. She was pretty in a pixie sort of way, but she kept clenching and unclenching her hands as though she wanted to do something but didn't know what. Or maybe she didn't want to get blood on her clothes. There was no wedding ring on the left hand, he noticed.

He cleared his throat, and the woman's wide eyes did a long, slow slide from the bloody scene to him.

"I'm Howard Datsko, and I'm looking for Theodora Russell," he said, noticing that her eyes darkened at the mention of Theo's name. "Do you have any idea where she could be?"

The woman's mouth twisted. "Are you a cop?"

"Yes, ma'am."

The woman shook her head and looked away.

"Well, then, can you tell me what happened here tonight?"

The woman's eyes glistened as she pointed limply to the man on the floor. "It was an accident. Something spooked her, and she pulled the trigger, but I know she thought the gun was empty. She didn't mean to shoot him."

"Who shot him?"

Silence.

"Where's the gun now?"

The woman shook her head. Her chin trembled as if she were about to cry.

Datsko turned to the victim. "Any idea, sir, of who shot you—or why?"

The man turned from the paramedic and gave Datsko a look of pained annoyance. "If you'd be kind enough to wait, Officer, I'll talk to you when I'm certain I'm not bleeding to death."

There was no fear in the man's eyes, no outrage. Like the woman, he wasn't going to say anything against Theo Russell. But Datsko would have bet his gold-plated cop's shield that she was involved. All the way up to her pretty little neck.

Taking a deep breath, Datsko sat on the edge of a chair facing the woman. "Let's start at the beginning," he said, taking his notebook from his coat pocket. "How about telling me your name and the name of the guy bleeding all over your living room."

"I'm Ann Dawson," she said, her voice a hoarse whisper. She pointed again to the man on the floor. "He's Dr. Ken Holman. Stacy, Theo's daughter, was sick, so she asked Ken to come over and make sure it was nothing serious. Theo had to go out—"

"Where'd she go?" Datsko asked, knowing the answer.

Ann Dawson shook her head again. "To meet some woman from the paper, I forget where." She fell silent as the technicians lifted the doctor onto a stretcher.

Datsko cleared his throat again. "So Theo came back here?"

Ann nodded. "Yes. Someone had left a threatening note on her car, and she was really upset. She came in and headed straight for the desk where I keep—"

She paused—her mental debate was evident on her face. She wasn't sure whether to trust him, whether he'd help or hurt her friend.

"It's OK, Ms. Dawson," Datsko said, trying to conjure up a smile. "I've met your friend Theo, and I like her. For what it's worth, I personally don't believe that she single-handedly did all the stuff she's accused of. But she's tangled up in some mighty serious charges, and it's my job to sort it all out. So if you could be honest and give me the truth, maybe I can help Theo before she gets into any more trouble."

Ann seemed to relax a little. "Theo came in," she said, pointing toward the front door, "and went straight for my gun—I keep it locked in my desk drawer over there—and then she pointed it at Ken."

"Why'd she think the gun was empty?"

The woman bit her lip. "I told her it was. I knew she'd flip out if she knew I kept a loaded gun in the house with the girls around." She looked down at her restless hands. "It was foolish, I know. But these are dangerous times."

Datsko glanced down at his notepad. "So why would Theo take out an empty gun?"

"I don't know. I think she wanted to scare him. She said Ken had set her up for the bombing of that clinic and that he was trying to keep her from working on her book. She had some crazy idea that he left the note threatening Stacy."

"Stacy's her daughter?"

Ann nodded.

"Where's Stacy now? And where's this note?"

Turning, Ann lifted a soggy slip of paper from an end table and dropped it in Datsko's hand. She then pointed toward a dark hallway. "Stacy's back there in my daughter's bedroom. I told both girls to stay away from this mess." She frowned as if she had suddenly remembered something. "Excuse me, I really should go check on them."

Datsko moved his legs out of the way so the lady could slip past him; then he carefully spread the wet paper over his palm. The threat had been scrawled on ordinary paper, probably from a spiral notebook, in blue ink from a typical ballpoint pen. He couldn't tell much; the rain had nearly softened the paper to mush.

While Ann was gone, he studied the room. Apart from the bloody scene in the center of the room, the place was a typical middle-class home: nicely furnished, clean, comfortable, homey. Several photographs of a pixie-faced teenager, a carbon copy of the mother, lined the piano.

"Clear the way, please; we're coming out." The emergency crew jostled the stretcher past Datsko's chair, then carried the doctor through the foyer and out into the night. From the window, Datsko watched them load the man into the back of the ambulance. Holman's face was lined with weariness but showed no trace of anger.

A crowd of neighbors had gathered in the street; the flash of red-and-white emergency lights punctuated the darkness like an eerie carnival. Datsko grunted when the blue-and-white squad car finally pulled up. "About time," he muttered.

Ann Dawson came out of the hallway and nodded gravely when she saw Datsko. "Is there anything else you need to know, Officer?"

"Yes. Why would Theodora Russell think the doctor was threatening her and her kid?"

Ann shook her head again and sank onto the couch. She stared for a moment at the bloodstains on her carpet, then gave Datsko a wry smile. "Do you guys clean up as well as you question?" she asked. "How on earth am I supposed to get this house back to the way it was?"

Datsko ignored the question. "Why'd she shoot him, ma'am? Surely you have an idea why she linked the doctor to this note. What was she thinking?"

"I told you," she sighed. "It was an accident. He lunged toward her, and she jerked." She stopped, distracted by two uniformed cops who came through the open door and glanced at the living room.

"Brother," one said. He nodded briefly at Datsko, then looked at Ann. "Is she the shooter?"

Datsko closed his notebook. "No, gentlemen, and thank you very much for finally showing up. Fill out your report if you have to, but this is part of an ongoing investigation centered at MPD headquarters. There was an accidental shooting, Dr. Kenneth Holman was wounded in the upper thigh, and if you check St. Francis Hospital, I think you'll find the victim awake and ready to talk in the emergency room. I doubt he'll file charges. But now I'd appreciate a few minutes alone with this lady."

The officers looked at each other and shrugged; he'd given them most of the information they needed for their report. They moved outside to the porch, and Datsko looked again at Ann. "You see, Mrs. Dawson, I'm not out to get Theo," he said, gentling his voice. "But if I'm going to help her, I need to know what she did with the gun and where she went."

"She took the gun," Ann answered, rubbing the side of her head as if she'd developed a migraine. "And I honestly don't know where she went, but I know she wouldn't go far without Stacy. I don't know what she was thinking—" She broke off the words, and Datsko thought she was going to break down. But she simply drew a shuddering breath and shook her head. "It's been a stressful week for Theo. She isn't herself."

The woman's words had the ring of truth Datsko had come to recognize, and he nodded and stood up. "Thanks. If we find her, I'll let you know."

Datsko turned to leave, but Ann reached out and held his arm. "It was an accident, Officer. I promise you it was."

"The guy's lucky she didn't kill him," Datsko answered. Ann Dawson released his arm, and he went outside to share his information with the cops from District Three.

✱ ✱ ✱

Back in his car, Datsko picked up the microphone and checked in with the dispatcher. "We had a ten-seventy-one with a possible ADW," he said, not quite sure whether to identify the situation as a mere shooting or an assault with a deadly weapon. "Suspect has left the scene."

"Unit fifty-two, we have a report for you on that eleven-fifty-four," the dispatcher's voice crackled. "Black Mercedes sedan, Maryland license number LIE-290, is registered to BioTech Industries, 159 Fifth Street, Hillcrest Heights, Maryland."

"Ten-four." Datsko slipped the mike back into its cradle, then massaged the Lincoln's steering wheel, thinking. According to a waitress at Pepe's, a black Mercedes sedan with a Maryland license plate had roared out of the parking lot after striking Victoria Elliott. If the woman he had seen in the driveway next door was Theo Russell, why would she willingly leave in a car driven by a hit-and-run killer? The woman he had met was no crusader, only a Sunday school teacher. Unless—

She had a gun. Datsko remembered the peculiar way the man and woman had entered the car: simultaneously, the woman in the back seat and the man in front. *As if she were holding a gun to his back.*

"Russell thinks she has the upper hand now," he whispered, turning the key in the ignition. The woman had watched too many cops-and-robbers movies; she was out of her league. He got on the microphone again to find Greerson and Stockton. It would be a long night, but his twenty-year, gold-plated gut instinct urged him to find Theo Russell. Quickly.

* * *

"Lady, I don't drive so good with a gun at my head." Scotty Salago glanced at Theo in the rearview mirror. "And since I want to take you to my bosses, and you want to go meet my bosses, why don't you put the gun down? We both want the same thing."

Theo lowered the gun to her lap, aware that her arm was trembling again. "OK," she said, taking pains to keep her voice strong. "But don't you forget that I've got it. Don't try anything . . . unusual."

In the mirror, she saw Salago roll his eyes, but he didn't answer. He had turned the car west on the beltway, and after a few moments Theo realized she had no idea where he was taking her. For all she knew, he could be driving her to a rock quarry to dump her body. She lifted the revolver again. "Where are we going?"

Salago saw the gun and jerked the steering wheel slightly. "Put that thing down, lady! We're going to a house in Falls Church."

"Whose house?"

"Dennison Reyes's."

She digested the name silently, but it meant nothing to her. "Who is Dennison Reyes? How does he know Ken Holman?"

Scotty made a face in the mirror and lifted his shoulders in a shrug. "Dennison Reyes is my boss, and I don't know any Ken Holman. I don't ask questions, lady; I just do what I'm told. If you're smart, you'll do the same thing."

"I'm better than smart. I've got a gun."

Salago chuckled. "That don't mean nothin', lady."

They rode in silence for a few minutes. Shining lights from an apartment complex towering above huge billboards for Wal-Mart and Burger King lent an eerie, dreamlike quality to the scene. She was an ordinary woman, a mother and housewife, as typical and tame as wheat toast. . . . What was she doing in a car with a murderer?

Theo looked down at the gun in her hand and turned it over,

half-frightened by the realization that she had actually sent a bullet through Ken Holman. How odd that a small steel contraption could cause such injury—or even tear the life from a man! Her free hand patted the bulge in her raincoat pocket. The gun she had taken from Salago was heavier than Ann's small revolver.

But there were other ways to take a life. She lifted her green eyes to the rearview mirror. "Why did you kill Victoria Elliott?"

Salago's eyes narrowed before he cracked a half-smile. "I told you; I just follow orders, lady. Reyes told me to knock her off before she got in the restaurant. They didn't want her talking to you."

"Holman tipped them off, right?"

"I told you; I don't know any Holman. Some muckety-muck from the paper called Rodenbaugh and told him there'd be trouble."

Theo leaned forward until the cold steel of the gun kissed the back of Salago's neck. He jumped; the car swerved in the lane. "Good grief, lady! Do you want us to wreck right here on the beltway?"

"Who's Rodenbaugh?"

Salago stiffened, eyeing the gun in the mirror. "He's some bigwig with the NCC. That's all I know, so sit back and relax. We'll be there in a minute, and then you can ask anything you want."

Theo leaned back, lowered the gun to her lap, and looked out the window. Salago took the Falls Church exit from the beltway, then drove into a development of wide streets. Luxurious brick homes sat far away from the thoroughfare, their brilliant porch lanterns pushing at the darkness. After following the winding road for three or four minutes, Salago turned into a long drive.

Theo looked out the window. The brick house, gloriously illuminated by security lights, was as immense as Texas and about as subtle as a parade. Salago parked the car in the circular drive, cut the engine, and glanced at her in the rearview mirror. "This is where we get out, lady."

"OK," she said, gripping the gun. She waved it slightly to remind him that she still held it. "I'll follow you. You take me in, Scotty, and introduce me to all your people. Then I intend to ask a lot of questions."

Salago grunted and got out. Theo moved in sync with him, keeping the gun pointed at his back. Though her heart pounded like a bass drum and adrenaline surged through her veins, still she had to struggle to keep up with him.

* * *

Dennison Reyes blinked in surprise when he opened the door. Scotty Salago stood outside, as greased and slimy as always, but behind him stood a petite, pale woman in a voluminous raincoat. In her hand she carried a steel revolver, and in her eyes Dennison could read determination distilled to its essence.

"Hiya, boss," Scotty said, waving and winking as he passed by Dennison to go into the house. "Guess who's got a gun?"

Dennison turned to the woman, who turned the gun on him without batting an eye. "Good evening," he said, grudgingly impressed by the unexpected turn of events. "You must be Theodora Russell."

"I am, and I don't know you," she said, her voice clipped and as cool as the October evening. "I know your name, but a man is more than a name, don't you think?"

"But of course," he said, opening the door wider. He extended his free arm into the foyer. "Let me offer my hospitality, and you can discover just how much more I am." He paused and pointed delicately at the gun. "There's no need for that, I assure you. That looks like a .22 caliber, my dear, and there are at least two men in my library who habitually carry .44s. You could take turns shooting each other, but that would accomplish nothing."

Her piercing emerald eyes never left his face, but she slowly lowered the gun and placed it in his outstretched hand. With forced casualness, he turned and dropped it into an umbrella stand in the foyer.

"That's ever so much better," Reyes said, folding his hands. "We're all convened in the library. We've been expecting you for some time."

"I would have come sooner, but I was busy shooting a man," she answered, moving calmly past him into the foyer.

Reyes felt a smile curve upon his lips. "Oh my. I can only hope we haven't underestimated you, Mrs. Russell."

Chapter 33

U NDER any other circumstances, the luxuriously paneled room would have taken Theo's breath away. A thick Persian carpet lay under her feet, a crackling fire roared in the massive stone fireplace, and the furniture gleamed with the patina of fine old woods and good taste. Two distinguished-looking men sat on a tapestried sofa, and Theo felt her face twist into a wry smile when she recognized Griffith Dunlap, the doctor whose clinic she had supposedly bombed. Scotty Salago stood at the bar, pouring himself a drink; two other men sat in a far corner of the room in dinner jackets that seemed too small. She gasped when she recognized the taller one as the man who shot Howard Datsko in the elevator; he grinned and winked almost playfully at her.

"Come and join us, Mrs. Russell," Griffith Dunlap called from the couch. "We were just discussing what we should do about you."

"Sorry we're late, boss," Salago said, jiggling the drink in his hand. "But she got a little trigger-happy back at the house."

"Yes, gentlemen," Reyes said, following Theo into the library. "Mrs. Russell says she has already injured someone tonight. And we, I might add, had nothing to do with it."

Dr. Dunlap lifted his brows in an elegant expression of pleased surprise. "Really?"

"Really," Theo echoed, taking a seat on the edge of a plush wing chair facing him. "And I wouldn't hesitate to do it again."

"There will be no need for violence," the older man on the couch inserted. "Reyes, will you make the introductions? Let's get down to business and send this enterprising young lady on her way. I'd like to be done with this as soon as possible."

"Certainly." Reyes straightened his posture and opened his hand to the silver-haired man who had just spoken. "Mrs. Russell, I'd like you to meet Dr. Burl Rodenbaugh, executive director of the National Committee for Choice. Seated next to him is Dr. Griffith Dunlap, founder of the Family Services Clinic and BioTech Industries. I believe you two have already met."

"Of course." Griffith Dunlap inclined his head slightly, and Theo shuddered as she remembered meeting him in the hall at BioTech. He had been no less calm and collected last night, right before sending her to jail. The righteous rage he had exhibited before Datsko must have been an act.

"We are three of the four board members of BioTech Industries," Reyes went on. "These other gentlemen work for us. Of course, you've met Scotty," Reyes smiled dimly at Salago, "and behind him are Brennan and Antonio. Their last names aren't important, but their faces may be familiar to you."

Theo looked warily from one man to the next. "I don't know what sort of game you are playing," she said, running her hand over the reassuring bulge in her raincoat pocket, "but it's not legal, and it's not right. You'd be wise to stop what you're doing and let me go."

"Let me remind you that you brought Mr. Salago to my door with a gun in your hand," Dennison Reyes said, widening his eyes in feigned astonishment. "And as a lawyer, I'm reasonably sure such an act constitutes kidnapping and abduction across state lines, a very serious felony. I'd be perfectly right to call in the FBI."

Theo sat back, stunned. Reyes took a seat on the sofa, then leaned forward, his elbows resting on his knees. "You see, Mrs. Russell, your problem is that you are half-informed. You know a few things, and a little knowledge can be very dangerous. So we hoped you'd come tonight and allow us to fill in the gaps of your understanding, thus lessening the likelihood that you'll injure yourself or your little daughter." He nodded in concern, but his cynicism was evident in the slight curl of his upper lip. "She's a very sweet little girl. We wouldn't want to see anything happen to her."

Theo couldn't answer. Her heart turned to stone within her chest; her legs felt like iron weights.

Reyes didn't seem to notice her paralysis. "So before you go running to the police with the incomplete knowledge that you've managed to glean, let us explain why you can't. And because you're an intelligent and rational young woman, I'm sure we'll be able to come to an amicable agreement."

Rodenbaugh had noticed her tenseness. "Relax, my dear," he said, a cool gleam in his eye. Theo wasn't sure, but when he gave her a lurking smile she thought he might be slightly drunk. "We've been waiting to meet the woman who has caused us such unexpected trouble."

"I'm not here to relax," she said, shifting in the chair. Her heavy raincoat was uncomfortably warm so near the fire, but she didn't want to take it off. Inside the pocket was Scotty's gun—the only power and control she had in this situation.

"Of course you're not," Reyes answered. "You're here to learn; we're here to explain." He glanced at his colleagues. "Where do we begin?"

"Tell me about Theodore Russell and *The Savage Breast*," Theo said. "My troubles all began there."

"Ah, yes," Reyes said, patting the arm of the sofa. "Burl, should I begin at that point?"

"It's as good as any," Rodenbaugh said, pulling a cigar from his pocket. "Tell her about Moreno's people."

Dennison Reyes closed his eyes for a moment, then leaned back and crossed his legs. "There is a great deal of money to be made in desperation," he said, his voice heavy with earnestness. "And it's legal money, free and clear. But any business requires capital to begin, and BioTech Industries required a lot of capital. We have connections in New York who loaned us the money. Unofficial partners, you might say."

A whisper of terror ran through her. "The mob?" she asked.

From the bar, Scotty laughed, and the men on the couch exchanged tight, uncomfortable smiles.

"Call the Moreno family whatever you like," Reyes said, leaning toward her again. "But these people know a sure investment when they see one, and they'll go to extreme lengths to protect their stake in the venture. One of these, uh, partners of ours has a niece who works for a publishing house in New York. The niece saw Russell's proposal and thought it was powerful stuff. The word came down that *The Savage Breast* would be bad for BioTech's business."

"Abortions might be curtailed, you mean," Theo said, forcing herself to meet his gaze, though her knees quivered beneath her raincoat. "Women would be afraid to risk breast cancer, the number of abortions would drop off, and BioTech's supply of fetal material would be severely curtailed."

Reyes shrugged. "I don't know if the number of abortions would actually decrease, but the climate would definitely change. And with a change in political climate, the courts, Congress, and the press would be affected. Things could get . . . complicated."

"Like he said, it would be bad for business," Dunlap said, growling impatiently. "Everybody's business."

"So you had Russell killed." Theo stated the truth as a fact, not a question, and no one in the room even blinked.

Reyes lifted his hand. "Mr. Moreno and his people warned Russell, but apparently he didn't listen. Brennan and Antonio took care of him in Washington, and we thought that was the end of that troublesome book."

Theo sat still in the chair, absorbing the insanity of it all. *Theo-*

dore Russell put words onto paper and died, and no one would ever have known why if I hadn't stumbled onto his proposal and continued to spread the truth. She glanced up at Reyes. "But my book was completely different from Russell's. It was supposed to be nonfiction, just facts and interviews."

"Our associates might have left you alone, but you stirred up quite a hornet's nest when you duped that editor from New York," Reyes went on. "Due to your little tête-à-tête in the hotel, Evelyn Fischer went to the police, and suddenly the cops were asking too many questions about Russell's proposed book. No one would have paid you any attention, but with the publicity—"

"Why didn't you just kill me?" Theo interrupted. She stiffened in her chair and pointed to Dunlap. "Why go through the trouble of blowing up this doctor's clinic and making trouble for me?"

"Please, Mrs. Russell," Reyes said, frowning as if she had just suggested that he eat filet mignon with his hands. "Murder is a distasteful last resort for people of little imagination and skill. There are more subtle ways of managing things." He shrugged slightly. "The police would never accept that two people named Theo Russell had died mysteriously. And we saw in you and your delightful naïveté an opportunity to take a few jabs at the political opposition. We invested a lot of time in our plan for you, and you've played along beautifully, going to the police, persevering in your self-righteous crusade with the persistence of a mosquito—"

"My office at the Family Services Clinic is highly insured," Dr. Dunlap spoke up from the center of the couch. "We get threats every week from antiabortion groups. No one was in the least surprised when my clinic was targeted." He shrugged. "In six months, we'll have replaced that old building with a new one."

"And Ken Holman will have put another of his competitors temporarily out of business," Theo added, her mind returning to thoughts of the handsome doctor. "Very neat, I'll admit."

"Dr. Ken Holman?" The corners of Dunlap's eyes crinkled as he grinned. "A partner? That's a laughable thought."

Theo closed her eyes for a moment. "Ken's not the fourth member of your board?"

Dunlap snorted, his abrupt laughter punctuating the stillness like gunfire. Reyes was smiling when she opened her eyes. "Holman is nothing to us," Reyes said, "but he has been useful."

Theo felt her heart sink. *God . . . O God, forgive me! How could I have been so wrong?* She'd assumed Ken was in on the conspiracy because only he and Ann knew she'd gone to meet Victoria Elliott. She'd never stopped to think that there might be a leak at the newspaper.

Father, I shot a man on an errand of mercy. The only man who's been even slightly interested in my welfare since Matt died. . . .

She lowered her head to her hand, trying to shake off the web of confused thoughts that whirled inside her brain. "And BioTech . . . let me guess," she said, looking at Dunlap. "You take fetal tissues from the aborted babies at your clinic and auction them off to the highest bidder under the auspices of BioTech Industries. You and your doctor friends do the surgery, you charge inflated fees—"

Dunlap's stone face rearranged itself into a grin. "Very good, Mrs. Russell. You heard more than I thought." He paused. "You shouldn't trespass in private buildings, you know. We were caught a bit off guard when you pulled that bit of law-breaking."

Theo ignored him. "You set it all up," she said, looking around the circle of men. "You called those protesters to come to my house today. One of you broke in and left that fetus in my bedroom."

"The protesters are all loyal NCC volunteers, all anxious to preserve a woman's right of choice," Rodenbaugh said, waving his hand. "They are as zealous for their cause as you are for yours."

"My cause is *life*, not murder!" Theo said, her eyes flashing hotly. "You have Theo Russell's blood on your hands."

"He died happy," Antonio called from the corner of the room.

"He asked for the final fix himself; then we let him go, just like we promised."

"How do you justify killing Victoria Elliott? She was no threat to you."

"Burl's office has contacts at the *Post*," Reyes explained. "One of the reporters was raising a stink with the editor in chief about Elliott's latent antiabortion bias. Seems this Pam-somebody-or-other was convinced that the sanctity of the press was about to be impugned. Editors can't take bomb-happy lunatics seriously, you see."

"And so you killed her?"

"A hit-and-run driver killed her. Drunk, no doubt," Rodenbaugh said dryly. "That's the story everyone will hear. Unless, of course, we need to change it. If that becomes necessary, then tomorrow, with a little luck and a major investment, we will find witnesses who saw *your* car strike the unfortunate Ms. Elliott." He laughed softly. "But I doubt that will be necessary."

Theo's mind whirled. For a brief moment she wished that last week they had shot her in the elevator instead of Datsko. If she had died, Victoria Elliott would still be alive. Ken Holman would be better off without her. And she wouldn't have put Ann and Stacy and Bethany through so much grief.

"You're much more useful to us alive," Reyes said, apparently guessing her thoughts. He leaned toward her again. "Now that we understand each other, let's get to the purpose of this meeting. What we want you to do, Mrs. Russell, is plead guilty to criminal trespass. Without our considerable influence against you, you will never be convicted of setting the bomb at the clinic; the evidence is all circumstantial. But you and I know you *are* guilty of trespassing at BioTech. As your lawyer, I could arrange a legitimate plea bargain. You'd serve no prison time, three months at the district jail, tops. Maybe you could even get a suspended sentence, considering that you have no criminal record."

Theo shook her head. "I don't understand."

"We want you to go away, Mrs. Russell, to stay out of the public eye for a few months. We want you to forget about the book, about the supposed link between abortion and breast cancer, about everything you've learned in the last two weeks. We especially want you to forget you ever even heard of Theodore M. Russell."

"You mean you want me to forget you murdered him. And Victoria Elliott."

Reyes smiled indulgently. "My dear, no one here has admitted to doing any such thing. Even if we had, it is your less-than-reputable word against ours. Whom do you think the officials will believe?" He paused for a moment to let the reality of his words sink in, then went on. "Serve your sentence, keep your end of the deal, and you won't have to leave your little girl. In time, you'll be a footnote on the back page of the local paper. No one will care about anything you have to say."

"And women will continue to have abortions, and many of them will develop breast cancer, and their babies' bodies will be used for spare parts," Theo whispered. "Nothing will cause a ripple in the tide; nothing will change."

"Why should it?" Dunlap's voice was curt. "Good grief, Dennis, I'm sick of hearing this self-righteous blarney. The operations of BioTech Industries are 100 percent legal, young woman. We have the right to use fetal cells, we have the right to tell women that their choice for abortion might mean the difference between life and death for someone else's kid."

"I've researched your 'rights'," Theo shot back. "I know that according to the NIH guidelines, a woman is *not* to be told of the possibility of fetal donation until *after* she's decided to abort. But you use it as a selling point!"

"There are no laws in effect here," Reyes interrupted. "The NIH guidelines are only suggestions."

"*Suggestions?*" Theo made a face. "I know that you're not supposed to sell fetal organs, but I heard you quote a fee of $500,000 to that desperate couple at BioTech."

Dunlap stiffened in indignation, but Reyes put out a soothing hand. "We're allowed to charge fees for the retrieval, preparation, and storage of biological material," Reyes countered.

"*Reasonable* fees," Theo said. "Half a million dollars isn't reasonable. And neither is murdering people." She glared across the room. "And women who fall into your trap, thousands of them, will pass the years in ignorance until they find that first lump. Then, in panic, they'll rush to their doctors and discover that they have breast cancer. Oh, some of them will be lucky and catch it at stage one, two, or even three, but others, like my sister, will suffer through stages four and five. What about *them*, gentlemen?"

There was a long, brittle silence. The gleam of subtle amusement disappeared from Reyes's eyes, and he regarded her with searching gravity for a moment, but then Dunlap broke the stillness.

"No one has ever died from breast cancer," he said, his voice ringing with reproach. "And this supposed link is a fantasy. No one will ever prove it."

Theo caught her breath, stunned beyond words. Of course, he was right in a literal sense; cancer in the breast spread to other areas in the body before the disease proved fatal. But his insolence and coldness were unbelievable.

No one argued his point. After a moment, Dennison Reyes picked up his drink and glanced at his companions. "I think we've discussed everything of importance." His eyes turned to Theo. "What we want from you, Mrs. Russell, is cooperation. Plead guilty to trespassing, keep quiet, and forget about this entire incident. Let things remain as they are. You haven't the expertise or the knowledge to resist us. The odds against you are simply too great."

"I can fight. I can write."

Dunlap smiled indulgently. "While I admire the tenacity of the young, dear lady, I'm afraid my colleague is right. BioTech Industries has a great deal of money and as much influence as money can buy. We are heavily involved in the campaigns of several congress- men and senators, for instance, and you can't fight Congress when the votes are against you."

"Quite true," Rodenbaugh said. "Abortion is here to stay. Taking away that right would destroy families, threaten women, put an end to promising research—"

"And bankrupt BioTech Industries." Theo slipped her hand into her pocket and felt the hard coolness of Scotty's gun.

"Accept our offer," Reyes said. "If you serve your time quietly, no harm will come to your friend Ms. Dawson or your little daughter. You might want to think about them, too. And when you get out of jail, BioTech Industries will offer you a cash advance to start out in a new life. Think about it, Mrs. Russell. You're not going to change anything; you're simply not that good. But we can make things easy for you."

"Remember the Morenos' niece in publishing?" Rodenbaugh inserted. "If you're still set on writing, we can get you a publishing contract. Name your topic; name your price. Name your slot on the best-seller lists, for that matter. The Moreno family could make it happen."

The mention of a book contract made Theo hesitate. *God, what do I do? I did trespass at the BioTech building. . . .*

Perhaps the righteous thing to do would be to plead guilty and pay for her crime. After all, she couldn't stand before a judge with a clear conscience and say she was innocent of the trespassing charge. Accepting their offer would keep Ann and Stacy from danger, enable Theo to atone for the wrong she'd committed, and ultimately free her to write whatever she wanted . . . even the book on Down's syndrome, which could help thousands of families. And what qualifications did she have to write the abortion book? Per- haps she had been foolish to even dream of adapting Theodore Russell's topic. Rodenbaugh was probably right. Abortion had been a part of American life for over twenty years; one measly book wasn't going to change anything.

And a cash advance. . . . It hurt her pride to admit it, but money had been much in her mind lately. With a hefty advance from the book contract they had promised, she wouldn't have to grumble about spending twelve bucks in a parking garage or worry about where she'd get the money for Stacy's next pair of shoes.

Don't be afraid. I will uphold you with my victorious right hand. You will be a new threshing instrument with many sharp teeth. You will tear all your enemies apart, making chaff of mountains. . . .

The words jolted her, and she looked at the men sitting in the room, watching her with supreme confidence on their faces. If she took their offer, she'd forever be in debt to murderers, at their beck and call, writing only what *they* wanted her to write. And that slot on the best-seller list wouldn't belong to her. Not really. She wouldn't have won it with hard work; it would simply be a payment for the blood of Victoria Elliott, Theodore Russell, and untold numbers of unborn babies and their mothers—even Janette. She'd had an abortion, and she had breast cancer. And no one would ever link the cause and effect if people like these men always won.

Time to make chaff of mountains. Pulling Scotty's gun from her pocket, Theo stood and backed toward the doorway. She moved the gun in an arc as they stared at her, and she almost wanted to laugh at the disapproving looks they tossed her way, as if she were a recalcitrant child.

"Thank you, but I'm going to write my book and tell the absolute and total truth when I have my turn in court," she said, her voice wavering despite her best intentions. "Including the details of your offer this evening. And I'm going to use everything I can to generate publicity. Maybe I'll even camp out on the sidewalk in front of BioTech with a poster of my own. Truth is on my side, gentlemen, and though you have money, goons, and influence, I'm doing what's right."

Brennan and Antonio stood and tensed. Theo had the distinct impression they were planning to rush toward her, but Reyes held up a restraining hand. "Mrs. Russell," he said, turning on the couch to face her, "are you quite sure about your decision? The offer is rescinded after this meeting. Tomorrow will be too late for a change of heart."

"I'm not going to *have* a change of heart!" Theo snapped, stepping back. "I'd rather watch for you over my shoulder than have all of you in front of me running my life."

Reyes shrugged and turned away, but Dunlap's mouth curved into a cruelly confident smile. "Think again, Mrs. Russell," he said, his gaze shifting to a point behind her. Theo's body tightened as a hand fell upon her shoulder, and she spun to see Adam Perry standing in the doorway.

"Adam, thank God!" she breathed, lowering the gun as relief swept over her. "These men—"

She broke off at the wry gleam in his eyes, and awareness slammed into her. Adam Perry had no reason to be in Dennison Reyes's home. He was the prosecutor in a lawsuit against Reyes. He would avoid contact with Reyes at all costs, unless . . .

"Thank you, Mrs. Russell," he said, calmly reaching forward to pry the gun from her hand. "But you're making my friends nervous with that thing. I hope you won't mind if I take care of it for you."

Theo stood helpless while he pocketed the gun and took hold of her arm, propelling her back into the room.

"You're the fourth board member," Theo whispered, her heart sinking.

Perry gave her a hard smile, then turned to the others. "Well, gentlemen, forgive my tardiness. I gather that Mrs. Russell has chosen not to accept our offer."

"A foolish mistake," Rodenbaugh said, his eyes narrowing as he studied Theo's face. She had the feeling he would find great pleasure in strangling her.

"You're Ken's lawyer," Theo said dully, glancing at Perry. "Why are you involved with these men?"

"Why not?" Perry raised a bushy brow. "I'm concerned with the issue and vitally interested in preserving a woman's right to an abortion."

"But Ken is suing an abortion clinic!"

Perry shook his head as Reyes laughed aloud. "A case, I fear, that he will lose. Given the lack of research and the present political climate, there's no way he could win. And when he loses, a precedent will be set in the courts, and other cases will undoubtedly refer to it throughout the years to come."

Theo sputtered in helpless fury. "What sort of war-zone ethics are those? You ought to be disbarred!"

Perry smiled again. "Probably. But I won't be."

"Well, gentlemen," Dunlap said, "we are now faced with an uncooperative young woman who knows far more than she ought to. What do we do with her?"

Reyes glanced toward the corner of the room where Brennan and Antonio were leaning against the wall with bored expressions on their faces. "I think it's time we called in our—what did she call them?—our 'goons'."

Chapter 34

THINK, Mrs. Russell, about what you've done," Perry said, casually slipping his hand into his coat pocket. "You're now publicly known as a right-wing antiabortion zealot. Probably 93 percent of people on the street believe you are guilty of bombing Dunlap's clinic; the other 7 percent are illiterate and don't care."

Burl Rodenbaugh picked up Perry's thought. "Don't forget that tonight you shot a man. I imagine that report is filtering through the local newsrooms even as we speak."

"You've also hijacked an innocent bystander's car," Reyes said, jerking his head toward Scotty, "and used a gun to force your way into a private home. We won't even have to elaborate on those facts, Mrs. Russell. In this situation, truth is on *our* side. If you don't accept our offer tonight, you'll be dead by tomorrow morning. Brennan and Antonio are quite adept at arranging suicides, and when we bring forth the witnesses who saw *you* driving the black Mercedes that killed Victoria Elliott, no one will doubt that the events of the last few days unhinged you and you acted in retribution for your bit of bad press. Then, if all of that wasn't tragic enough, you took your own life when you couldn't handle the guilt. You see, young woman, although your options are perhaps more limited than you thought, you always have a choice." His smile vanished. "Make yours now."

Theo closed her eyes and spoke the words that reflexively sprang to her lips: "Oh God, help me now!" One of the men in the room snickered, but Theo's mind raced in a frantic prayer: *Oh God, I'm sorry. I'm sorry I read the proposal. I'm sorry I went into BioTech. I'm sorry I shot Ken. I've made a real mess of things, but if you can make a way out for me, I'll take it.*

The library was as silent as a church as Theo waited for her answer. No police burst through the door; no one rose to defend her with a miraculous change of heart. She had come to the end of herself, and God was offering—*silence*. Only one thought came to her mind: God was the author of justice, of life, of *truth*.

"I'll plead guilty to trespassing because I did wrong," she said, lifting her chin and gazing steadily at Dennison Reyes. "But I can't be silent about atrocities masquerading as medicine that are actually accomplished purely for profit. And I can't conveniently forget what happened to Theodore Russell and Victoria Elliott. You are asking me to do what God detests: acquit the guilty and condemn the innocent children who are sacrificed to abortion. Do to me what you will, gentlemen, but I won't be a part of your plan."

"Feisty little thing, isn't she?" Perry remarked offhandedly.

"Well—" Reyes nodded toward Scotty, who put down his drink and stepped forward—"I suppose that's our answer." He gave Theo a polite smile. "It's been a pleasure to meet you, Mrs. Russell. A genuine delight."

For a moment, Theo thought he would actually shake her hand, but he stood and gestured to Brennan and Antonio. The two came toward Theo and stood on either side of her, waiting.

"So sorry to have seen the last of you, Mrs. Russell," Griffith Dunlap said, peering up at her through his glasses. "You have enlivened the past few days with a real sense of adventure."

As Brennan and Antonio each gripped one of Theo's arms, Reyes's tone became immediately clipped and businesslike. "Holman's office," he said, nodding to Scotty. "Use the plastique again, and look for chloroform to knock her out. We don't want any bruises or swelling, no telltale marks. It's got to look like she decided to remain behind."

"No problem, boss," Scotty said. He adjusted the lapels of his suit and swaggered through the double library doors while Theo struggled uselessly in Antonio's and Brennan's iron grips.

H OWARD Datsko crossed his legs at the ankle for the hun-
dredth time and stared down the gleaming hospital hall.
Ken Holman had been in the curtained emergency cubicle
for nearly an hour, and Datsko was anxious to talk to him again.
Ann Dawson's story had made little sense, and Datsko wanted to
hear from the horse's mouth why Theodora Russell would shoot
the man doing his best to help her.

A nurse backed into the corridor, guiding a wheelchair, and the
detective sprang to his feet when he recognized Holman in the
chair. "Hey, Doc Holman," Datsko called, rushing after the nurse.
"I've got to talk to you."

The nurse, a sturdy woman with fiercely graying hair, frowned as
Datsko cut in front of the chair. "Excuse me, sir, but this man is
being examined."

"Just a minute." Datsko pulled out his shield and flashed it before
her angry gaze. "Dr. Holman, can you hear me?"

Holman's eyes were closed, but he mumbled something.

"Is he lucid?" Datsko asked the nurse.

"Yes, but he's not in the mood for conversation," she snapped.
"Can't this wait until tomorrow?"

"No." Datsko moved aside to let her proceed but kept up with the
nurse's determined pace. *Good grief, this lady must be training for a
sprint relay.* "Holman," he shouted, bending toward the doctor's ear.

The man's eyes opened as if on a spring. "Yes?"

"I need to talk to you about Theo Russell. Why'd she shoot you?"

The doctor turned to Datsko with a puzzled look in his eyes; then Datsko saw memory crash into his consciousness with the force of a careening vehicle. "I don't know," he answered after a moment, a weight of despair on his bearded face.

Datsko put out his hand to stop the nurse again. "Look," he said, kneeling before the wheelchair, "something's up, and if you want to help Theo Russell, I need you to talk to me. I saw your lady friend getting into the car of a known criminal, and if you can tell me why she'd do that—"

An earsplitting electronic beep shattered the stillness of the corridor, and Holman's eyes widened as he fumbled for the belt he was no longer wearing. "My beeper. The alarm."

Sighing in exasperation, the nurse withdrew the beeper from a bag on the back of the wheelchair. "I've got it with your personal effects, Doctor," she said. She pressed the button and the alarm silenced. "I don't think you're going to be answering calls tonight, Dr. Holman."

"No—no," the doctor shook his head.

"You go through that kind of noise every time a patient beeps you?" Datsko asked. "You gotta be kidding, Doc. That kind of electronic leash I don't need."

"That wasn't a patient," Holman said, reaching for the beeper. He took it from the nurse's hand and studied the message box carefully. "That's a special code from my security system. Someone has cut the wires to the alarm."

Datsko stared at the doctor for a moment as an idea whipped in among his thoughts. *Yeah. Of course.* Grinning his thanks, he left Holman in the hall and sprinted for the doorway.

* * *

Brennan waited until Theo stopped struggling, then removed the chloroform-soaked handkerchief from her nose and mouth. She'd been stubborn and uncooperative right until the end, and his skin still stung from where she'd scratched his neck while he held her down to tape her wrists and ankles. As fierce as a banshee, that one. He was glad they'd soon be done with her.

He pulled her to the small bathroom off the main hallway, then flicked on a light. "Hurry up out there," he called to Antonio, who knelt by the doctor's desk with a timer and a bundle of plastique in his hand. "I'll have her cleaned up in a minute. Mind you, she's not going to stay knocked out for long."

"Almost done," came the muffled reply.

Brennan stripped the gray duct tape from Theo's wrists and scrubbed the sticky residue from her arms with paper towels and soap from the bathroom sink. As an afterthought, he grabbed a cleaning brush and rubbed it over the edge of her hands to scrub under her nails. Not that there'd be anything left for the police to find, but one could never be too cautious.

When he was certain the police would find nothing unusual about Theodora Russell's body, Brennan grabbed her under the arms and dragged her into Holman's office.

"This place is a dump!" he said, looking around. "How can anyone work in this mess?" Shaking his head, he let Theo slump to the floor and bent to study Antonio's handiwork. As usual, the Italian had done quick work, but this time he left the wiring a bit askew. They'd learned that from the job at Dunlap's place: The police hadn't seriously considered the woman a suspect because the work had been a little *too* professional.

"There," Antonio said, looking at the explosive with an almost reverent expression on his face. "I've set the timer for ten minutes."

"And what if she wakes up before that?" Brennan frowned. "She could get away."

"If she moves, she'll trip the bomb herself," Antonio said, grinning. He pointed to a three-foot-long wire hooked into the timer. A loop had been twisted into the end. "Bring her over here next to the sofa. We'll slip this over a finger. If she moves her hand, this place blows."

Brennan arched an eyebrow. "And if she moves her hand in her sleep?"

Antonio grinned wickedly. "That's why we're outta here as soon as we put this loop on her finger and arm the bomb."

"Well, naturally," Brennan murmured, gritting his teeth. He didn't appreciate Antonio's fondness for walking the knife edge of danger, but so far their luck had held.

He dragged Theo closer to the desk and lifted her arm. Her hand was warm and small in his, and Brennan quietly rubbed his thumb over the fragile skin. Too bad. He thought about her wee little girl. Well, women with small children shouldn't be messing around with things that'd get them into trouble.

Antonio tightened the wire noose around the woman's little finger, then attached the wire to the explosives. Holding his breath, he pressed a button on the timer. The red numbers shifted immediately to nine fifty-nine, and Brennan felt his stomach tense as he lowered the woman's head to the floor.

Theodora Russell groaned. Brennan froze for a brief moment, then muttered a low curse as he sprinted toward the doorway, Antonio's frantic breathing in his ear every step of the way.

✳ ✳ ✳

Howard Datsko had called for backup on the way: code two, no red light or siren. A blue-and-white police car met him in the parking lot outside The Women's Center on Reservoir Road, and the cops crouched behind the open doors of their car and scanned the outside of the neat brick building. Trouble was definitely afoot. Shards of glass glinted darkly on the sidewalk; one pane of glass had been broken out of the door.

"Whaddya think?" one of the uniformed cops called to Datsko, his hand hovering near his holster. "Dopers after a quick fix?"

Datsko shook his head as he pulled his gun from his shoulder holster and shifted his weight behind the Beast's door. "No. I'm betting we find a woman inside. A couple of hours ago she shot her boyfriend and drove away from the scene arm in arm with that slug Scotty Salago. This is the boyfriend's office."

The officer cursed softly and drew his gun. "Nice lady, huh? Just the kind you want to take home to Mom. Is she still armed?"

"Could be." Datsko squinted through the darkness toward the building. A loose wire flapped against the brick wall—telephone wires? the security system? He was surprised Theodora Russell would know which wire to cut, but he'd been surprised at everything the woman did.

Rain began to fall again, streaking the Beast's windshield like tears, and Datsko wrapped his coat closer. The wind chilled him to the bone, and for a moment he wished he had stayed at his desk instead of venturing out on his wild hunch. But this case was about to break. He knew it. Whether Theo Russell was working with other people or alone, he could almost smell her presence inside Holman's office.

He was about to venture out from behind the security of the Lincoln's heavy door when the front door of the building crashed open and two men ran out. Forgetting the rain, Datsko fell into the crouched shooter's position. "Stop or I'll shoot!" he yelled, practically in unison with the other cops.

The two men on the sidewalk hesitated a moment. The taller one immediately laced his fingers atop his head—an old prison position—while the other reached into his coat.

Datsko pulled the trigger.

* * *

Brennan saw Antonio go down. *Stupid move, Tony,* he thought, but he didn't move. He stayed as he was, his hands on his head. "Don't shoot!" he called loudly, standing as still as he could and facing the light from the squad car's headlights. "I'm not going to move, mind you. I'm going to stand right here. I'll be wanting to stay alive to talk to you."

One of the uniformed cops came out from behind his car, his gun still smoking. "Put your hands against the building," he barked, his eyes bright with adrenaline and fear.

Brennan did as he was told, counting the seconds it took the officer to reach him.

"Don't budge," the policeman said, patting him down and removing his gun. "Don't even breathe."

"Whatever you say," Brennan replied quickly, "but I'm thinking we should move—"

"What you're thinking doesn't really matter, friend," an older cop in a trench coat replied as he knelt to press his fingers to Antonio's throat. "Now, you mind telling me just exactly why we should give a rat's tail whether you're dead or not?"

"Information," Brennan answered, feeling a fine sheen of sweat breaking out on his forehead. He couldn't remember the last time he'd broken a sweat! "I have a lot of it, and I'll talk, haven't I said so? But I strongly suggest we move away from the building. Now. It's going to blow."

Doubt flickered in the cop's eyes, but the detective stiffened suddenly and jerked his head up. "The building's wired? How long till it blows?"

"In seven, maybe six minutes, maybe sooner." Brennan's hands trembled like a man with palsy as he held them up. "Truth to tell, I wouldn't joke about it. I'm serious. Get me out of here."

"Where's Theodora Russell?" the older guy asked, wiping a wet strand of gray hair from his forehead. "She was with you, right?"

Brennan jerked his head toward the front door. "The lass is inside. Antonio wired the bomb to a timer and a trip wire to her hand. She's out cold, but if she wakes up—" He shrugged.

Datsko's expression suddenly shifted, and his face seemed to grow pale. "Take this scumbucket in," he told the uniformed cops as he holstered his gun. "Read him his rights, and get him out of my sight." He took a tentative step toward the building and peered through the broken glass in the door.

"I wouldn't go in there, if you take my meaning," Brennan said, his voice dripping with sarcasm. He ignored the younger man who approached with a set of handcuffs. "Antonio rigged it to look like the woman set the bomb, and chloroform doesn't last very long. If she comes around—"

"Son of a gun!" the older cop said, staring at the pair of doors like a mad bull.

"I wouldn't go—," Brennan repeated, but before he could finish his warning, the cop had run into the building.

❋ ❋ ❋

Puffing with every breath, Datsko ran through a waiting room and a corridor, then peered into dark examining rooms. The place was a maze of closets and cubicles, but one light burned from a room at the end of the hallway. As Datsko neared, he thought he could see the form of a woman's body on the floor.

It was Theodora Russell, and beside her, under the edge of the desk, the numerals of a cheap digital timer glowed red in the gloom. Terror stole his breath, which came in short, painful gasps as he raced into the room and knelt to reach her. As he felt for her pulse, he glanced at the flashing red digits. Four minutes twenty-eight seconds. Not even time to call the bomb squad.

Theodora Russell's head moved, and he reached over and firmly patted her cheek. "Theo," he said, grasping her chin in his hand. Her eyelids fluttered weakly, and Datsko suddenly remembered that the perp outside had said something about wiring her to the bomb. *How?* He glanced quickly over her body. No wires at her waist, her feet, her arms. A metallic gleam caught the light, and then Datsko saw the wire.

A cold lump grew in his stomach as he studied the wire knotted securely around the woman's finger. He couldn't leave to get his wire cutters because if Theo woke up or even stirred, it was a sure bet she'd move her hand. But if she didn't wake up, they would both be as dead as bedposts in—he looked up—three minutes, fifty-nine seconds.

Datsko patted her face again, harder. "Theo, you've got to wake up, and you can't move. Listen to me. There's no time to sleep." He pressed his palm over hers, stilling any movement in her wired hand. Her eyelids fluttered again, then opened. She frowned when she recognized him.

"Your right hand has been wired to a bomb," he said, knowing from the stricken look in her eyes that she understood completely. "I can cut you loose, but I've only got—" he glanced at the timer— "three minutes and thirty-nine seconds to do it. I'll have to go to my car for my wire cutters. You mustn't move. Do you hear me? Don't move an inch! If you do, you'll trip the bomb and kill us both."

"OK," she whispered, her body rigid.

With a quick intake of breath, he lifted his hand from hers, then turned and sprinted for the door. The uniformed officers were waiting in their car, probably radioing for an ambulance and a crime-scene unit, but Datsko ignored them as he dove into the Lincoln and fumbled with the latch on the glove compartment.

"There's a bomb!" he yelled through the open window, struggling to make his mouth and his fingers work at the same time. "It's wired to a woman inside. Get away, give me a minute to cut the wire, and I'll get her out."

There was silence from the other officers; then the blue-and-white's engine roared to life.

As the sound of Datsko's pounding footsteps faded, Theo gulped back the sob that wanted to rise from within her. She wouldn't blame him if he didn't come back; why should he risk his life for hers?

God had brought her to this place, but why? Hadn't he promised to be her victorious right hand? Hadn't he promised to make chaff of her enemies? But she was the one who would be mincemeat in a few minutes. There were no angelic supermen hovering near to save her. She had no choice but to lie on the dusty floor of Ken's office and watch a clock dimly count down the last minutes of her life.

She'd made a royal mess of things, blundering into every trap the enemy had set for her. How Reyes and his cronies must have laughed at her mistakes! She was naive and foolish; she probably deserved the headline Pamela Lansky would write for tomorrow's paper: *Anti-Choice Zealot Killed in Bomb Blast.*

She balled her free hand into a fist, fighting back the tears that swelled hot and heavy in her chest. Tomorrow's newspaper would be her final legacy to Stacy and Janette—a pitiful collection of clippings to explain her mysterious death. Not even Ann would ever know the complete truth.

Her life was finished unless she could loosen the wire on her hand. She turned her head, trying to see what connected her to the bomb. Every nerve in her body leapt and shuddered with the urge to *do something.* She could yank her hand free and run, she could rise up and try to loosen whatever held her, she could twist and try to bite the wire so she'd be doing something during her last living minutes. Throughout the last week, throughout her entire life, her mantra had been *With God's help I can do this!*

She closed her eyes, picturing herself as a little girl, holding tight to God's hand. Two weeks ago she had been full of confidence that he led her, but in the past few days she had frequently slipped and fallen as she rushed ahead.

What a fool she'd been. She'd played the game her way, telling Ann that God had dropped the proposal into her lap and that he would take care of her because she was working for a righteous cause. But as she stared into the stark face of death, Theo suddenly realized that she'd nearly left God out of the equation. Like a headstrong little girl, she had independently plunged ahead, trusting in God to pull her back from the edge, never stopping to ask for his direction. Even back at Reyes's house, she'd glibly apologized for her misdeeds like a misbehaving child who thinks that saying "I'm sorry" *really sweetly* will cancel the spanking she deserves.

In a breathless instant of clarity, she understood her problem. She was too determined, too independent. Part of the problem sprang from her own nature; part was the self-reliance she'd forced herself to adopt since Matt's death. But ever since Theodore Russell's proposal had fallen into her hands, she had dashed ahead with her plans. She was like a little girl walking with her loving father, her hand resting confidently in his until the path became rocky. Then she had stubbornly pulled away, fallen and hurt herself, and wondered why God had let her go.

Her struggle—now, as always—was not against a bomb and its merciless timer, but against her own self-will. God had allowed her to stumble into an extraordinary circumstance, perhaps to help change the world, but mainly to change herself. Theodore Russell's proposal was the mirror in which God had revealed her ambition and pride, her overwhelming *self*-confidence, her foolish independence, even her foxhole faith as she cried out to God in a string of apologies only because she did not know what else to do.

God might have let her fall . . . but he hadn't left her side.

Now she faced another, much more nerve-racking choice than the one posed to her by Reyes and his colleagues. She could rise up and try to save her own life . . . or lie still and pray that God would send an overweight, balding, out-of-shape cop to rescue *her*, an alleged felon.

Unbidden, another snippet from Isaiah ran through her mind: *When the poor and needy search for water and there is none, then I, the Lord, will answer them. Everyone will see this miracle and understand that it is the Lord who did it.*

"Oh, God," she whispered, closing her eyes. "Forgive me for trying to do it by myself. Please, Father, give me another chance."

* * *

Datsko grabbed the wire cutters—*Thank you, God!*—and shimmied backward out of the car. *I wish I were fifteen years younger. My rear's too big, and my heart's too weak for nights like this.*

He tried not to think about the timer as his unwilling feet carried him back into the building. Theo Russell was lying as motionless as a statue on the floor, but tears streamed from the corners of her eyes into her hair.

"Don't worry," Datsko said, eyeing the wire and the timer. Twenty seconds left. Too late to turn back now. "One little snip and we're out of here, honey."

He positioned the cutters, held his breath, and pressed downward. The satisfying bite of the cutters broke the wire, and Theo Russell gasped as he gingerly pulled her hand free and helped her to her feet. "Now we run like bandits," Datsko yelled, grabbing her hand. Together they sprinted through the hall, spurred by fear and the certainty of the blast to come.

The rooms, the desk, the foyer, the door, almost home—

The sound of the explosion roared just after Datsko felt the breath of fresh air on his face; the concussion hurled them several feet from the doorway. He was aware of the woman's scream, his own hoarse yell, falling debris, and the roar of flames that seemed to lick at his heels.

A moment later, he lay in the grass on the far side of the parking lot. His feet were bare, his shirt unbuttoned. Theo Russell lay next to him, a long smear of dirt running along the side of her face and neck. She, too, was barefoot, and her jeans were torn below a bloody cut on her knee.

He sat up and rested his hands on his knees. The Lincoln had been slightly thrown back from the blast but seemed undamaged. He grinned. It would take more than a bomb to dent the Beast.

"Are we alive?" Theo Russell whispered, sitting up. She wiped her nose with the back of her hand and gave Datsko a crooked smile. "Are we really alive?"

"You bet," he said, watching flames consume the building. "It's a bloomin' miracle."

Chapter 36

THE keening wail of sirens pierced the roar of the flames, and soon emergency technicians were racing toward Theo and Datsko, their eyes wide with concern. One of them knelt by Theo's side and peered anxiously at the cut on her knee.

"I'm OK," she said, a tremor in her voice. She tried to stand but swayed into the medical technician's arms, her legs as weak as a baby's. That was OK. She was alive. She could hardly believe it, but God had brought her through.

Next to her, Datsko grunted as an EMT tried to examine him. "I may be too old for this, but I'm young enough to know I'm OK," he barked, slapping the man's hands away. "Leave me alone; I've got work to do." He pointed a shaky hand toward Theo. "I have a few questions for you, young lady."

"Good," Theo answered, steadying herself. "I have a lot to tell you. As long as we can talk sitting down."

Datsko nodded. When the EMT had finished cleaning the cut on Theo's leg, the cop flailed his arms and rose to his shaky feet and helped Theo up. Leaning forward a little, he led the way to his huge, tanklike car.

"Am I under arrest?" she asked, pausing at the rear door.

"Shoot, no," Datsko said, moving toward the passenger side of the car. "Sit in here. With all we've been through, lady, you could almost be my partner."

He opened the passenger door for her, and Theo slid into the seat, touched by the unexpectedly polite gesture. "That's a new tack for you, Detective Datsko. What changed your mind?"

"Let's just say that I see things from a different vantage point now," Datsko answered. He groaned and pressed his hand to his back as he grumbled his way to the other side of the car. "I'm too old for this stuff. I think I pulled something."

A fire truck pulled into the lot, and a team of firefighters in bright yellow suits sprang into action. Datsko settled in behind the wheel of his monstrous car, and for a few moments they said nothing as they watched the firefighters battle the blaze devouring Ken Holman's clinic.

WEDNESDAY
October 30

Chapter 37

OURS later, her eyes heavy with exhaustion, Theo told her story from beginning to end for Datsko, a couple of other cops, and a little tape recorder perched on the edge of Datsko's desk.

"So basically these guys were upset because Russell's proposal threatened their supply of fetal tissue," Datsko said when she had finished.

Theo nodded wearily.

"And they were going to pay you off rather than deal with two dead Theo Russells. Any idea how much money they would have offered?"

She shook her head. "They didn't say. I just knew I couldn't do it."

Another cop approached and pointed to Datsko. "There's a guy downstairs asking to see you and Theo Russell," he said. "Some doctor named Ken Holman."

"Send him up," Datsko said, his chair squeaking in protest as he leaned back. As the officer left, Theo covered a yawn with her hand and caught Datsko grinning at her.

"What?" She dropped her hand. "Can't I be tired?"

"I couldn't figure you out, lady," he said, slamming a stack of notes into a manila file. He crossed his hands on the file and shook his head. "I had you pegged as a housewife who considered gardening living on the edge, but you kept showing up in the oddest places. I still haven't figured out how you broke through the security at BioTech."

"Perfect pitch," Theo said, shrugging. "I overheard a guy punch in the key codes. I knew what the pitches were, so I just matched them to the keypad." She felt a blush burn her cheeks. "And my methods of investigative research are going to change, Detective. No more trespassing, no more pilfered papers."

Datsko gave her a smile of grudging admiration. "They nearly nailed you, you know. You played right into their hands at every turn. And they'd have beaten you tonight—"

"No, they wouldn't have," Theo answered, lifting her chin. A warm kernel of happiness occupied the center of her being. Couldn't he understand it? "They'd have only beaten me if I had given in to them. If things had ended differently, if you hadn't come along, they still wouldn't have beaten the truth. Ken knows the truth; so do Ann and Janette. They won't keep silent. People are going to learn about the abortion lie . . . eventually."

The detective seemed preoccupied for a moment, as if a memory had suddenly surfaced and overshadowed his awareness of their conversation. Then, slowly, he grinned at her. "Yeah, I think you're right," he said, the warmth of his smile echoing in his voice. "And I'll bet you'll be the one to tell them."

Theo smiled her thanks. "Will you do me a favor, Detective Datsko?"

"What did you have in mind?"

"Call Pam Lansky at the *Post*. Give her as many of the facts as you can. Enough, anyway, that she can write the story and restore my reputation. I don't want people on my street thinking I'm the criminal element in the neighborhood."

"We can do that." Datsko scribbled a note on his calendar. "Anything else?"

"No." Theo yawned again. "I just want to get home, crawl into bed, and forget that all this ever happened. These have been the longest two weeks of my life."

"Hang on a minute," Datsko said, looking toward the elevator, which had just opened. "We have to talk about what comes next."

Theo turned to follow his gaze and saw Ken hobble through the elevator doors. Maneuvering carefully on his crutches, he wended his way through the sea of desks until he stood in front of her.

Swimming through a haze of feelings, Theo looked up at him, not sure what to say.

"Hello," he said, smiling grimly. "I was hoping I'd find you here."

"I didn't think you'd ever want to see me again," Theo answered, looking down at her dirty and scraped hands. "And yet last night when I was sure I was about to die, I wanted to see you. I wanted to tell you how sorry I was for doubting you."

"Tell him you're sorry for putting a bullet in his leg," Datsko suggested, a wry smile curling his mouth.

"It's out now," Holman answered, his eyes never leaving Theo's face. His brows lifted in a silent inquiry. "I believe we have a few things to discuss."

Theo swallowed, feeling her breath quicken. "You're right. We do." She looked down at the floor as shame washed over her. "I'm sorry, Ken—" Her voice broke, but she pushed on, "I jumped to a conclusion that shouldn't have made sense. All I could think was that you and Ann were the only ones I'd told about my meeting with Victoria. I was stupid, I know, because I know the kind of man you are." She lifted her eyes to meet his steady gaze and saw that his quick gray eyes were humorous and tender. "Just like I know you're the kind of man who will forgive me. It was an accident. And I'm terribly sorry."

Ken closed his eyes and shook his head. When he finally spoke, it was to Datsko. "You know, Detective, all night I've been telling myself that life would be a whole lot simpler—and safer—if I went home and forgot about this woman." One corner of his mouth turned upward. "And I probably could put her out of my mind for a few hours. But after a while, I'd have to go to work, and then I'd remember that I no longer have an office. So I figure it's impossible to forget her for the long term, right?"

"Right," Datsko replied, crossing his meaty arms. "Kinda hard not to think about her when you look at your burned-out building."

"That's what I thought." Ken's dark eyes moved to meet Theo's troubled gaze. "And it would be hard not to think about her when I eat in Italian restaurants, and when I walk under the stars, and every time I pick up a newspaper. And I'd miss those invigorating discussions and her endless questions. Not to mention the thrill of bailing her out of jail every now and then."

Theo's smile was watery. "And my obstinate independence," she added, caught up in the warmth of his gaze. "Maybe, if you think it's a good idea . . . I should make a point of leaning on someone."

"So," Ken shifted his weight on his crutches, "what do you think? Could I apply for the job?" His eyes held hers, waiting for her response.

"I'd make her promise not to use me for target practice," Datsko inserted, his voice dry.

"I promise," Theo whispered, her lips trembling.

"OK, then." Ken hobbled a step closer. "I'm yours, if you want me."

"I need you." The tears began in earnest now.

"Well, this has all been very touching," Datsko blustered as Ken leaned forward and kissed Theo's tremulous smile. "But you two don't know what you're talking about. Theo can't go back to life as usual."

"Why not?" Ken asked, a glittery challenge in his eyes. "The bad guys are going to be caught, right?"

"Yeah, sure," Datsko answered, tapping the eraser of his pencil on his desk. "Even though their little operation at BioTech may not be technically illegal, the gang that was after Theo will be nailed for criminal conspiracy to commit murder, kidnapping, arson, felonious assault. . . ." He shrugged. "And a few dozen other charges I think we'll manage to make stick."

"Won't Stacy and Theo be safe?"

"We'll post a guard around her house until Salago, Dennison, Rodenbaugh, Reyes, and Perry are in the pen. With Brennan put away and Antonio in the morgue—"

Theo shivered as another thought struck her. "But what about that crime family in New York, the Morenos? Does it ever end?"

Datsko pressed his lips together in a thin line. "No, it doesn't," he said, his voice clipped. "Evil never stops, Theo. It just keeps on rollin', taking innocent people with it. And that's where this crusade for truth is going to cost you something. You'll be safe, but we can guarantee your safety only as long as you're in the Federal Witness Protection Program."

"The Federal Witness—" Theo's mouth went dry. "Stacy and I would have to leave this place? Change our names? But I grew up here, Detective!"

Datsko leaned forward and rubbed his chin, his eyes softening. "I know, Theo. I didn't say it'd be easy."

Not easy! She looked at Ken, afraid that her eyes revealed too much of her heart. To lose him after just finding him would be unbearable, but she couldn't ask him to give up his patients, his home, even his *name*. . . .

"You're going to have to do it, Theo," Ken answered, his expression growing serious. "It's the only way you and Stacy will be safe."

She felt as if there were hands on her heart, slowly twisting the hope from it, but she nodded dumbly.

"And of course, someone will have to go with you," Ken went on, looking up at Datsko. "My building is destroyed, but I'm a pretty good doctor. I guess I could start over someplace else with a new name."

A cry of relief broke from Theo's lips, but Datsko ignored it. "Sorry, but the protection program is for material witnesses only," the detective said, idly scratching his chin. "And their spouses and families, of course. But I'm thinkin' you'd have some time to remedy that problem. Theo will have to stay here in protective custody long enough to testify, and I don't expect the trial will happen for at least another six to eight months."

Ken looked at her then, a look of mingled eagerness and tenderness on his face. "What do you say, Theo?" he asked, leaning hard on his crutches. "Do you think we can settle this little problem of not being married in six to eight months?"

"I think so," she whispered, slipping her hand over his. "There are a few things we haven't discussed, but I'm willing to try if you are."

"Well, now," Datsko said, standing. He thrust his hands into his pockets and pushed his bottom lip forward in thought. "You two can pretty much pick where you want to go. It will all be kept quiet, of course, and the program administrators will set you up with a decent house and a job."

Theo's mind hummed with happiness. She could see them in a little house somewhere in Florida, some quaint and cozy town close to John and Janette. Ken would keep busy bringing babies into the world, and she'd write books, sitting under the trees with Stacy, tapping on her laptop computer. . . .

"My book." Her mind came to an abrupt halt, as if hitting a wall. She turned to look at Ken. "I went through all this just so I could write the book about abortion and breast cancer. And if I write it, the mob will know who I am. My name—whatever name I use— will be on the cover, for heaven's sake! They'll read the story, and they'll figure out how to find me."

"Unless," Ken said, watching her with a keenly observant gaze, "you approach the problem from another angle. Which is more important, Theo, getting your name on the cover or getting the truth out?"

"Why, the truth, of course!" she answered, but even as the words left her tongue she felt her heart sink. The truth did matter most, but the recognition would have been . . . nice.

"You could always write it like that famous political novel," Datsko offered, his mouth twitching with amusement. "You know, the book by 'Anonymous.' I hear it did real well."

Theo stared at Ken for a moment, and the sympathetic concern in his eyes made her heart swell with a feeling she had thought long dead. She smiled. "Why not? I can always write other books. As Mrs. Ken . . . Whoever you decide to be."

Datsko cleared his throat and shuffled papers and files on his desk. "Uh, I think it's time you two cleared out of here. We have real criminals to apprehend, you know."

"I can go?" Theo asked, turning to the detective.

"Go," he said, dismissing them with a shooing gesture. "All charges against you have been dropped. I'll be in touch very soon to get you in contact with the agents who will ensure your safety. You'll be called to testify when they're ready to convene a grand jury."

"I'll be here," she answered, standing up.

"Come on," Ken said, his dark eyes warm and protective. "I've got a cab waiting outside."

"We'll call you," Datsko said, standing behind his desk.

"Don't take too much of her time," Ken said, waiting for Theo to join him. "I don't think she'll have much to spare in the days ahead."

"Oh?" Theo asked, an odd surge of gratitude and happiness running through her. "And why is that?"

"Because you need to spend time with the people you love, namely Stacy and me," Ken said, moving toward the elevator. "And because you have a book to write."

Theo stopped and searched his face. "I think you're right," she said, turning to wave good-bye to Datsko. "And I think it's going to make chaff of a few mountains."

NOTES

1. Mona Charen, "Studies Link Breast Cancer and Abortion," *Tampa Tribune,* 19 October 1994.
2. Material from Theodore M. Russell's proposal based on research data contained in Scott Somerville's brochure *Before You Choose: The Link between Abortion and Breast Cancer* (Snowflake, Ariz: Heritage House, 1976).
3. "Abortion-Cancer Link Studied," *World,* 11 September 1993, 10–11.
4. Somerville, *Before You Choose.*
5. Seattle Post-Intelligencer report, "Researchers Report Link in Abortion, Breast Cancer," as quoted in the *Tampa Tribune,* 27 October 1994.
6. Kenneth L. Woodward with Mary Hager and Daniel Glick, "A Search for Limits," *Newsweek,* 22 February 1993, 52.
7. Ibid.
8. Sharon Begley with Mary Hager, Daniel Glick, and Jennifer Foote, "Cures from the Womb," *Newsweek,* 22 February 1993, 51.

The plot and characters in the novel you've just read are fictitious, but the message the "bad guys" wanted to stifle is all too true. By working real medical journal citations into the story line, Angela Hunt has skillfully crafted an entertaining vehicle for the delivery of the true story that medical associations, the media, and the federal administration do *not* want you to hear—that abortion *is* a cause of breast cancer. In truth, half a century of worldwide published medical research has shown that when breast cancer is not conveniently left out of the equation, abortion is more than a hundred times more deadly to women than childbirth.

Abortion is the single most avoidable known risk factor for breast cancer. Angela Hunt has performed a remarkable service for women everywhere by revealing what they need and have a right to know.

Joel Brind, Ph.D., Professor of Biology and Endocrinology
Baruch College of the City University of New York